PIAU

PIAU

Journey to the Promised Land

BRUCE MURRAY

Foreword by Anne Murray

DUNDURN
TORONTO

Cover painting: David MacIntosh
Printer: Webcom

Library and Archives Canada Cataloguing in Publication

Murray, Bruce (Bruce Joseph Robert), author
        Piau : journey to the promised land / Bruce Murray ; foreword
by Anne Murray.

Issued in print and electronic formats.

ISBN 978-1-4597-3845-4 (softcover).--ISBN 978-1-4597-3846-1 (PDF).
--ISBN 978-1-4597-3847-8 (EPUB)

1. Belliveau, Pierre, 1851-1922--Fiction. 2. Acadians--Fiction. 3. Historical fiction. I. Title.

PS8626.U7748P53 2017   C813'.6   C2017-903279-8
                                                C2017-903280-1

1   2   3   4   5   21   20   19   18   17

Conseil des Arts du Canada **Canada Council for the Arts** Canadä **ONTARIO ARTS COUNCIL CONSEIL DES ARTS DE L'ONTARIO** an Ontario government agency un organisme du gouvernement de l'Ontario

We acknowledge the support of the **Canada Council for the Arts**, which last year invested $153 million to bring the arts to Canadians throughout the country, and the **Ontario Arts Council** for our publishing program. We also acknowledge the financial support of the **Government of Ontario**, through the **Ontario Book Publishing Tax Credit** and the **Ontario Media Development Corporation**, and the **Government of Canada**.

Nous remercions le **Conseil des arts du Canada** de son soutien. L'an dernier, le Conseil a investi 153 millions de dollars pour mettre de l'art dans la vie des Canadiennes et des Canadiens de tout le pays.

Care has been taken to trace the ownership of copyright material used in this book. The author and the publisher welcome any information enabling them to rectify any references or credits in subsequent editions.
— *J. Kirk Howard, President*

The publisher is not responsible for websites or their content unless they are owned by the publisher.

Printed and bound in Canada.

VISIT US AT

 dundurn.com | @dundurnpress | dundurnpress | dundurnpress

Dundurn
3 Church Street, Suite 500
Toronto, Ontario, Canada
M5E 1M2

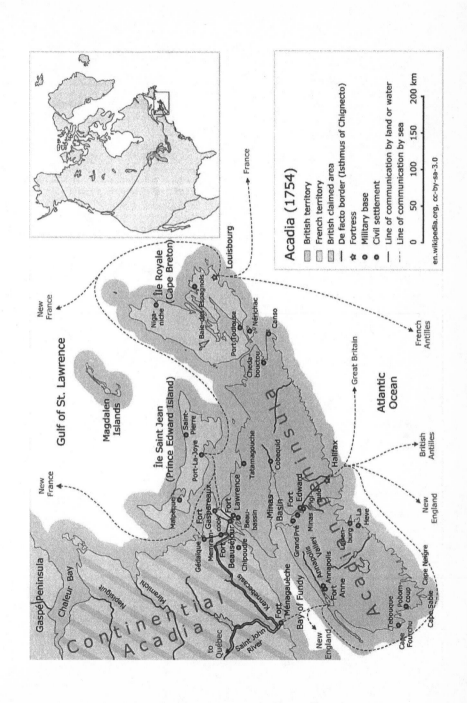

Acadia (1754)

- British territory
- French territory
- British claimed area
- De facto border (Isthmus of Chignecto)
- ★ Fortress
- ● Military base
- ⊙ Civil settlement
- —— Line of communication by land or water
- ---- Line of communication by sea

en.wikipedia.org, cc-by-sa-3.0

0 50 100 150 200 km

Gulf of St. Lawrence

Magdalen Islands

New France

Île Royale (Cape Breton)

Louisbourg

France

Niga-niche

Baie-des-Espagnols

Port-Toulouse

Nérichac

Canso

Cheda-bouctou

Île Saint Jean (Prince Edward Island)

Saint-Pierre

Port-La-Joye

Tatamagouche

Cobequid

Tabamagouche

New France

Malpèque

Gédaïque

Fort Gaspereaux

Memram-cook

Fort Beauséjour

Beau-bassin

Chipoudie

Fort Lawrence

Minas Basin

Fort Edward

Pisi-guid

Cobequid

Halifax

Great Britain

Atlantic Ocean

British Antilles

French Antilles

New England

Gaspé Peninsula

Chaleur Bay

Napisiguit

Miramichi

Continental Acadia

to Quebec

Saint John River

Kennebecassis

Fort Ménagouèche

Bay of Fundy

New England

Fort Anne

Fort Annapolis

Annapolis Valley

Grand Pré

Minas

La Hève

Lun-burg

A c a d i a n   P e n i n s u l a

Trebouque

Cape Foutchu

Pobom-coup

Cape Sable

Cape Nègre

Foreword

Even as a young child, my brother Bruce had an insatiable curiosity. It wasn't unusual to see him rummaging through drawers, peering into our family's old cedar chest, or sneaking into the attic to discover untold secrets and treasures.

He loved the company of older folks, who would regale him with stories of their childhoods and family history while he peppered them with questions and begged to see pictures.

He was fascinated with graveyards and visited them every chance he could get.

So, it was no surprise to anyone when he chose to study history in university.

By the time my brother had made the decision to enter show business, after six years of university, he was already a trained historian. He sang back-up for me both on tour and on several of my albums. In the years we toured the world together, he carried his passion for history with him, seeking out landmarks of significance everywhere we performed. Celebrity had made me reclusive and he would drag me from my hotel room and insist that I accompany him. Each tour was a fascinating history lesson and his enthusiasm was infectious. He singlehandedly changed my lonely life on the road.

I remember him forcing our chauffeur to stop at a churchyard in the English countryside so that he could stand over the gravesite of Winston Churchill. I must say that I was caught up in that special moment, too.

So when Bruce informed me that he was writing a historical novel based on the life of Piau Belliveau, it seemed like the natural thing. After all, Piau had been part of our family folklore for as long as I can remember.

In the book, my brother summons our Acadian ancestors, skillfully weaving their stories into the fabric of the novel and lacing them with such passion and detail that they are hard to resist. Knowing that the majority of the characters existed, and the events actually occurred, allows the reader to be easily transported back in time, unconcerned about which of them is fictional and which is historical.

I felt it was very courageous of Bruce to allow Piau to tell his own story. It is a risky business to channel the thoughts and words of a main character. It reads as a memoir but has the sense of a journal being written. Allowing Piau's voice to be heard makes the narrative sound more authentic. Seeing the historical players in the story through Piau's eyes allows the reader to penetrate his character and experience the people around him in an almost mystical way.

And there is Piau's singing voice, a personal touch, coming from an author who himself has an extraordinary singing voice. We were told that our great-grandfather Damien Belliveau, a descendent of the novel's hero, was famous throughout the Acadian community for his magnificent singing voice. Using song in the novel to add the special meaning that music provides in the everyday lives of people everywhere is a nice touch and resonates to my very core! The times of celebration and sorrow in *Piau* are accompanied by French songs from the period, songs that tug at the reader's heartstrings. And of course, the unique sound and tone of my voice and that of my brother's had to have come from somewhere. Why not from Piau?

I cannot ignore the perilous and heartbreaking journey that the Acadians were forced to endure during the Acadian Expulsion. When I filmed a music special for television several years ago in my native Nova Scotia, one of the filming sites was the Church of St. Charles at Grand Pré, the place where Acadian men were torn from their families, homes, and lives, were locked up in the church, and finally packed off on to ships and inhumanely exiled to far-off places. As I toured the museum, I found myself imagining the hopeless cries of the mothers and children. I became so overcome by the feeling that this place created in me that I found it difficult to proceed with the taping. I recovered, however, and proceeded to tell Piau's story on camera: of his capturing of a British ship and the violent encounter that event created. I will leave that story to the storyteller here but I must say reading the novel resurrects those intense emotions in me.

The story my brother has told is not only an Acadian story; it has a universal message. Those who were affected by this tragic story and survived, have descendants in all parts of the globe. Because this is such a momentous event in our history, its story is remembered by hundreds of thousands of people of Acadian descent throughout the world. *Piau* represents just one of these amazing stories and the tale of his courageous journey has been long overdue in the telling and deserves to finally be heard.

— Anne Murray

Introduction

This novel is closely based on the life and times of Pierre Belliveau, an Acadian folk hero and also an ancestor of mine. Known as Piau, Pierre was a central figure in Acadian history, helping some of his fellow Acadians to escape the British expulsion of his people in the 1750s. He was the leader of a group that eventually settled in what is now New Brunswick, establishing a settlement there.

You may wonder what motivated me to resurrect an Acadian patriarch 210 years after his death. Why not leave him to the world of cultural myths remembered by those whom author Antonine Maillet describes as "the Acadian nation"? Is it because I am a direct descendant of Piau and therefore I feel an obligation to tell his story? Perhaps. After all, he has been part of my consciousness for most of my life. I have collected a lifetime of stories about him and the Acadians from my maternal grandparents, whose own parents and grandparents and earlier ancestors had never married outside the Acadian community; from stories passed on by word of mouth by others; and from other stories published by uncles and cousins who happened to be Acadian historians. So it is natural that I, as a trained historian myself, should want to explore and relate the story of Piau's life and great achievements. It may sound odd, but I have the mystical feeling that it was not I who chose Piau, but, rather, it was Piau who chose me. This claim requires a leap of faith on the reader's part, I know, so I will leave it at that. My own journey to discover Piau deserves some explanation, however.

Surprisingly, the seed for this book began with my unearthing of an ancient Protestant Bible in the dresser drawer of my Acadian grandmother.

A budding historian even at the age of ten — some, however, might think I could be better described as a snoop — I intuitively had a distinct impression that the Bible was forbidden fruit. According to my grandmother, who eventually caught me red-handed perusing the well-worn volume, this was the King James Bible that had been passed down to her through her father. Ironically, although the book was a treasured family heirloom, those into whose hands it had come were forbidden to read it, because it was not approved by the Roman Catholic Church. This Bible plays an important role in *Piau*. To my supreme sadness, the Bible was burned when my grandparents' home went up in flames in the late 1970s.

My Uncle Harry, who was an author and Acadian historian, informed me that the Bible had belonged to one of our ancestors whose name was Piau Belliveau. It was he who first told me of the exploits of this ancestor, famous for leading his people during the expulsion of the Acadians. Not only was my uncle obsessed by our illustrious ancestor, but he was also an authority on Colonel Frederick DesBarres, who was connected in history with Piau. Their story also appears in the book.

My family, ever rich in historians, produced a written account of Piau's life that was published in a reputable magazine while I was still in my teenage years. The author was my cousin Edward "Ned" Belliveau. Inspired by his account, I set about to find out everything I could about my famous forebear. This pursuit has continued to this day. What a journey it has been, reading about Piau in nineteenth-century histories and listening to personal accounts of his life from centenarian cousins of my Acadian grandmother.

So, there existed a considerable amount of written material on Piau, not to mention the great amount of oral history that was available about him. Still, I felt that Piau's life hadn't yet been properly told, and I knew that I was the person to tell it. So that is what I set out to do. Why, though, you may ask, did I write a work of historical fiction based on a lifetime of research rather than produce a non-fiction account?

I believed, as I channelled the life and accomplishments of this great Acadian figure, that hearing Piau's voice and those of the people in his life was essential to the telling of this remarkable tale. It would allow for his story to unfold in an emotional way for the reader — Piau's struggles could be relived as he experienced them. It would be possible to see, almost firsthand, his joys and disappointments, and to feel the hopelessness the Acadians must have felt time and time again as they were perpetually challenged by the arbitrary behaviour and decisions of the British soldiers and their officers.

So, I decided that the story of Piau's life needed to be told not as a non-fiction history or biography but as a work of fiction. Nevertheless, despite the fact that this is a novel, all of the main events really happened, and all but two of the characters in the book are real — the only fictional characters in the book, Captain Tyrone and Madame Thibideau, play at best only minor roles in the story.

Piau is not just the story of one man's life and his struggle for survival, however. It is a far greater story, one of an exiled people, fifteen thousand souls driven from their lands, many displaced by force and stranded in unfamiliar lands around the world. This is a case of ethnic cleansing and forced human migration on a large scale, possibly the largest of its kind anywhere until the twentieth and twenty-first centuries. This story deserves to be known. It should provide universal lessons not only to Canadians but to people everywhere.

PART I:

THE EARLY YEARS

Chapter 1

I am Pierre Belliveau but my people call me Piau. I am in my hundredth year. My spirit has embraced this land and its ancestry for nearly a century. Every possible joy and calamity has come upon me because I am Acadian. Like Moses and the Israelites, who escaped the mighty pharoah and his army, my people and I escaped the British and their army and have wandered through the wilderness, searching for the Promised Land. The North Star guided me into exile and on my return I crossed the River Jordan into the land of Canaan. I am my own master here, and those I love are with me; therefore I am one with God, who has protected me, and one with my ancestors, who bore great hardships in order that I should survive, procreate, and live in this land. I was a witness to the resurrection of my people and I surrender my spirit happily in the knowledge that my descendants will forever remain in the land of their forefathers.

I speak of the British as if they are other than me, but I have forever been a man with a divided spirit. I have witnessed the atrocities inflicted on my people and my family by British soldiers, but I must confess that I myself am part English.

My mother was half French and half English. Her father, Charles Melanson, was an English Protestant, born of a French Huguenot father and an English mother. He sailed into Port Royal on the ship *Satisfaction* at age fourteen with his British parents and his brother, Peter (my great-uncle Pierre), when Acadia became an English colony in 1657. Her father was to become the patriarch of Melanson Village.

In 1664 my grandfather Charles married my grandmother Marie, daughter of Abraham Dugas, the gun-maker to the king of France and armourer at the fort. Following their marriage, my grandfather decided to adopt his mother's family name Melanson, doing so (I was told) to distinguish himself from his older brother, Pierre Laverdure. The influence of this English blood flowing through my family's veins has been profound. Because Acadia has been a British possession for most of my life, I was inclined and encouraged to embrace both my heritages.

If the influence of the English blood in my veins has been strong, even stronger has been the influence of the French blood. Perhaps this is a result of my father's death. I do not remember that event — I was only a year old. However, I have heard so many tales of his courage fighting General March and the British that I have absorbed others' memories of him as my own. In my own conflict with the conquerors, I heard my father's whispers in my ear inspiring me to lead my people to a land of exile so that our survival would be assured. He has walked with me my entire life, whispering to me that I am the reason he lived. He has always been part of my journey.

My mother, Madeleine, who spoke both French and English perfectly, realized that teaching the English language to her children would grant them special privileges in this life. No one embraced the English language more than I. My great-uncle Peter, called Pierre Laverdure, who lived in Grand Pré, announced when I was a boy, "Piau speaks the King's English with the eloquence of a proper English gentleman." I basked in his praise. Under his tutelage I learned to read and write English with considerable fluency. French and English had no nationhood for me. I do not remember not communicating in both tongues. But French was the language of my father. And was not my father killed by an English musket? There lies the conflict.

Looking back on my life and the deportation of my people, I am aware that the actions of both the French and the English, with little concern for the well-being of the Acadians, shaped our tragic history, and each was responsible for our betrayal.

As I have said, it was Pierre Laverdure who taught me to read and write English. My first recollection of Uncle Pierre (he was really my great-uncle)

was from when I was eight years old. He visited us with his wife, Aunt Marie-Marguerite, an elegant woman, the daughter of Sieur de Pobomcoup. They arrived by vessel from Grand Pré, the settlement they founded. My uncle's arrival was met with much fanfare in Port Royal.

Because he was an English gentleman, he was received with the utmost respect by Lieutenant-Governor Caulfield at Annapolis. My uncle had a noble carriage but he had an easy way with people. His children he called his seeds, and he never failed to remark that the wind had blown them to all parts of Acadia, boasting that he had in excess of sixty grandchildren. He had arrived to celebrate the end of the harvest with the family of his deceased brother, Charles, at Melanson Village and to deliver his crops and produce to the English soldiers of the garrison at Annapolis.

After doing business with the new British lieutenant-governor and spending several evenings in the company of the officers at the fort, he joined his family for a week of harvest celebrations. It was at this time, not too many years after the Treaty of Utrecht had established British rule in Acadia, that Uncle Pierre spoke to my mother about my spending the winter with him and Aunt Marie-Marguerite. He remarked to my mother that his home lacked the presence of children and he would like the opportunity to spend time with me, something he believed would benefit me.

"I have noticed in Piau a rare intelligence in one so young. I can imagine he has a great capacity for learning," he told my mother.

I was the youngest child and she believed that she could spare me for the winter season. My grandmother was less easy with my leaving, however. She did not easily give me up for the winter. I was Grandmama Marie's first grandson born after the death of my grandfather and she had pampered me from birth; I gave her love and affection in return. She was responsible for my French education. On parting with me she declared that every day she would blow kisses into the wind hoping they would find me in Grand Pré. I asked her how that could be possible and she replied that they would be soaring on a warm breeze and that they would find my cheeks and caress them.

Uncle and I sailed with the tide and the wind to Grand Pré, journeying so that I could begin my education, an event that would change my life irrevocably. This was my first long trip by boat. We followed the shoreline of the mighty Bay of Fundy, witnessing the riot of colours from the sugar maples along the shore. We floated swiftly past Blomidon, the majestic mountain of the Great Spirit Glooscap at Cap Baptiste. As evening approached, I could see the autumn sun setting over the valley at Minas. The richness of the golds impressed me as a young boy — I believed I was entering paradise.

As we sailed into Minas Basin, Uncle pointed to a stone building being constructed in the distance. With considerable pride, he declared, "There is the new church of Saint Charles rising up from the ruins of the old. It was destroyed by the English during the great battle of 1704. I am a master stonemason and I will resurrect the old chapel stone by stone in defiance of the British conquerors."

I was puzzled by the emphatic nature of Uncle's comment.

"But Uncle, you are English. You are friends with the lieutenant-governor and all the officers at the garrison."

"Piau, you must learn to see beyond appearances. It is true I was born in England — yes, I was educated there, I became a journeyman stonemason in Yorkshire, and my parents were English. However, I have lived in Acadia for over fifty years. I married your aunt, who is French, embraced the Roman Catholic faith as my own, and have more often than not been in the service of the French king. The blood that flows through my veins was at one time English but now it is Acadian. My English ways have stood us in good stead during these times of British rule, but there remains no more to it than that."

Over time, I, too, was to cultivate these skills, which had taken Uncle Pierre fifty years to perfect.

On our arrival at the jetty in Grand Pré, there was a large vessel, flying the flag of the king of France, awaiting our arrival. When Uncle Pierre disembarked he encountered three officers dressed in French uniforms, spoke a few words to each, and slyly passed a roll of manuscripts to one of them. This was the first time I witnessed Uncle delivering dispatches to the French. This transaction completed, Uncle met my aunt and me on the dock and we continued to our carriage. Looking back, I saw the French ship lift anchor and drift into the bay, where it remained until the following morning. I was too young at the time to comprehend that Uncle Pierre was spying for the French. I was to witness similar events time after time over the years.

I clearly remember riding slowly through the village of Grand Pré for the first time and witnessing the respect and homage paid by its inhabitants to Uncle, the patriarch of their community. This regard was amplified by the sight of the seigneurial home at the western end of the village. It was grander than anything I had ever seen, a huge stone structure with two levels. Our homes in Port Royal were modest in comparison. On our arrival at the front gate a man greeted us.

"*Bonjour, René, comment allez-vous?*" shouted Uncle. "*Dites bienvenue à mon petit-neveu, Pierre, dit Piau Belliveau. Il va rester avec nous pendant l'hiver.*"

"*Bienvenue à tous et à toi, Maître Piau.*"

The young man who greeted us was René LeBlanc, Uncle Pierre's son-in-law, the husband of his daughter Isabelle. Even as an eight-year-old, I was struck by René's extraordinary presence, for he truly was a force of nature, one of those beings who exudes a boundless energy even on first meeting.

"It is a pleasure to meet you, Piau. I have a son named Benjamin — perhaps he can be your companion during your stay. I am certain that both of you will get on famously."

I was comforted by this news for I had feared I would be living exclusively in a world of adults. It was a prediction that turned out to be true — Benjamin and I became great friends and remained so for years.

The comfort of my uncle's home wrapped its arms around me in a way no human had ever done. The grand armchairs by the fire were finely carved and covered in tapestry. They always welcomed me on cold winter days and nights. The main room of the house was miraculously laden with books of every kind and size. These would be my refuge for the next ten winters of my life. Hidden amongst the books was a large ancient volume. On first discovering it, I realized it was written in English, a language I had yet to master, and it was filled with sacred images of the life of Jesus and other unknown characters that had some connection with the divine. Uncle often noticed my fascination with these printed images and one day revealed the true nature of this special volume.

"I see, Piau, you have become enraptured with the holy book. It is the King James Version of the Bible. As you see, it tells of the life of Jesus and all

those who went before. My parents brought this English Protestant Bible to
Acadia when we arrived over fifty years ago.

"You notice in the centre of the book that my parents have signed their
names and written the dates of their births, the day of their marriage, and
my birthdate and that of your grandfather as well. See Father — Pierre
Laverdure, born in La Rochelle, France, in 1606; and Mother — Priscilla
Melanson, born in Bradford, in Yorkshire, England, in 1613. And there I
am, Peter Laverdure, born in Bradford, England, in 1636, and your grandfather Charles Laverdure, born in Bradford in 1643.

"When my parents moved to Boston with my brother John in 1667
when the French regained their governance of Acadia, they left the family
Bible with me. Over the years, I have returned to this book many times
because it is the only thing that connects me to my parents and my distant
past. This is not the Bible of the Roman Church but it still holds the secrets
to our humanity and God's divinity. I give you permission to read passages
from the great book when your English improves."

Chapter 2

Not only were my uncle and René welcoming when I first arrived, so, too, was my cousin Isabelle. She spilled a torrent of greetings when my uncle first introduced me to her and Benjamin.

"Could this be little Piau? How wonderful to finally meet you! I trust your mother is in good health. I have not seen her since the British took over the garrison at Port Royal, which I hear is now known as Annapolis. You certainly seem to take after her. And my father has boasted to me of your precocity. Here is your cousin Benjamin. He is just beginning his education, too. Together you will be learning the language of those who govern us."

"I am pleased to meet you, Cousin Isabelle. My mother is in very good health, thank you, and she has told me all about you. And, yes, the town is now called Annapolis but we choose to call it Port Royal as we always have."

I shook Benjamin's hand.

"It is a pleasure to meet you, Piau. I look forward to spending the winter in your company."

Benjamin's greeting was extremely formal in its delivery but unmistakably genuine.

"What did I tell you, young Piau," interjected Uncle. "Like you, Benjamin is an extraordinary child, mature and intelligent beyond his years."

Benjamin was also a handsome child. His eyes sparkled in a way I had never witnessed before. He seemed a most interesting person and I felt immediately that we would be bosom friends. The prospect of having a fellow student to share my learning filled me with a confidence I had not felt before. And, of course, I relished the prospect of having a playmate.

And so began our daily learning sessions. René and Uncle were responsible for my studies, and Isabelle oversaw Benjamin's English and French lessons. While I practised my lessons, I listened to Uncle's heated debates with René. They spoke of the constant indecision of whether to leave Acadia for Île Royale or Île Saint Jean, or to stay. The issue of whether or not to take the oath of allegiance to the British Crown seemed to riddle their discussions. I was made aware of the willingness of the Acadians to leave with their worldly goods and livestock and sail to the surrounding French colonies. But however much the British wanted us to leave, they feared us more in exile. The increased power of the French surrounding Nova Scotia should eight thousand of us enter the neighbouring French colonies was far too threatening. There was also the question of who would feed the one hundred and fifty British soldiers at Annapolis should we leave our farms. I heard that Lieutenant-Governors Nicholson, Vetch, and Caulfield all decided to prevent us from emigrating by denying us the sails necessary to wind our vessels.

Over time, Isabelle became a mother figure to me. She was everything one would hope for in a mother. She was beautiful, warm, comforting, and charismatic. She took me under her wing and was as kind to me as she was to her own son. She informed me of my family history, all the stories that were too painful for my own mother to relate. One day she sat on the floor before Uncle's hearth and talked about my mother's tragedy.

"Piau, your father was a great man and very heroic. When Colonel March and the British attacked Port Royal on two occasions in 1707, your father fought bravely to defend the fort and his property from the invaders. He became a victim of their treachery after holding out against many days of attacks. British retribution rained down upon your home and your family. They shot your father, burned your house, and killed and confiscated your livestock.

"Your mother fled with her children. You were a babe in arms. Your grandmother Marie took you in. When the British left Port Royal in ruins, Captain Pierre Morphan and the French privateers, who had fought alongside the Acadians in the battle, felt such compassion for your mother and such respect for your father's courage in the face of the enemy that they presented to her a British vessel they had captured off the New England coast. You all were to live on that ship until your new home was constructed in the village. Your brother Charles's passion for shipbuilding began at that period. He transformed his grief into something constructive. The ship was confiscated when the British arrived at the garrison five years ago.

"This is a story I believe you must hear and one you will in time pass on to your descendants so they can be proud of those who went before them."

"Isabelle, it is true I was a baby when we lived aboard the British ship, but I have heard many tales told of those times living below decks. We never sailed her but I am certain it was fun to pretend we were at sea for my older brothers. Poor Mother never speaks of that time, though. But you are correct, my brothers Charles and Jean remember it all as a great adventure, raising the sails when they chose to and climbing to the crow's nest to stand on guard for the first sight of an imaginary enemy fleet.

"Even though he was only ten at the time, Charles was forced to become the man of the family. Living on the ship made the finest ship-builder in all Acadia!"

"How you boast, Piau!" said Isabelle.

We all began to laugh. I suppose I was a budding storyteller even then.

That first autumn, I learned more of my family and witnessed their life in their village. I saw the completion of the new church, observing how René instructed the men of the village how to place the stones. Uncle supervised from his seat in the churchyard, but it was René who made certain each stone was placed and mortared properly. They completed the construction of the roof before the first snowfall and prepared the church interior for the Christmas season. Although I was very young, I was able to absorb their joy and pride at midnight mass on Christmas Eve. Not even the British lieutenant-governor at Port Royal could threaten what they had rebuilt, for they had learned to savour each moment of this life as if it were a precious gift. The church was the gift they had given themselves and no one could steal that from them.

During that winter of 1715, I was to discover that René was no ordinary overseer. He was René LeBlanc, and, although only twenty-seven, he was a very influential person in the community at Grand Pré. I discovered that, at a very young age, René's genius had been recognized by my uncle.

Uncle Pierre had placed him under his patronage just as he had now placed me, and had educated him in English so that someone in the community could be a liaison with the English as Uncle grew older. Stonemasonry had been only a small part of his education. In later years his position as notary at Grand Pré would secure him a major role in the exile of our people. He became my teacher and mentor. He was married to Uncle Pierre's daughter Isabelle and therefore he was also the husband of my mother's first cousin. Even at my tender age, I was struck by Isabelle's extraordinary beauty and vibrancy. She, too, became a part of my English world during those early years. Their son, Benjamin, only six at the time, became my closest friend.

When the spring arrived at Grand Pré I was anxious to return home to Port Royal. I was returning to my family at Melanson Village an altered person and far more enlightened. The influence of Uncle, Isabelle, René, and even little Benjamin was to survive each summer and spill over into my life with my brothers and sisters. My mother perceived a great change in her youngest son both physically and mentally.

"You have changed, Piau. You have grown and I notice a difference in your eyes. Perhaps they are wiser. We all missed you but I see that your winter with Uncle Pierre has been a benefit."

She embraced me in a more meaningful way than I could remember. From that time on she never took me for granted again.

During the summer we received a visit from Uncle, Isabelle, and Benjamin. For a week Benjamin and I enjoyed the freedom of the hot summer days, swimming in the river and scaling the ramparts of the dikes. Occasionally we would find a shady spot in the town where I would read aloud from one of the English books from Uncle's library.

One day, as we sat outside the blacksmith's shop engaged in our usual pastime, a distinguished-looking officer chanced by and heard me reading aloud. He spoke to me with a sound of amazement in his voice: "Young man, where did you learn to read English with such fluency? That is remarkable for an Acadian boy and one of such a tender age."

"My uncle taught me and has allowed me to choose some English books from his collection."

"And who might your uncle be, young master?"

"Uncle's name is Pierre Laverdure, of Grand Pré."

"Indeed! I am acquainted with your uncle. He is a venerable English gentleman and you are a very fortunate young man to have access to your uncle's library. I am Lieutenant-Governor Caulfield. I am pleased to make your acquaintance. And to whom am I speaking?"

"Pierre Belliveau, but they call me Piau. This is my uncle's grandson, Benjamin. He speaks English as well."

Despite my mistrust of the British at Port Royal, I felt proud that I was able to communicate with them in their own language. That being said, I always felt a degree of remorse after each encounter with the British soldiers of the garrison.

The lieutenant-governor appeared to be genuinely good-natured, though. My discomfort began to dissipate when he spoke.

"Come to the garrison tomorrow. I have something I wish to give to you. I will expect you after the noonday gun. Until tomorrow, young Piau."

The following day at noontime, the soldiers guarding the gate at the fort were amused at the sight of two young Acadian boys requesting to see Lieutenant-Governor Caulfield. They were even more amazed that one of them spoke perfect English. Just as promised, the lieutenant-governor appeared at the gate with a book in hand.

Ignoring the guards, Lieutenant-Governor Caulfield spoke to us in a congenial and familiar manner.

"Good day, Master Piau and Cousin Benjamin. Recently, my wife forwarded to me a book newly published in England. It is a story of great adventure on an exotic island in the South Seas. The author is a Mr. Defoe and the title is *Robinson Crusoe*. It is a fascinating story, and although it will require much effort on your part to read it, I am certain in time you will find it most entertaining. It is my gift to your continuing education. Keep it. I am able to get another should I wish in future."

He shook both our hands and sent us on our way. I have never forgotten his kindness, and history has shown him to have been the gentlest and most sympathetic of all the British lieutenant-governors of Acadia.

One winter followed the next, and the summers followed each other as well, and I enjoyed my two lives — winters at Grand Pré and summers at Port Royal.

My education continued under the tutelage of many. At Grand Pré, Uncle Pierre, René, and Isabelle each felt responsible for contributing something to my knowledge — sometimes, admittedly, my fog of knowledge. Absorbing all they hurled at me was daunting. It took my summers to digest all they chose to send my way during the winters.

Isabelle made certain that Benjamin and I perfected our penmanship, encouraging us to practise in both French and English. This was not an onerous task for us, because we rallied back and forth between languages on a regular basis. I don't believe we were even conscious of which we were speaking at any given time. Certainly, in our community, however, we spoke to our neighbours in French.

René was responsible for our practical use of numbers, allowing us to create imaginary ledgers of goods one might purchase or trade. He instructed us in measuring the size of properties, particularly community fields, weighing bags of grain produced in those fields, and predicting what each was likely to yield in a growing season.

He instructed us also in stonemasonry. This skill I was not to perfect until much later in life, for I was only in residence at Grand Pré in the winter. Benjamin, on the other hand, became a master stonemason like his father and grandfather before him.

As for Uncle Pierre, he supervised what we read in both languages and was able to produce any number of volumes from his massive library to improve our reading. He encouraged us to practise incessantly so that we should become competent in French and English.

It was Uncle's knowledge of history that captured my imagination most. In telling his own story he was able to bring to life a great web of stories that described the history of France and England over a period of close to a hundred years. One such story told of the execution of the English king.

"When I was thirteen, the king of England, Charles I, was beheaded. Can you imagine that, a monarch being executed by his own people?"

Benjamin and I sat there in total wonderment.

"Why would they cut the king's head off, Uncle?" I asked.

"That is a good question, Piau. Well, the answer is clear. He went to war against his own subjects and lost that war. He was tried and executed.

The stubborn King Charles believed he was only answerable to God, not the people of England, and it is a known fact, especially in England, that a monarch reigns only by the good graces of his subjects."

"Who became king after the execution?" inquired Benjamin.

"That is also an excellent question, Grandson. There was no king. The commanding general of the army was a man named Oliver Cromwell, and he governed for ten years as Lord Protector of the Commonwealth. He did not wish to be king but he certainly was an able leader. My father was a member of Cromwell's New Model Army. It was because my father was on the winning side that he was given land at Port Royal in 1657. That is how I came to live in Acadia."

"How is it that we have a king now, Uncle Pierre?" I asked.

"Well, three years after my family arrived in Acadia, in 1660, to be exact, the English Parliament, the elected assembly where all the laws are created, invited the old king's son to return to England as their new king. King Charles II happily agreed but he was forced to relinquish many of the powers his father had enjoyed. After he was crowned, we heard little news of His Majesty in the colony."

"Tell us about our French history, Grandfather," Benjamin requested.

"My father told me many tales of his growing up in France. He was a master tailor, you know, from a place in France called La Rochelle. He grew up in a family that was very religious, but they were not Catholics, they were referred to as Huguenots. They believed that a person could have a direct relationship with God through prayer and by reading the words of the Bible. Their church services were conducted in French, not Latin like the Roman Church. The Huguenots were mistrusted by many of the French Catholics, including the king of France himself. They were persecuted for their beliefs even to the point of being hunted down and murdered. The infamous St. Bartholomew's Day Massacre is an example. Under the leadership of the Duke of Guise, thousands of Huguenots were hunted down in one day and butchered like wild animals. My father always became very emotional when he related the story of that gruesome day."

"Why was your family spared?" I inquired, horrified by what I was hearing.

"In La Rochelle the citizens were further away from the seat of power, and most people living in the walled city were Huguenots. With the fortress to protect them, they were able to defend themselves time and time again. Of course, my father was not born at that time and by the time he was, King Henri IV, a man raised a Huguenot, sat on the throne of France. Unfortunately, Good King Henri was assassinated in 1610, three years after my father's birth, and things became difficult for those who were practising the Protestant religion. By the time my father reached adulthood, he had decided to immigrate to Yorkshire to avoid persecution. That is where I was born."

Benjamin and I often sat spellbound as Uncle Pierre retold these stories again and again, each time embellishing them with more details for the entertainment of his captive young audience.

During the summers, there were many days when I sailed from Melanson Village the short distance to Annapolis with my brother Charles, who worked daily in the shipyards constructing and repairing ships and boats. Many of the soldiers and officers of the garrison at Annapolis adopted me as their special pet. They valued my ability to communicate with them in English, and I thrived on their attention.

Although I chose conscientiously never to enter the fort, not even when Uncle Pierre inhabited the garrison during harvest time, I sought the company of the British soldiers whenever they sauntered through the town. Acting Lieutenant-Governor Caulfield continued to share his library with me, but for some reason I always made an effort to return the books to their owner. Perhaps it ensured more contact with him, or perhaps it was that nagging guilt that was never far from the surface when I cavorted with the conquerors.

One day in early March of 1717, following my return from Grand Pré, I was passing the gates of the fort when I noticed the Union Jack flying at half-mast. I inquired at the guard post as to its meaning. The soldiers solemnly informed me that the lieutenant-governor had suddenly and unexpectedly passed away during the night. I turned about-face and ran down the street of the lower town sobbing uncontrollably. I wished to escape the horrid news, hoping that if I ran far enough the truth of it would disappear. I followed the path along the river to a place of sanctuary. How could someone just die? I was eleven years old and could not remember ever losing someone to death — my departed father I had never known. This was only the beginning of a series of tragedies that plagued my life in those early years.

With the death of Caulfield came the usual unsettled feeling among the Acadians that the new lieutenant-governor would force the issue of taking the oath of allegiance to the British king. Caulfield's replacement, like every new lieutenant-governor, took the hard line at first and insisted the Acadians swear without any qualifications. Uncle's dealings with the new lieutenant-governor were more circumspect and less cordial despite the usual acceptance of Uncle Pierre's "Englishness." Uncle railed about the new lieutenant-governor's lack of understanding of the situation in Acadia. On his annual visit to Annapolis he told his family how he had pressed his case with the new Lieutenant-Governor Doucette.

"We have ever been loyal to the British Crown, Your Excellency, but abandoning our neutrality in times of war would force us to take up arms against our kinfolk who live in the French colonies surrounding Acadia. It would force me to take up arms against my own children. That part of the oath can never be sworn by His Majesty's loyal French-speaking subjects. The remainder of the oath is agreeable to us. I represent the wishes of Acadians throughout His Majesty's colony in this matter."

Over the next two years Uncle Pierre's efforts with Doucette did eventually reap the benefits he so desired to achieve. Overhearing his discussions on the matter with René and Isabelle, I sensed, though, that his success would only survive the time of the current lieutenant-governor.

During the summer of 1719 Isabelle permitted Benjamin to spend the summer with his cousins at Port Royal. He was now ten years old and able to be taken in for a season by my family. I was overjoyed, and we both relished the idea of the warm days of summer when we could mix the carefree life by the river with the chores of the farm and fields. The purpose of this arrangement was to allow Isabelle a more relaxing summer as she prepared for the arrival of a new child. It was strange for me to imagine her with child, and I experienced benign feelings of jealousy that the new baby would eclipse me in Isabelle's affections. However, I kept these thoughts in check, forcing myself to be joyful for the new life inside the woman I cared for more than any other.

Chapter 3

Days of mists and fog delayed our departure for Grand Pré in the autumn of 1719. After several days of waiting for the fog to lift, Uncle made the decision to risk the lack of visibility, fearing that to wait too long might cause us to be marooned at Port Royal for the winter. Our vessel sailed blindly through the mist, filling all those aboard with the same uneasiness Odysseus must have felt on his journey home to Ithaca. I pondered this as I sat wrapped in a blanket at the bow of the boat.

As our vessel finally sailed into the bay at Grand Pré, I could see a ghostly figure standing at the edge of the pier in the distance. As we approached the dock, I realized that it was Isabelle awaiting our arrival wrapped in a cape and hood.

"Welcome home." The sound of her voice filled me with a familiar joy and a relief that now we were safe in the bosom of Grand Pré.

Isabelle had chosen to spend the remainder of her confinement in the big house under the watchful eye of her mother, Aunt Marie-Marguerite. The house was, therefore, filled with laughter and stimulating conversation: Uncle's stories of dealing with the new lieutenant-governor at Annapolis; my tales of my widowed grandfather, Jean Antoine Belliveau, courting my mother's sister Aunt Cecile, a woman a full generation younger than he; Benjamin's recounting of our summer exploits in the forests around Port Royal; and general family gossip.

After four years of struggling with *Robinson Crusoe*, I now was able to read the story with some fluency and understanding. During the days of inclement weather, I lounged by Uncle's warm hearth reading chapter after chapter to the entire household. I held my audience captive, especially

Isabelle who wondered at the possibility of there being such a paradise on earth. One evening she remarked pensively, "Crusoe's sense of survival seems to be as strong as that of the Acadians. I sometimes lament that we cannot be left alone in our little paradise called Acadia, free of the capriciousness and unpredictability of the British who govern us."

In the coming weeks, Isabelle was to remark how active the baby in her womb was and that he or she would become a great Acadian warrior, judging by its energy and constant movement. However, one day I heard her comment casually to Aunt that the little one inside her had been sleeping a great deal in the past several days. I suspected nothing in what she said. Then the pains arrived and suddenly my world was turned upside down. Aunt instructed me to find René and tell him to come quickly. I was to remain at his house with Benjamin and the other children until further notice. I suspected nothing. The child was about to arrive into this world, I thought. Again I suspected nothing. Several hours later Uncle sent for us.

When we reached the Manor House, we were informed by Uncle that the baby, a girl, had been born and had mercifully survived, considering her early birth. She was now nestled in the arms of her grandmother. The priest was with Uncle as he delivered the news, but their grave expressions seemed to reveal something far more sinister. We were all told to congregate in Isabelle's room immediately, where the priest was to perform the necessary prayers for such an occasion. We solemnly mounted the stairs to Isabelle's room. Isabelle lay quietly in her bed, pale and lifeless, with René staring on. Her breathing was laboured. Her spirit appeared to have vanished from her body. I hoped she was resting after the ordeal of giving birth. The priest continued to pray as we all looked on in disbelief. Was this the face of death? Before long, Isabelle's grasping for each breath ceased. I stood paralyzed on the spot, oblivious to the sobs and crying around me. I could not run away from the presence of death this time. I stood completely still — not able to grieve, not able to believe. That day, in the late autumn of 1719, I became a man.

For the next five years I continued to spend my winters at Grand Pré, not yet willing to abandon the memory of Isabelle nor the education that Uncle Pierre and René provided me. In addition, I felt a certain responsibility for Benjamin.

Sadly, Aunt Marie-Marguerite died within months of Isabelle's death. With the passing of her beloved daughter, she seemed to lose the will to live. René remarried within six months of his wife's demise, thus beginning a new life and a new family. In my mind his grief evaporated while Isabelle's body was still warm in the ground. But who was I to say such things? I was a fourteen-year-old, and at that age I was rash in my judgments for lack of experience. Uncle hired a widow, Madame Thibideau, to run his household. Benjamin, his sister, Marie Josephe, and the newborn baby remained in the Manor House in the house-keeper's care. They never lived with their father again.

Lessons abounded during the final winters of Uncle's life. Besides giving us the use of his growing library, he provided experiences that broadened our knowledge of the world. Every autumn, on our return to Grand Pré, we were greeted by a French vessel and we witnessed the annual delivery of dispatches in exchange for crates of books, furniture, and foodstuffs not available in the colonies — all these for the secret documents he gave to the French officers. There were friendly greetings between Uncle and the French captain, but no more than pleasantries. For years Benjamin and I were present at these exchanges, but it was not until a year before his death that Uncle Pierre was forthright in describing the nature of the written dispatches.

"Piau and Benjamin, you have been witnesses to my annual trade with the French and you have been very patient with me, not asking me to explain the true nature of these mysterious dealings. Well, because I am old and my time on this earth is coming to an end, I feel it is only fair that I share the truth with you both. Since the British began to rule Acadia or, as they call it, Nova Scotia, I have been relaying secret information to the French. That is true. When I visit the fort at Annapolis each year, I keep my eyes and ears open to any privileged information that might cross my path, and believe me, when you are in the company of soldiers who are under the influence of drink, much confidential information emerges. That which I hear, I write down in dispatches once I arrive at Melanson Village for the Harvest Festival. If I have noticed changes to the battle-ments at the fort, I draw those also. If British or New England ships arrive during my visit, I mention them and observe any cargo they bring ashore or put on board their vessels. Over the years I have had an accomplice in this enterprise, for I am only present at the fort of Annapolis for one week a year. This does not provide a great deal of information. Because your brother Charles works daily in the shipyards, Piau, he long ago agreed to be my second pair of eyes in the town. And, may I say, his enthusiasm for the task is prodigious, for he has a profound distaste for the British, primarily because he witnessed your father's murder at a young age. This fuels the hatred building inside his soul."

I had often speculated about the nature of the secretive dispatches, but the disclosure of Charles's involvement in their creation shocked me. How could I not be aware of such subterfuge? As usual, this provoked an instant response from me.

"Why would you engage in such a spying operation, Uncle Pierre? What did you have to gain from such a dangerous enterprise? Why would you put my brother in such a position of jeopardy? For what reason, Uncle, tell me?"

Uncle did not appear to be surprised by my sudden outburst. Benjamin grasped my shoulder to contain my surging emotions but he remained calm.

I could feel this anger rising in me but I knew to keep it in check, for it would be unacceptable to show disrespect for a patriarch.

Uncle was quick to respond. "I am not surprised that you are angry, Piau. However, it is necessary to place these things I have related in a perspective you can understand. Acadia has existed for more than a hundred years. For only twenty of those years have the British ruled here. I have lived in this colony for almost seventy years. Where should my allegiance lie? Think carefully about this last question!"

I stood there speechless, seriously pondering the question put to me by Uncle. My understanding was insufficient for an intelligent response so I remained speechless.

"The fact that you are unable to answer my question is a tribute to your intelligence, Piau, for it is not an easy one to answer, not even for me. Therefore, I have chosen not to answer it myself. The only answer I will put forward is that I was motivated by a desire to engage in good commerce — call it trade, if you wish. Trade does not involve allegiance, only fair exchange. The French required confidential information about the British in Acadia, and I wanted those things I could not acquire any other way but through trade with the French. There you have it. The French books you have enjoyed at the Manor House for all these years were provided by this commerce.

"As for your brother, he is a man who needs an outlet for his anger. That is essential; otherwise he may act upon it unwisely."

Benjamin interjected into the conversation as a means of defusing the emotions surrounding Uncle's revelation.

"Thank you, Grandfather, for entrusting us with your secret. We may not completely comprehend this business you have had with the French, but we respect your judgment in these affairs and hope in time we are able to grasp what you have done."

Uncle responded by kissing Benjamin on the forehead and patting me gently on the back.

"Thank you, Benjamin. You are very gracious to respond as you have. And Piau, may you continue to contemplate these things so you can truly understand the workings of the people around you. Bless you both."

During my Grand Pré years I witnessed the wedding of my brother Charles to Marguerite Granger. He was nine years my senior, and because of this and my frequent absences from Port Royal, our relationship only grew as I advanced into adulthood. Since he had witnessed the death of our father and the brutality of the British in 1706, he was never inclined to embrace his English side, except when it was useful for him to do so. In fact, he had a benign contempt for my English education and he disapproved of my associations with the officers at Annapolis. This was so, even though his wife was the granddaughter of Lawrence Granger, a sailor from Plymouth, England.

Following the marriage of Charles and Marguerite, my mother decided that, as the firstborn, Charles was to inherit the family farm. My grandmother Marie lived alone in her homestead at Melanson Village, and since my brother Jean was still unmarried, as was my seventeen-year-old sister, Madeleine, we all moved in with my grandmother to start a new life. My mother was to live with her mother for the remainder of her life.

My grandmother was elated that we were coming to live with her. Our relationship blossomed because she had many life lessons to teach me and she had many stories to relate about my forefathers both in Acadia and France.

Often she spoke about her father, Abraham Dugas, who was a man of great importance when France governed Acadia in the century before. He was a gunsmith by trade, and she prided herself in commenting that his title while in France was Gunsmith to His Majesty the King. The Dugases were from Vaucluse in Haute Provence. Abraham's parents moved to Toulouse just before he was born; there he was educated and trained as an armourer.

One day after our arrival at my grandmother's house, she caught me in a pensive moment. "Piau, you know that your great-grandfather, Abraham Dugas, was an eminent man here in Acadia and in France. He was sent here by the king of France to Port Royal, and he held the position of lieutenant-general and armourer of Acadia."

"I know all of this, Grandmama," I said, feeling a little frustrated thinking that my grandmother would be repeating an oft-told tale to me.

"Of course you do, my dear," she replied. "And you know that he met my mother here and married her not long after. And not long after that, I was born. But that's not what I wanted to tell you today. What I wanted to share with you is one of the stories that my father shared with us when I was young.

"My father often spoke of his days in Toulouse and especially relished telling us stories of the family's ancestral home, Fontaine de Vaucluse, in Provence. He told us how he and his family travelled over a great distance every summer to Vaucluse, which was at the foothills of the Alps, to escape the crippling heat of the city. He referred to it as a pilgrimage to his ancestral home.

"Now, Fontaine de Vaucluse is famous for these things: the presence of the famous Italian poet Petrarch centuries before, and its miraculous fountain in the hills above the town."

Having caught my imagination, I inquired, "Grandmama, what was magical about this fountain? Did it shoot water into the air?"

"In answer to your question, no. What is special about this fountain is that no one knows its source and no waterfall provides its deep pool. The mystery lies in the fact that the pool high on the mountainside forever remains filled and yet perfectly still. From this still pool come a hundred waterfalls that flow down through the town into the Sorgue River and ultimately into the mighty Rhone. The waterfalls fall fiercely, never running out of water."

I responded with disbelief. "But how is that possible? Every deep pool must be fed by a waterfall, and no spring could provide such great amounts of water."

"The fountain gathers its strength from within," Grandmama assured me, "and its power only shows itself in the hundreds of waterfalls that fall from its still pool. Have you never heard the old saying 'still waters run deep'? Remember, Piau, that the strength of your character, like that of the water, gathers itself from within, and you draw your power from it in times of trouble. My father told me this when I was a little girl, and this lesson has served me well throughout my life in Acadia."

I pondered this awhile. Over time I have come to see the true wisdom of her words.

Grandmama and I had many other conversations over the next few months. Always curious about our family history, I inquired one day, "How was it that you came to marry an Englishman? There are those who have said that my grandfather Charles Melanson was an English spy, which is quite impossible, given that I am certain his brother, Uncle Pierre, spies for the French."

"And how would you know these things?" she declared, surprised.

"I have witnessed Uncle passing documents to the French each fall on our arrival at Grand Pré."

"You cannot be certain of the contents of these documents."

"I have only come to this conclusion because of the manner in which they have been delivered and the veil of secrecy surrounding how they are received. The exchange always occurs out of the sight of people." I deliberately withheld the details regarding the knowledge I already had of the contents of these documents out of respect for Uncle Pierre.

"But not out of your sight. You are truly an observant young man, Piau.

"Well, all I can tell you is that when my husband, Charles, was alive, whatever his dealings with the English may have been he kept them to himself. I always respected his privacy as you must do with your Uncle Pierre. He is a wise man and much respected by both the English and the French in Acadia.

"And to answer your first question, many English settlers arrived when the English Crown took over Acadia in 1657. At that time, the new settlers fit in quite nicely with the French-speaking Acadians. And, of course, your great-grandfather, my father-in-law, Pierre Laverdure Senior, was raised in France but moved to England to avoid persecution because he was a French Protestant."

"Were they known as the Huguenots, Grandmama?"

"Yes, your great-grandfather was a Huguenot and he continued to practise his religion throughout his life. When the English left Port Royal in 1667, he moved to Boston so he could continue to live amongst the Protestants of the colonies to the south. He never returned to Acadia. He, your great-grandmother Priscilla, and your great-uncle John remained in the English colonies."

"And grandfather and Uncle Pierre remained behind in Acadia."

"Yes, Piau, they both married French Acadians, adopted the Catholic religion, and raised their children here. Your grandfather Charles, my husband, also changed the family name to Melanson, which was the family name of his English mother."

Chapter 4

As I grew older, I became fascinated by my brother Charles's obsession with the sea and with shipbuilding. From the earliest days of our misfortune aboard the captured British ship we called home in 1707 and 1708, he had relished the science of ship construction. He was able to design and construct vessels of all kinds: simple fishing boats, small sailing vessels, and even large ships. He became a master mast-maker and his skills were often used when British ships sailed up the river from the sea, looking for a repair of their sails and hulls. As he approached adulthood, he insisted on being well paid for his efforts. He would later become famous for these marine skills that had been nurtured out of his own adversity. They would in time serve him well in a formidable act of revenge against those he considered to be our father's murderers.

I never had a deep understanding of building a boat, but I often became a second pair of hands when Charles was in need of them. I marvelled as he crafted the spine of the vessel from sturdy lengths of oak using the tools he had collected over the years from Uncle Pierre and from the British at the garrison. These often engaged him for repairs and to create new masts from the massive white pines we felled. Benjamin became the assistant's assistant during the summers at Port Royal, and we mixed this work with occasional fishing along the river. While Benjamin and I enjoyed the fish we caught, the news and gossip that I was able to pick up during my time working with Charles by the harbour would prove to be of greater value.

One day in early September of 1726 news arrived that a new lieutenant-governor was arriving at Port Royal. The word quickly spread throughout the Acadian communities and beyond. The Acadians knew Lawrence Armstrong from previous visits, and he was as unpopular among them as he was among the soldiers and officers at the fort. Armstrong had never endeared himself to Governor Philipps, who spent most of his time away from Acadia; in fact, Philipps complained to the Board of Trade at Westminster about Armstrong's behaviour elsewhere in Acadia, forcing Armstrong to sail to London to defend himself more than once. Now that Armstrong had become acting lieutenant-governor, a position he was to hold for the next fourteen years, he turned his attention to the matter of the oath of allegiance. Refusal to swear the oath had been a long-standing problem in Acadia, but a compromise had always been reached. It was soon evident that he had chosen to take a hard line with those he considered obstinate.

Not long after Armstrong took up residence at Annapolis, he began visiting the various communities in the district to survey the farms, live-stock, community activities, and, much to my brother Charles's conster-nation, the local shipyard. To say that the lieutenant-governor's perusal of Charles's work on a newly constructed *chaloupe* was an intrusion was to understate the anxiety we all felt by his sudden presence.

As the lieutenant-governor looked on, we continued with our task silently. It was he who broke the silence.

"Your reputation as a shipbuilder has reached as far as England, Monsieur Belliveau. I have some commissions I wish to discuss with you."

Charles purposefully gave Armstrong a blank stare, pretending not to understand what the lieutenant-governor was saying. We all were aware of the antipathy that lingered beneath the surface of that blank stare. There was a moment of uncomfortable silence. I was the one who decided to respond to the lieutenant-governor, being the most fluent in English of all the Acadians present.

"I speak on behalf of my brother, Excellency, that at a convenient time for him you may discuss the time, compensation, and design of any projects to be completed in future."

Taken aback by my forthrightness, the lieutenant-governor responded quickly and authoritatively: "Young man, I sense a certain impertinence in your tone. You will in future speak to your lieutenant-governor in a respect-ful manner. Furthermore, any discussion of commissions will be at my con-venience, not yours."

Sensing that I had overstepped, I softened my response. "I meant no disrespect, Excellency. The abrupt tone of my English is explained by my lack of a true understanding of the language. My mother tongue is French."

Armstrong stood motionless, not knowing whether this young man of twenty was being sincere in his response or taking advantage of him.

"We will talk!" Armstrong turned about-face and strutted away. Major Cosby, who attended the lieutenant-governor, followed him for several yards and then glanced back, giving us a knowing smile and an informal salute.

Feeling we had achieved a minor victory over an oppressor, we quietly resumed our work.

Chapter 5

The month of September 1726 was one I remember as a time when fate began to manipulate our lives in ways we never imagined. Only a few days after our unsettling encounter with Lieutenant-Governor Armstrong, a vessel flying a French flag floated through the thick and impossible mist like a ghost ship carrying no one but the dead. Eerily approaching us at the shipyard at Annapolis, at first it appeared to have not a living soul aboard. Looking back on that day, I realize that Benjamin, in watching that ship sail into our lives, was facing his own destiny.

It was he who first noticed the tall, faceless apparition at the wheel of the ship. He became so mesmerized by the vision, he was not aware of the commotion surrounding him. Soldiers rushed to the shore with muskets pointing at the mysterious vessel. The lieutenant-governor waded into the water, pushing officers and troops aside. We waited breathlessly on shore as the tableau unfolded. To this day, I can clearly remember the two men facing one another for the first time: Armstrong and Mangeant.

An unlikely alliance was about to be forged. In hindsight, an unholy one!

Armstrong barked an order in the direction of the figure behind the helm, "All persons on board must show themselves unarmed on deck immediately or my soldiers will commence firing on your vessel."

Not completely certain his message was being understood by the captain of the ship, he called to me on the shore.

"Young Belliveau, come here at once."

Running as fast as I could, I shouted: "Yes, Excellency. I am at your service."

"Did you hear my orders just now?"

"Yes, Excellency. You were quite clear in your directions."

"Deliver them to the captain of the ship in French."

I nodded in agreement, and then translated his command into French, loud enough for all to hear. A quiet descended on the scene.

The captain's voice broke the silence. "I understood you the first time, Monsieur le Gouverneur." There was only a hint of French in his accent but no sign of fear or deference.

The captain spoke to his unseen compatriots below deck, but no one ashore heard his utterances or their reply. The small group who came up from below were a surprise to all watching.

If anyone had witnessed this scene not knowing what had gone before, they would have believed it to be an almost farcical scenario. One hundred and fifty muskets directed at one tall, unarmed man, an elegant woman, and two small children, a boy and a girl. The only possible threat was from the first mate, who followed them on deck. His simple dress and lack of a weapon diffused any sense of menace he may have posed.

The captain shouted to those on shore: "We come in peace. My family and I wish to seek sanctuary."

"You have no other crew aboard?" inquired Armstrong.

"None, I assure you, Monsieur le Gouverneur."

Armstrong's tone and demeanour relaxed and he seemed to be more intrigued than alarmed by his new visitors.

"Come ashore then and we will talk."

On being given permission to disembark, the first mate activated the pulleys to lower the lifeboat into the water. A seat suspended by ropes appeared to accommodate the captain's lady. She was lowered into the small vessel. The others descended a ladder after the swing was lifted.

Once ashore, the captain and his wife and children engaged in the formalities of gentlemanly bows and curtseys.

"Monsieur le Gouverneur, I am François St. Germain Mangeant, and this is my wife, Marguerite, and my children, Samuel and Louise. Jacques is my first mate."

"You say you are here seeking sanctuary. Why would a French gentleman and his family enter an English colony seeking protection? And protection from what?"

"If you would permit me a private audience, Excellency, I will relate my story. There are too many sensitive details to describe here amidst so many."

"Sir, you must present yourself formally to my council and describe fully the circumstances that have brought you here. You may take up temporary residence in the priest's quarters at the garrison. At present, he is absent from Annapolis."

"You are more than generous, monsieur."

The soldiers were instructed to disperse, and Armstrong personally led the visitors toward the fort, giving the impression he was about to entertain honoured guests.

The oddity of this event did not escape us as we continued our tasks in the shipyard. Although we were not privy to Mangeant's presentation to the council nor the telling of his story, the details would be revealed to us in good time. My great-uncle on my father's side, Abraham Bourg, was an Acadian delegate on the Lieutenant-Governor's Council and he would enlighten us.

True to our prediction, Uncle Abraham began his visits to the Acadian homes throughout the Annapolis community to reveal the nature of Mangeant's mysterious arrival at the colony. When he finally arrived at our home in Melanson Village, the fantastic story Uncle related was far more unusual than even we could have imagined. He spoke of how Mangeant, having immigrated to Acadia from Paris several years back, had arrived in Beaubassin, married one Marguerite Caissie, and then moved to Quebec, where he proceeded to amass a considerable fortune in the shipping industry. Apparently, Mangeant's fleet grew to such a size that he became one of the wealthiest men in New France.

The extraordinary details of the story were delivered with great ceremony by Uncle Abraham, who tended toward the histrionic.

"Mangeant explained that on board one of his own ships, after being at sea somewhere close to the entrance to the River St. Laurent, his captain, one Joseph Alphonse Lestage of Quebec, did, and I quote, 'most basely and heinously insult, affront, and provoke' him, forcing him to attack and wound said captain. The captain's wounds were so severe he died two days later. Evidence was submitted to the Admiralty Court at Quebec, where

Mangeant was found guilty of murder. Shortly after, he escaped on one of his ships with his family and a first mate, sailing continuously until he reached Annapolis. He has made a formal request to settle in our colony. And the most astounding development is that, in the presence of the council, he declared he was prepared to swear the oath of allegiance to King George without qualification.

"Could you trust such a man?"

He paused for dramatic effect, and then he resumed. "Apparently so, for our lieutenant-governor not only accepted Mangeant's story but declared that his actions against his captain were justified. Can you imagine? He believed every word of his story without question! Armstrong has assured his safety in Acadia, allowing him to settle here. I believe the lieutenant-governor was quite taken by the gentleman. Mangeant does have an exquisite carriage and impeccable manners."

My grandmother interrupted as expected. She had an opinion on most things.

"The lieutenant-governor got the consent of all those present, without any dissent?"

"Madame Melanson, the lieutenant-governor did not request our consent. Major Cosby seemed very suspicious of Mangeant, however, and not certain of his story or his motives for settling here, other than it was clear he was not able to flee to any French colony because of his murder conviction. Cosby cross-examined him relentlessly. I believe it was more to vex Armstrong than on account of any feelings he may have had against Mangeant."

"It is well known that the lieutenant-governor and Major Cosby share an enmity for one another," I interjected, wanting to contribute to the conversation.

"The fact is, Major Cosby is the brother-in-law of our ever-absent Governor Philipps, and Lieutenant-Governor Armstrong sees him as both a threat and a spy. He feels Cosby's opposition at every turn. God bless Major Cosby."

"Amen," we all chanted in unison.

Chapter 6

With the arrival of Mangeant, we experienced a change in the atmosphere of the town. Darkness seemed to descend. Those living in the lower or upper town readied themselves for the next reign of terror and, therefore, the next round of negotiations with the British rulers. With little warning, Lieutenant-Governor Armstrong insisted that an unconditional oath of allegiance to the newly crowned King George II be taken by every French-speaking subject in Acadia. He publicly admonished Ensign Wroth, who had been sent to Grand Pré and Pisiquit to administer the oath to the French inhabitants, for accepting a conditional oath. When the Acadian delegates at Annapolis requested that the clause allowing the French to maintain their neutrality in wartime be accepted by the ruling council, the lieutenant-governor jailed the lot of them, including poor Uncle Abraham. In such times of trouble, most Acadians distanced themselves from the British as best they could until the storm passed.

This was easier for us at Melanson Village. We were at a distance of eight miles from Annapolis by road and four by river. My grandfather, Charles Melanson, had established our settlement close to the mouth of the Dauphin River, later known as the Annapolis River, in 1664. Our family farm faced directly across from Goat Island, known to us then as Île aux Chèvres. Grandmama always declared that the distance between us and the fort was a blessing from God. For the time being, she was correct.

Benjamin came to stay with us during this period because René had purchased land in the lower town and was building a stone residence to rent out. He travelled each day by boat to and from Annapolis with my brother Charles to work on this structure.

Now a young man, like me, Benjamin had retained the good looks he had possessed as a child. In truth, he was inordinately handsome. However, unlike many blessed with fine features, he had a profound inner toughness and a strong character. He also had a great commitment to fairness and justice, which would help define the rest of his short life.

Having been raised at Grand Pré, Benjamin had little contact with the British and had little fear of those that governed his community from a distance. He had been influenced by his grandfather in all things and chose to live with him in the last ten years of Uncle Pierre's life, thus insuring his inheritance of the ancestral home in Grand Pré. His father had remarried and had produced a household of new children. Benjamin was tutored in the ways of the English by a man born in Yorkshire, but he had learned from him that the British were not to be trusted. It was a matter of getting along, taking advantage when you could, and enjoying your freedom while it lasted.

One Sunday, after we had returned from mass at St. Jean Baptiste in Annapolis, Grandmama pointed to a huge wooden chest in the corner of the room. It was covered with an ancient woven rug. She directed Benjamin and me to use the key she was grasping tightly to unlock the chest. She then instructed us to lift the lid and discover what was inside. To our surprise, it was filled with muskets of every design and size.

"These were weapons my father designed and constructed over his lifetime," she remarked with pride. "Some date back to France some seventy years ago when he was gun-maker to the king. Do you know he invented muskets for King Louis's own musketeers? I wish to make you responsible for maintaining these weapons. Clean them and ensure that they are in working order. Promise me, Piau."

Benjamin and I were stunned by the appearance of this arsenal of vintage muskets.

"It would be a great honour, Grandmama. You can rely on me to get them in good working order." I could feel the privilege that was being bestowed upon me.

One day, while alone in the house, I decided to remove all the muskets from the box for cleaning. To my surprise I found documents at the bottom that were not the property of Abraham Dugas, my great-grandfather, but papers belonging to my grandfather, Charles Melanson — official letters, deeds, letters of appointment, and, startlingly, several journals written in English.

I should not have been surprised, I suppose. After all, my grandfather was born and raised in England and his mother tongue was not French but English. However, they were not writings from a time of English rule. They were more recent, dating from 1691 to 1695, when France was struggling to hold on to Acadia. I remember being told that this was a tumultuous time, plagued by English raids at Port Royal, a decade before the battle that took my father's life and brought Acadia under English rule for the final time.

My recollection of the rumours associated with my grandfather being a British spy resurfaced. I hesitated to discover the contents of the writings in case they confirmed the truth I had already suspected. I would leave them for another day, postponing the inevitable revelation that he was an English informant. I would wait until I felt prepared to learn their secrets. Nevertheless, only a lifetime of hardships and misery have allowed me to accept them in the context in which they were written.

Curiosity and fear were my constant companions over the next few weeks. I could not erase the thought of my grandfather's letters, nor the fear of what they contained. This feeling was only heightened by the troubles in Annapolis.

I stole moments of solitude when I could and began to read the personal correspondence first. My mother's oldest sister, Marie, had moved to Boston when she was a girl to live with her grandmother Priscilla Laverdure, following the death of her husband. Marie never returned home; she was educated there and married a Boston merchant, David Basset. Judging from the letters, it was her father, Charles, who made regular visits to his mother and daughter in New England. I had not known this.

By the time I had completed Aunt Marie's letters, I felt I had known her all my life. A person's character reveals itself in his or her writing. After Marie had married Basset, she moved her grandmother into her husband's home to live out the remainder of her life in a warm and loving household. Judging from her responses to the letters she had received from my grandfather, he was keeping her well informed of all the goings-on at Melanson Village and, more importantly, the movements and policies of the French at Port Royal. It was apparent that her husband was relaying this information to the governor in Boston. The details could only be imagined.

I decided to question my grandmother about Marie and Basset without giving away that I was secretly reading her husband's correspondence.

"Grandmama, what can you tell me about your son-in-law David Basset? I have heard his name mentioned several times in connection with Aunt Marie in Boston and I am curious about the nature of his business."

A look of fury appeared on the old woman's face. "I do not mention that name in my home. He was a scoundrel and as close to the devil as anyone I ever set eyes on. I will only tell you that three years ago he was found aboard his ship in the West Indies with his throat slit from ear to ear — a fitting end for someone who had caused only misery to those close to him — especially my daughter Marie, who is an angel!"

"But what of his business?" I persisted.

"I will say only this. He was a privateer, and although he made plenty of money for his efforts, most of it was earned illegally. Every British pound he pocketed was soaked in blood. Where there was trouble, you could expect Basset to be there. For certain he is eternally damned!"

I never mentioned Basset again, but the contents of the letters and journals now made sense.

Complicity! Complicity! Complicity! That was what I thought as I read my grandfather's journal entry dated May 20, 1690. He spoke of having been taken at daybreak to a British command ship by his son-in-law David Basset, having already seen seven English ships dropping anchor at Goat Island the night before. Basset apparently was in command of one of the New England vessels. He described a meeting he had with the commander, Sir William Phips, where he was questioned about the state of the fort at Port Royal and the number of soldiers and cannons present there. He admitted to delivering the requested information hoping that no resistance would come from the French garrison and that a peaceful surrender would be achieved, thus sparing the town and his own settlement pillaging and destruction.

He wrote that Phips had warned that he possessed seven hundred and fifty armed men at the ready to attack the fort and had urged him to deliver such warning to Governor Meneval at Port Royal. Grandfather said he had met with the French governor later that day and the governor had reluctantly agreed to surrender without a fight.

He described how agitated Meneval had been on hearing the British threat. The French governor lamented that of the seventy soldiers in his command, half were out game hunting and those left behind were without arms. He despaired that he was sitting in a fortress that was barely constructed. The old fort had been destroyed earlier in the year in order that a newer stronger one could be built. The governor had fumed at Grandfather out of sheer frustration. He had insisted that there be honourable terms of surrender.

His next journal entry was dated May 21, 1690. Grandfather wrote that he accompanied Father Petit to Sir William Phips's ship to discuss the terms of surrender. The terms agreed upon were that the troops at Port Royal were to retain their arms and personals and be permitted to return to France. The church and its properties were to remain as they were and the priests were to continue to serve the Acadian community. The people living in and around the town were to be left in peace. Grandfather seemed overjoyed with the results of his efforts. "We are so blessed at the outcome!"

His entry on May 22, however, described the horrible reality of the previous day's negotiations. News from the fort had been grim. Some Acadian residents of the town had fled to Melanson Village to escape the pillaging. They informed Grandfather that Phips had broken the terms of surrender, had imprisoned Governor Meneval and his soldiers in the church, levelled and burned the fort, removed the cannons, destroyed the cross, looted the church, killed the livestock, and emptied His Majesty's storehouses. They had confiscated china, pewter, and even the priest's vestments. They took everything they could find.

Grandfather's written response to these events seemed to contain a small dose of bewilderment with a large dose of resignation. Can you imagine such quick resignation? Was he happy with the outcome? I could not detect any feelings of remorse from his journal. I stopped reading immediately. I was filled with such strong feelings of indignation. To think this man's blood ran through mine and was mixed with the blood of my heroic father. I immediately felt I had been poisoned by the things I had read. And at that point I craved the sage advice of old Uncle Pierre, who regrettably was no longer with us. I realize now that he would have simply said his brother was a misguided man.

Chapter 7

The spring at Annapolis released the natural urges of the young and awakened romantic feelings in all of us. I was no different. After the planting was completed, free time along the river brought us into contact with the young Acadian girls. It was essential for me to have Benjamin along. His beauty and charisma meant that wherever Benjamin walked so also did a parade of young ladies of varying ages. He also had an ease about him that I lacked. I considered myself quite presentable but I felt greater comfort in the company of men. The one thing I was not tutored in was wooing the opposite sex.

My mother kept reminding me I was twenty-one and single, but I thought, well, my brother Jean was still unmarried although he was four years my senior. However, because he was the senior male in a household of two widows, he was exempt from the pressure that my mother was putting on me. He operated the farm and fulfilled the duties of the man of the house for Mother and Grandmama. I was expected to find a suitable wife from outside Melanson Village — finding a spouse in my community was impossible since everyone was related where I had uncles, aunts, and cousins by the dozens. Arrangements had to be made to unite several communities so the young people could socialize and eventually pair up for marriage.

An opportunity arose in June. Grandmama was soon to celebrate the eightieth anniversary of her birth, and given her status as matriarch of not only Melanson Village but all the Acadian communities along the Annapolis River, a huge celebration was planned to coincide with the summer solstice. It was to be held at our settlement. The day of the event, fishing boats and schooners transported hundreds of families along the river to our village opposite Goat Island. They arrived early in the day and set up tents to accommodate those who would stay overnight. Many came from as far as Gaudet Village, twenty miles up the river, and Belle Isle, Paradise, and, of course, neighbouring Annapolis Royal.

It was a perfect day for the festivities. A hovering cloud of pink apple blossoms formed a brilliant backdrop above the village; a warm northwest breeze sent an intoxicating aroma from the orchards on the hill, wrapping everyone in a cloud of delirious floral scents. The cloudless sky was a deep blue, and the sun shone well into the evening, welcoming the summer solstice.

Grandmama appeared younger than her eighty years, with her youthful spirit defying her aging body. She paraded proudly through Melanson Village, the settlement she had helped found, stopping to chat with each of her descendants and friends, never forgetting a single name, always spreading her pearls of wisdom as if she had an endless storehouse of experience to convey. Sometimes she feigned a scolding manner, if only to make the children laugh.

The day was filled with fine food placed on tables in everyone's front garden. Games were played in the streets, and the music that accompanied the singing and the dancing seemed to emanate from every corner of the village. On such a day, everyone was united and filled to the brim with the warmth of the Acadian community.

The evening was ignited by a huge bonfire at the water's edge, and the young and the old danced about the fire to the music of violins, spoons, triangles, and jaw harps. As midnight approached, it was my turn to pay tribute. I chose to sing the song I had learned on Grandmama's knee when I was a small child. A silence came over the crowd as I began to sing the first notes of "À la claire fontaine," a song about that magical place in Provence and lost love.

> À la claire fontaine, m'en allant promener
> J'ai trouvé l'eau si belle, que je m'y suis baigné.
> Il y a longtemps que je t'aime,
> Jamais je ne t'oublierai.

That evening my voice soared hauntingly over the night visitors, surprisingly casting a spell on all those present, especially the guest of honour. By the light of the fire, I could see the tears in my grandmother's eyes, noticing she was not the only one. It was the first time I had felt the power of my singing voice. And it was the first time I noticed Jeanne, staring mysteriously into the bonfire as I sang. She appeared to be in a world of her own, quite separate from the hundreds of people humming to the sound of the music. It was then I knew she was my destiny.

Destiny, however, requires persuasion. Jeanne Gaudet was not someone I knew. She lived as far up the Annapolis River as one could sail by boat. If I was to make an impression on her, I would have to use all the resources I could muster. It was necessary for me to seek the counsel of someone who was acquainted with her. Then I had to arrange a face-to-face meeting.

All those participating in Grandmama's celebration seemed to evaporate by noon the following day. One of my cousins who had been seated beside Jeanne the previous evening told me her name and the name of her parents.

I solicited Benjamin's help, hoping he might assist me in tracking her down. It was far easier than I could have hoped for.

"I know her father, Bernard Gaudet, very well," Benjamin volunteered. "He and his brother Denys are managing the timber construction on my father's new house in the lower town. I work with them daily."

You could imagine my excitement at that moment. I saw this as an unexpected opportunity. The first steps in my plan to court Monsieur Gaudet's daughter would be to acquaint myself with her father and then to garner his favour.

"The Gaudet brothers are masters of timber construction, which we call *la charpente bois*," Benjamin continued. "My father knew of their expertise and hired them to construct the timber frame for the roof of the new house. I am responsible for the stonemasonry below. Their uncle, Pierre Gaudet, did the *charpente bois* construction on the fort. Bernard and Denys were his apprentices."

"Could you use an assistant mason?" I asked with a wry smile on my face. "I learned some lessons in masonry from Uncle Pierre and your father at Grand Pré."

Benjamin understood my intentions immediately. "I would enjoy your company and, of course, I would appreciate your assistance." He then proceeded to laugh uncontrollably.

Chapter 8

Overnight I became a mason's assistant. I joined my brother Charles and Benjamin the following morning and sailed into the harbour at Annapolis to begin my quest. Charles proceeded to the shipyard while Benjamin and I walked to René's building site in the lower town. When we arrived, Bernard Gaudet and his brother were already directing the workers where to place the large pieces of timber. Benjamin hesitated to interrupt them, but the Gaudets were vigilant enough to note the presence of a new worker on the site. Before we could utter a word, Bernard Gaudet spoke.

"Bonjour, Benjamin. It is a perfect day for laying stones. I see you have a new assistant. Young Pierre Belliveau, I believe."

I could barely contain my surprise. I stood there motionless.

"You made quite an impression the other evening. Your grandmother was much pleased with your gift of song and, I would say, exceedingly proud. Allow me to introduce myself and my brother. I am Bernard Gaudet and this is Denys."

We shook hands, and he continued, "I knew your father very well when we were young boys. He was a very courageous man who ended his short life a hero. You look very much like him."

The only response I could muster was, "I appreciate your kind words, monsieur."

That being said, we proceeded to do our work.

As the day progressed, I realized I had the situation and the goal but not the plan. How was I going to manage an introduction to Jeanne Gaudet?

When we finally completed our work for the day, I took the opportunity to question Gaudet about his family.

"Monsieur Gaudet, did your family accompany you to my grandmother's celebration or did they remain in Gaudet Village? It is quite a distance to travel." My tone was intentionally one of casual interest.

I noticed a quizzical look come across his face, perhaps in response to a question that appeared to come right out of nowhere. But his response was congenial.

"Indeed, my wife and children all sailed downriver for the occasion. Living so far away, we do not often have the opportunity to attend large community gatherings. They thoroughly enjoyed themselves and now have returned home. You may have noticed them and not known who they were."

Benjamin smiled but remained silent. Gaudet began to sense something from the conversation, and he certainly noticed my cousin's knowing look.

"Perhaps you caught sight of my three beautiful daughters." He paused to study my reaction. "Isabelle is the most beautiful by any standard. Perhaps, if you are unmarried, you might be able to wait a few years and court her."

The unfamiliar name left me speechless. I began to feel uncomfortable.

"In twelve years you will be how old? Thirty, perhaps? Isabelle is only seven years old. For certain every girl grows to be a woman. Are you in any particular hurry to find a bride, young man?"

At that point, I was aware that I was being trifled with, but with a playful spirit. This fed my courage. I thought at this point it probably would be the best policy to be honest about my intent. That should be evidence of my good character and honourable motives.

"I must be perfectly honest, monsieur, that it was your older daughter, Jeanne, who caught my eye. She appeared to have such a sense of mystery about her. At the party, she was conspicuous by her reserve and calm."

Gaudet seemed stunned by my honesty. And for the first time that day, he was the one who was speechless.

Sensing his sudden lack of ease, I continued without restraint. "I realize you must find my manner and words extremely forthright, even a bit impertinent. But I have always been afflicted with bold speech. It has more than once gotten me into trouble but it is not something I find easy to contain. In my family, speaking your mind is encouraged. My grandmother insists on it."

Gaudet looked at his brother, then Benjamin. He suddenly burst into a laughter that could be heard as far away as the fort.

"Your grandmother insists on it, does she?" He continued to laugh so uproariously that I thought he might collapse from apoplexy.

Benjamin and I returned home that day, not having resolved the dilemma I had found myself in. But there would be another day. Bernard Gaudet was without a doubt aware that I had put a stake in the ground where his daughter was concerned.

Chapter 9

Days passed with mere pleasantries at the work site. But ominous murmurs from the fort changed all that. Lieutenant-Governor Armstrong was on a sacred mission to have the entire colony take the unqualified oath. Mangeant's willingness to take the oath of allegiance without qualification only encouraged Armstrong in his quest. The royal favourite, as he was called by those at the garrison, was getting under everyone's skin. It was then that Bernard Gaudet began to rant.

"I don't know why I did not relocate to Île Royale years ago. Denys and I had the opportunity to move to Louisbourg. We could have had a good life there. At least we would have been saved from this continuous oath business. And that demon Armstrong, he could unsettle the patience of a saint, *mon Dieu!*"

"Hold your tongue, brother!" Denys cautioned. "We do not need trouble. The walls of the buildings in this town have ears. You made your choice to return to Annapolis years ago. Remember, we still have the advantage of distance from the fort. Gaudet Village is our refuge. Life is wonderful there. Continue to work and keep your opinions to yourself!"

Later, I asked Gaudet about Louisbourg.

"Monsieur, you visited Île Royale?"

By this time, he had calmed himself sufficiently and was able to manage a civil answer to my question.

"We not only visited, we lived there for close to two years. Our departure to Île Royale is a fascinating story." His enthusiasm for storytelling seemed to return. "Thinking we might move to Louisbourg, we decided to visit there and investigate the land and the people's life. We had heard that a group of Acadians from Annapolis had travelled to Île Royale to make an official investigation for those who might wish to migrate. We were not authorized to join the group, but we obtained a passport to fish in the bay as a pretext for joining the delegation. Denys and I hid our fishing boat at St. Croix and boarded the ship and sailed to Port Toulouse, where we spent a short time. Then we continued on to Louisbourg."

I was captivated.

"To our great good fortune, our building skills were much prized in the French colony. We practised our beam construction on the governor's house at Louisbourg, can you believe it, and on many other homes of import-ant Frenchmen there. The building trade kept us busy and it became quite profitable. However, the land beneath our feet was made of solid rock. One could walk on the water, there were so many fish in the sea, but the land was barren. And the fogs were so thick you could barely see the sea or the land for days on end. As for farming, such an enterprise was impossible. You could plant nothing but turnip and cabbage. We considered ourselves build-ers, but more importantly we saw ourselves as keepers of the land, much as our ancestors had at Port Royal and in France. A man has no soul if he is not tilling the soil or rescuing the salt marshes from the sea. This is what makes one an Acadian. His dikes and his fertile soil mean everything to him!

"So we returned home after two years abroad. Our boat was still safely hidden at St. Croix." He began to laugh. "I am not certain anyone at the fort noticed our long absence. Perhaps those who granted us our passports thought it was a particularly long fishing expedition!"

We all began to laugh. The company was merry. I liked Bernard Gaudet — exceedingly!

Chapter 10

The business of the oath began to heat up to such a degree at Annapolis that most of the men at René's building site agreed it would be prudent to escape the flames flickering around them. Gaudet declared he was leaving Annapolis and was returning home to Gaudet Village.

"My friends, it is time to leave here before we are forced to do what we know we cannot possibly do. And you all know what that is. I was wondering, young Belliveau, whether we might impose on your brother Charles to transport us home in his *chaloupe*. We have no vessels, since ours returned home when our families sailed upriver after your grandmother's birthday celebration. Perhaps you could stay on at my home as a guest. It is summer, and life in the upper river is especially pleasant at this time of year. And there are many amusements which you might find attractive."

Gaudet was giving me his blessing to court his daughter Jeanne. It was an invitation I could not refuse.

A short time later the mood was altered by the sound of approaching soldiers. They appeared in the lower town, led by the lieutenant-governor himself, who was, in turn, accompanied by the royal favourite, Mangeant, and Major Cosby, chief officer of the military. They carried with them a sense of fear and intimidation as they made their way through the streets of Annapolis to the town square.

Everyone was ordered into the street to hear Armstrong's proclamation. Mangeant acted as translator, which gave the order an even more sinister tone.

"Be advised that all adult inhabitants of the town and surrounding areas must gather at the church no later than tomorrow at noon to take the oath of allegiance to the newly crowned king of England. Those who fail to do so risk imprisonment in the garrison jail. Members of the Acadian Council are still in custody there as an example to the rest of the community."

The tone in Mangeant's voice matched the vehemence in Armstrong's. The royal favourite appeared to enjoy his superior status in the square.

Soon after the regiment returned to the fort, I volunteered to go to Charles at the shipyard to arrange a hasty departure. Charles was already aware of the proclamation and quickly agreed to my request to leave for Gaudet Village. I believe he was as relieved as the rest of us to have an excuse to get as far away from Annapolis as possible, if only for a short time. We Acadians had cultivated a variety of escape routes to avoid the will of the lieutenant-governor.

Our exit went unnoticed. Although we evacuated the building site with great speed, no one in the fort could have suspected our destination. Charles carried passengers to and from Melanson Village daily, so our departure caused no suspicion. We were fortunate in our timing. The direction of the tide was in our favour. Not only did we have the advantage of a southwest wind, but the river was approaching its high tide. Charles would be able to drift downstream with the tide when he sailed home.

Our journey up the Annapolis River was a revelation to me. Along the way the rich grain fields danced in the breezes and filled our sails with the warmth and energy of late summer. The river meandered through the verdant valley protected by the North Mountain on its left side and the South Mountain on its right. This protection created a natural haven for growing and grazing. We sailed by Belle Isle and Paradise, apt names for both communities. The further we floated upstream, the freer I felt. Nearing Gaudet Village I was seized by a sense of peace I had not experienced since my winters at Grand Pré with Uncle Pierre and Isabelle — and by a new awareness of the path I was to take on my life's journey.

As Charles's *chaloupe* approached the shore at Gaudet Village, I felt like Moses being greeted by the daughters of Midian. Every woman and child of the colony came out to meet us. I presumed it was because of the unexpected return of their patriarch, Bernard.

It was a unique experience for me to witness so many unfamiliar faces. Arriving at such an isolated community was not something that many experienced in their lifetime. For an unmarried young Acadian man it was particularly poignant. I searched the faces of the young women, hoping to spot Jeanne's. Would I recognize her in the light of day? Would the memory of her profile lit by the light of a wood fire fail me? My self-doubt was interrupted by Bernard Gaudet's hardy cry.

"Bonjour, my lovelies! I come bearing gifts. I bring two handsome young men to brighten your day and stimulate romance in our little village!" He broke into his familiar laughter while embracing his wife and daughters. Benjamin and I cautiously disembarked, leaving Charles at the helm of his boat.

"Join us, Charles Belliveau, and rest a while before returning downriver. Perhaps you can catch tomorrow's tide or possibly the next day's. Each day away will soften your arrival back at Annapolis."

Charles understood that this was wise advice.

"If you have sufficient room for all three of us, Monsieur Gaudet, I will accept your kind invitation."

"That is excellent, monsieur. It is the least I can do to repay you for transporting us home."

Gaudet continued to shout. "Attention, everyone! Allow me to introduce our honoured guests, brothers Charles and Pierre Belliveau, grandsons of Madame Marie Melanson, and their handsome young cousin, Benjamin LeBlanc from Grand Pré, grandson of the venerable and now deceased Pierre Laverdure. I beg you to make them feel welcome."

The growing crowd of villagers spontaneously began to applaud. This was an unusual way of welcoming visitors, and it caught us quite by surprise. Although I was aware of receiving considerable attention, once Benjamin was introduced all eyes were on him. I was, however, not slighted in the least. His beauty and presence demanded such attention, no matter where he went.

We followed the crowd along the road to Gaudet's impressive timbered home. It stood as a model of the building construction he had perfected over the years. It was a more sophisticated and elaborate version of what I had seen at Annapolis — truly a monument to his life as a master builder.

As the crowd reached the threshold of the Gaudet home, the front door slowly opened and there appeared Jeanne. My heart skipped a beat as I stood there nervously gazing at her. Until this day, the image of her standing there remains vivid in my mind. Her bright eyes startled me. Her beautiful face was luminous in the evening sun. She was statuesque and dignified. I thought at that moment, *How can I make myself deserving of such an angel?*

Jeanne greeted her father with a warm embrace and a kiss on both cheeks. "Welcome home, Papa. We were not expecting you for at least another week."

"My dear, Annapolis became far too hot for us so we decided to come home to the cool and peace of our little valley."

He paused and smiled with an impish grin. "Daughter, I wish to introduce our guests, Monsieur Pierre Belliveau, his brother Charles, and their cousin Benjamin LeBlanc. They will be visiting with us for a time. The two young men are masons from Melanson Village and Grand Pré. Perhaps we will put them to work while they remain with us."

Jeanne stood before us but did not appear surprised to be in the presence of strangers. Her look was of someone who regularly received visitors. With a polite curtsy, she gave us a smile that seemed to me to illuminate the entire village. Such was my feverish state of mind.

There was a certain expectation in the air. Time had suddenly stopped. The players were all present, but how things would work out was still a mystery to me. I was faced with a situation that I couldn't control; nor was I assured of the outcome. Was my future here or would I be forced to float downriver to a different one? As always, I decided to jump into the deep water of uncertainty and swim relentlessly until I reached my goal.

Jeanne closed the door of the Gaudet home and joined the crowd gathered in the courtyard. She was accompanied by her sisters, Madeleine and Isabelle. They were as their father had described them. Madeleine sought out some of her cousins, but Isabelle was quite intent on investigating Benjamin and me.

Isabelle curtsied to us and was the first to speak. "I am Isabelle. Welcome to Gaudet Village."

She demonstrated a self-assurance that was beyond her years. She and Benjamin bonded immediately. Sensing this was an opportunity for me to be alone with Jeanne, he asked Isabelle to show him about the village. She was overjoyed to comply.

Now face to face with Jeanne, I was unexpectedly aware that she appeared to know exactly what role she was to play in the scenario we were about to act out. She was the first to speak.

"Monsieur Belliveau, I remember you from your grandmother's birthday celebration. The song you sang under the stars was beautiful. '*À la claire fontaine*' is my favourite love song. I do not believe I have ever heard anyone sing it so magnificently."

A sudden warm sensation overtook my body and I blushed.

"You are very kind to say so, mademoiselle. And please, call me Piau. Everyone does."

"Then, Piau, you may call me Jeanne."

Chapter 11

For the next month our spirits soared. The exhilaration Jeanne and I felt being in one another's company transcended the life we were experiencing each day. She performed her daily chores, and I helped place stone after stone on the new storehouse. Jeanne and her sisters visited the work site at regular intervals to provide the workers with food and refreshments. We found excuses to stroll along the river alone, not that anyone took particular notice. Courtship was a common ritual. These stolen moments allowed us to discover one another's innermost thoughts, relishing those unexpected brushes of our hands that sent shivers through my body. Other contact of any kind would be considered inappropriate before the courtship was formalized by a promise of marriage. Jeanne and I had to content ourselves with the intimacy that comes from deep conversation.

In the evening, I recounted stories from the Old Testament, ones seldom heard by those who did not possess a Bible. I had a captive audience. Jeanne requested that I retell the story of Ruth on several occasions. She loved the idea that a woman could be the central character in a book of the Bible. Bernard particularly enjoyed the story of Job because, as he said, patience was not one of his virtues. And I loved to glorify the story of Moses and the flight of the Israelites from Egypt. This was an important story for me, one that would inspire me throughout my life. I have always relished the strong message of hope it conveys.

Benjamin and Charles stayed at Gaudet Village for only four days. Both had to return to their lives and work at Annapolis. Charles would relay to my mother the message that I had decided to stay upriver for at least a month. At the end of that time he would return to retrieve me to help gather the harvest at Melanson Village. Benjamin had to revisit his father's building site in Annapolis to complete the masonry. René would arrive there in the early autumn and transport him home to Grand Pré, where he would remain for the winter at the Manor House.

Poor little Isabelle was distraught when Benjamin departed. She was only seven years old, but she was still hopelessly smitten. Their paths would cross again.

The autumn winds seemed to breathe life into my growing love for Jeanne. Not even the chilly evenings could cool my ardour. And although we never spoke of our feelings, we did not doubt them. As the month's end approached, I almost wished the tides would fail Charles in his journey to Gaudet Village. Such fancies had to be set aside and a decision had to be made if I was to capture the woman I loved. It was time to get Bernard's permission to seek Jeanne's hand in marriage. One day I asked to meet with him in private. We met in the garden.

"So, young Piau, what is it that requires such privacy? I suppose you are going to tell me you are leaving soon. This is not unexpected, but I must say you will be missed when you are gone. You have been more than helpful in constructing the storehouse. I would venture to say that because of your efforts it is the most magnificent one in all of Acadia. Furthermore, you have charmed many in this community. They, too, will regret your departure."

As he spoke, my emotions began to paralyze me, leaving me momentarily speechless. When I regained my composure, I was able to get right to the point, as was my custom.

"Monsieur Bernard, I know you are aware, and have been since before I arrived at Gaudet Village, of my intention to court your daughter. In our time together I have discovered that, for me, a life without Jeanne would be unimaginable. I believe she feels the same, although she has never said so in so many words. It is time for me to marry. I request permission to ask for Jeanne's hand. If you are so kind as to grant it, I promise I will strive to make her happy."

There was a deep silence. I saw tears in Bernard's eyes. After a pause, he spoke.

"Piau, you had my permission back in Annapolis, the day we met. I felt a sense of destiny in our first meeting. To unite our families by marriage is beyond anything I could hope for. God will bless both our houses with this union."

He then embraced me wordlessly. Bernard turned and walked toward the storehouse.

Ecstasy, ecstasy! I was free to express my feelings to Jeanne. My desire now was for her to share her feelings with me. What a romantic I had become!

When Jeanne and I sat on the garden bench under the harvest moon that evening, I wasted no time in getting right to the point. "Your father has given me permission to ask for your hand in marriage. I told him you would most certainly accept my proposal. Was that presuming too much?"

She rose from where we were seated and slowly walked to the garden gate. Gazing up at the night sky, she spoke. "Do you see the Big Dipper, there?" She pointed to the constellation I knew as the Big Bear. "It is filled to the brim, much like my heart."

Jeanne did not look at me when she uttered those words. There was a deafening silence between us, but I had said all I was able to say short of declaring my love outright. There was no need. She turned to me and smiled that extraordinary smile of hers, and our eyes met. She broke the silence and declared in a quiet voice, "Where you go, I will follow, where you lodge, I will lodge, and your home will be my home."

"The Book of Ruth!"

"*Certainement.*"

She placed her arm in mine and nonchalantly suggested, "Shall we go into the house and make the announcement?"

Charles returned to Gaudet Village as planned at the end of September. His arrival filled me with mixed feelings. The news he brought did not.

Charles reported that since I had been upriver things in Annapolis had gone from bad to miserable. The Acadian members of the council were still locked up in the jail, and many in the colony had chosen to spend long periods away from the town. They had sought excuses to be out at sea fishing or hunting in the woods. Many found reasons to assist the most distant villages with their harvests, neglecting their own. Their women and children became responsible for collecting the crops and managing the farms.

Armstrong was living up to his name. He was determined to have his way on the oath, and Mangeant was always at his side to reinforce his position. As an interpreter, the royal favourite intimidated the Acadians because he shared their language. It was difficult to hold their ground when everything they said could be adversely interpreted.

The most astonishing news was that the lieutenant-governor had declared the church upriver, the Chapelle St. Laurent, henceforth closed. The parishioners there were to be refused the services of a priest, forcing all Acadians to worship at St. Jean Baptiste, the parish church in Annapolis. This required the people to hold all their baptisms and marriages, and to receive the Eucharist, under the watchful eye of the lieutenant-governor. His spy, Mangeant, attended these functions.

The impact was felt strongly in the Gaudet home. My marriage to Jeanne now had to be celebrated in Annapolis. Given the disruption in the timing of our ceremony, we would have to postpone it until after Christmas, causing problems with winter travel. As the river froze and the snow collected in the woods, the coming together of the communities to celebrate our marriage would be impossible. We would begin our life together faced with the first of many challenges we were to endure. Looking back, I now know that it was the least significant one.

How were we to ensure that all the family members were there? The only solution was to have the Gaudet family sail with Charles and me to Melanson Village. It meant moving closer to the fire of the lieutenant-governor's wrath, but at least we all could be together for a Melanson Christmas. Grandmama and my mother knew how to celebrate the birth of Jesus in grand style, and the settlement had grown so large there would be no problem accommodating everyone. This was an opportunity for the two families to get to know one another. Our marriage would be attended by relatives and close friends. My only regret was that Benjamin would not be present. Given our love for one another, I would feel his absence keenly.

The sail down the Annapolis River was particularly pleasant in the fall of 1727. Acadians in the valley were enjoying an Indian summer, and the leaves were late in revealing their colours. The North and South Mountains were dressed in a riot of hues made more spectacular by the autumn sun. We floated with the tide in two vessels. Bernard believed that two boats were more comfortable than one — the second carried provisions to last through the winter season. Brother Denys remained at Gaudet Village with his family and promised to mind the two farms. He gave his niece Jeanne and me his wishes for good fortune in our future life together.

Any anxiety I may have felt as we travelled closer to the fort was relieved by Jeanne's presence seated at the bow of Charles's *chaloupe*. She faced into the wind like the figureheads one sees on grand ships, elegant and dignified. One could only imagine what she was thinking as we sailed down the river. Perhaps she was imagining her new life, perhaps her new family. As we journeyed past the garrison we noticed it was caught in a thick mist, a ghostly, abandoned-looking place. With any luck no one inside the fort would even notice our boat.

As our vessel came within sight of Goat Island we knew that home was near. Would my family know we were coming? Would they be surprised by the arrival of our visitors? Would they have guessed that I would return home betrothed? Certainly Charles must have informed my family and relatives at Melanson Village of my engagement. I was filled with excitement at all the possibilities our arrival would bring!

As we approached the shore at Melanson Village, we could see men in the fields harvesting with their scythes and sickles; in the distance we could make out the white-capped women and the children at the top of the hill collecting apples from the orchards. The entire settlement was a beehive of activity … I had not realized how much I had missed being home.

Our arrival took on the appearance of a tableau. On sighting our vessel, everyone in the settlement seemed to freeze on the spot. Were they curious to see who was arriving? In the distance, I spotted a lone white figure ambling down the main road of the village, coming from the direction of the Manor House. There was little doubt who that person was. My grandmother grew closer and closer, never slowing her pace. Even at her advanced age, there was such a determination in her gait. As she approached us near the shore she went directly to Jeanne. Then, with a permission she bestowed upon herself, she raised her arms and embraced the younger woman, leaving everyone spellbound.

"My dear, you are a blessing on our house. The Lord favours both our families with this betrothal. Your union with my grandson will enrich our bloodlines. The Melansons and Gaudets are among the most ancient of Acadian families."

Turning to face Bernard, Grandmama declared, "Welcome to our community, Monsieur Gaudet. You and your family honour us with your presence. May you and your kin be with us until the marriage has been solemnized before God at the church." There was little doubt that she was referring to St. Jean Baptiste in Annapolis. Every Acadian now knew that the Chapelle St. Laurent upriver was closed.

"Madame, it is *you* who honour us. We come bearing gifts of food from our harvest. They will benefit us all through the cold months of winter. If you would allow us, we will also use our skills to build an annex onto your house that will permit us all to dwell under your roof until the spring arrives. With strong young hands and my knowledge of construction, we can double the size of your Manor House."

"You overwhelm me, monsieur. We have barely spoken a dozen words and you are offering to enlarge my home. That is an offer I am unable to refuse. Bless you, Monsieur Gaudet."

"Call me Bernard, madame. We are now families united. Allow me to reintroduce my wife, Jeanne, my daughters Madeleine and little Isabelle. And my daughter Jeanne you are acquainted with."

The women curtsied politely and my grandmother addressed the group. "Come, let us be off to enjoy a warm hearth. You will become acquainted with my numerous descendants in the coming days."

Unexpectedly, as if everyone had suddenly evaporated, Grandmama embraced me, kissing me on both cheeks.

"I have missed you, Piau. When you are gone, part of my heart goes missing." She chuckled quietly. "Did your cheeks catch my kisses from the wind?"

"Indeed they did, Grandmama, indeed they did." I placed her arm in mine and we all sauntered up the hill to greet my mother.

Our entourage marched up the main street of the village, moving slowly toward the Manor House and receiving greetings from everyone we passed along the way. My mother was already strolling down the hill from the apple orchards. She was followed by a parade of children carrying baskets filled with apples. The pounding of their little wooden shoes on the ground boldly beat out the time to the song they were singing. Their fresh young voices serenaded us as we arrived at Grandmama's stone gate.

My mother was always known for her reserve, but on that day her face exuded love and joy. I took Jeanne by the hand and approached Mother, who was still surrounded by the excited children. Their instincts told them they were witnessing a special moment. The moment did not fail them. Taking our joined hands, my mother raised them up and kissed them, tears moistening her eyes. Then with a simple welcome she led us all through the gate and into the Manor House.

So began the uniting of the Gaudet clan with my own. It was decided that all the men should take up residence in Charles's home, with the women lodging at the Manor House. This situation continued until the annex was built in the final days of the harvest festival. We met every evening in the Manor House for food and entertainment. My family enjoyed the company of the Gaudets, especially Bernard, who was able to create a festive mood at work and at leisure time.

The temperate autumn weather helped make the construction of the annex fairly routine. Bernard had done this so many times that, with the huge number of cousins and uncles assisting with the timber work, the Manor House was expanded in very short order. The women of the settlement provided the workers with food and drink, and the children set about completing the smaller tasks of harvesting to pick up the slack. This kind of collective effort filled us all with a joyous sense of purpose and a belief that, working together, we could accomplish just about anything. We would be sustained by the memories of such times when we were called upon to endure incredible hardships.

By Christmas we were all settled into our daily routines, and the annex was complete. Once the snows arrived everyone was back in their homes, and the Gaudets were comfortably enjoying their separate quarters in the annex. Our new extended family added to our feeling of togetherness, especially during the season of light. We made and lit additional candles to honour the coming of the Christ Child, and hung spruce garlands laced with dried red cranberries along the ceiling to add to the festive mood.

In the evenings I would recite stories of the Nativity to our family as we warmed ourselves by the crackling fire. My audience was awed by the stories of the wise men from the east and the star that guided them to the baby Jesus. I left out nothing in my narrative, and even added additional details that were more a part of my personal inspiration than divine revelation.

It was also the season for all to raise their voices in song, me more than anyone else. We sang:

> *Il est né, le divin enfant,*
> *Jouez, hautbois, resonnez, musettes;*
> *Il est né, le divin enfant;*
> *Chantons tous son avènement!*
>
> *Depuis plus de quatre mille ans,*
> *Nous le promettaient les prophètes;*
> *Depuis plus de quatre mille ans,*
> *Nous attendions cet heureux temps.*
>
> *Il est né, le divin enfant …*

Whether it was the stories I told or the songs I sang, over time Jeanne came to look at me as if I were her own personal revelation. Her eyes would light up and her smile would broaden, inspiring floods of emotion that I could barely contain. Everyone surrounding us was caught in the warmth of our love, somehow believing it belonged to them as well.

Chapter 12

The wedding day was set for January 12. Preparing for the celebration at Melanson Village was easily accomplished, but getting into Annapolis where our union was to be solemnized presented problems. Travel by boat had become impossible as soon as the snows arrived. The guests who wished to be at the matrimonial mass would have to travel the road to the Chapelle St. Jean Baptiste by snowshoe. Most of the residents of the village decided they would remain behind to prepare for the later festivities.

Grandmama was not among them. She vociferously insisted on attending the ceremony at the church. Nothing on this earth could deter her from attending my marriage. Therefore, on the day of the wedding her grandchildren pulled the sled she had been harnessed into. She was the vision of a Snow Queen wrapped in furs from head to toe and topped by layers of rabbit fur blankets. Transporting my grandmother was a human team of snowshoeing youths, who synchronized their movements for the better part of five miles. Along the way, they sang to the rhythm of their snowshoes on the crusted snow.

The abbé met us at the front door of the church — Grandmama, Madame and Bernard Gaudet, my mother, Charles and his wife, Marguerite, Jean, my sister Madeleine, Jeanne's sisters, Madeleine and little Isabelle, and Grandmama's team of snowshoers. As the abbé led us into the chapel, we were surprised and overwhelmed to discover the church was filled to capacity with friends and relatives from the town, there to honour me, my family, and perhaps the memory of my father. Their smiles, as we walked in procession down the centre aisle, lit up the church with goodwill and joy.

Once we were all settled at the front of the church, the abbé spoke, "Welcome, everyone."

Out of deference and respect for my grandmother, he added, "Madame Marie, you honour us with your presence."

The abbé then began the marriage ceremony: "Every time two people enter into the sacrament of marriage, it is a special time of rejoicing. God looks down upon their union and bestows his divine blessing on them as we witness their commitment with our support and love. Let us —"

The abbé's address was interrupted by a sudden commotion from out-side the church. The expression on his face changed from joy to concern. The sound of marching feet, becoming ever louder, paralyzed all those present. Everyone exchanged agitated looks: they knew this could have only one meaning. Silence reigned. Suddenly the door at the rear of the church swung open with no regard for the solemnity of the event.

Soldiers from the militia filed into the church. Filling the aisles all the way to the front, they took their positions and stood at attention.

"Make way for His Excellency, the lieutenant-governor!"

The parishioners turned in their seats at the sound of the command-er's voice.

Lieutenant-Governor Armstrong appeared in the doorway. He strutted imperiously up the centre aisle. Mangeant followed. Armstrong ignored the congregation in their seats, directing his gaze precisely at me. He smiled a sinister smile, but I was determined not to show any uneasiness. Once he reached Jeanne and me standing before the altar, he turned and faced the congregation, never changing his expression. The favourite was by his side, prepared to translate.

"It has only come to my notice this very hour that a wedding was taking place here. With a large gathering such as this, I, as lieutenant-governor, take particular notice, when, in the past four months, Acadian families seem to have been scattered to the eight winds. This is an indication there is a grand avoidance going on in this colony. May I remind you that the matter of the oath has not been resolved, and on any occasion that I have demanded your appearance in this very church, you have failed to comply with my commands. Father Saint Poncey is presiding here because your former pastor, Breslay, was a vile traitor, conspiring with the French col-onies and the Native peoples, undermining British rule here. And I wish you to know that many here today have failed to demonstrate loyalty to His Majesty the King. This disloyalty is all too apparent as I observe the villages and the towns of this British colony.

"Monsieur Belliveau, you and your family have been particularly elusive these past months. I congratulate you and your bride on your marriage, but I wish you to know that you and your family will not escape my notice in future."

Before Mangeant could translate the lieutenant-governor's final sentence, my grandmother rose from her seat and boldly addressed Armstrong in English with such power that he was rendered speechless.

"Sir, we accept your presence here as a guest, to witness this important event in our community, but the alarming tone in your voice shows a gross lack of propriety and it offends everyone here. I have lived in Acadia for more than eighty years, both under French rule and under English governance. My deceased husband was a proud Englishman to his core and a loyal subject to their majesties. Because we are French-speaking does not mean that we are disloyal. Perhaps, in time, those who govern us at the garrison will understand this most important truth."

She turned to face the altar and demanded, as only a matriarch could, that the priest proceed with the ceremony.

Those looking on saw that the lieutenant-governor had met his match in my grandmother. She had swept him aside like a horse would a fly on a hot summer's day. He bowed to my grandmother and marched down the aisle, containing his rage as he exited the building. Mangeant lagged behind. The military guard obediently followed their superior, but no one could ignore their smiles as they left the church.

Grandmama and Father Saint Poncey exclaimed in unison, "Let us proceed!"

So began our life together, Jeanne and I, a life filled with great joys and incomprehensible hardships. Through it all, we would never lose hope. Our faith in one another sustained us through the worst calamities imaginable.

Our first year of marriage was a time of personal discovery, both physical and spiritual. The annex that Bernard and my family built was to be our nesting place in the coming year, 1728. In the spring, the Gaudets returned home by river, having forged an unbreakable bond with my family. Over the six months they lived in Melanson Village, they contributed to settlement life, insuring a safe haven for Jeanne and the children she was to bear.

Following the wedding, Jean began showing a quiet interest in Jeanne's sister Madeleine, but both were too shy to proclaim their feelings for one another. Of course, their attraction was not lost on Bernard. He got considerable pleasure from teasing them when they were around one another. Some relationships require a long incubation period, and theirs was not to hatch for a few more years. Their sweet natures were destined to meld into one, but like some birds, they would fly away all too soon.

The next year, God granted us two blessings: the first was the birth of our daughter Marguerite on January 18, 1729, and the other was the departure of Lieutenant-Governor Armstrong, who left our colony in the spring. Plagued by discontent in the rank and file of the military and by what he considered the insubordination of his second-in-command, Major Cosby, he decided to return to England to lodge complaints and discuss his governorship with the Board of Trade at Westminster.

Mangeant sailed with him. This signalled the return of the long-absent Governor Philipps. A collective sigh of relief passed over the towns and villages of the colony when the news arrived. The king's French-speaking subjects descended on Annapolis from every part of Acadia to greet the governor, who had not been in residence for nearly ten years. As his ship arrived in St. Mary's Bay, a flotilla of schooners and *chaloupes* from all over Acadia was there to hail his return. This was the start of a much welcome period of peace for my people.

PART 2:

BENJAMIN

Chapter 13

Some lives burn more brightly than others, and their light shines on those who have been fortunate enough to bask in its illumination. My beloved cousin Benjamin possessed such a light. He exuded not only goodness but unfaltering determination, fearlessness, intelligence, and an uncompromising sense of justice. Such a person can inspire many things: admiration in some and resentment in others, courage in some and fear in others, understanding in some and skepticism in others, moral rectitude in some and guilt in others.

Despite all of Benjamin's outstanding qualities, his father seemed little interested in the remarkable son that he had sired. Indeed, after René LeBlanc remarried and began his life with a new wife, Benjamin seemed to be largely forgotten by his father. René's new children — one child seemed to be born every year for the next fifteen years — instead occupied his attention.

Given this situation, Benjamin decided it would be more to his liking to remain with his grandfather, my Uncle Pierre. Uncle Pierre was a widower, and although his mind was keen to the end, his old body began to seriously fail him. At twelve, Benjamin began to take on duties that were far beyond his years. His two younger sisters, the children of Isabelle, also remained in the great Manor House. The old mansion became a place for the very young and the very old. Madame Thibideau, the housekeeper, rounded out the occupants of Pierre's home.

When Uncle Pierre died at Grand Pré some years later, he left his entire estate to Benjamin. Overnight, young Benjamin LeBlanc became one of the wealthiest landowners in Acadia. The estate was so well managed and the income so secure that Uncle Pierre's property ran itself. Despite being put in the odd situation of now working for his son, René, the notary at Grand Pré, continued to manage Uncle's business, as he had when the old man was alive. The estate continued to trade with New England merchant ships, French merchant ships, schooners from other communities in Acadia, and the garrison at Annapolis. With the arrival of Governor Philipps, Benjamin's prosperity seemed to know no bounds. He was only nineteen years old.

In the early summer of 1729 I met up with Benjamin again. A group from Melanson Village was to join Charles and his wife on his newly built schooner sailing for Grand Pré. They were visiting her parents at Minas. Since Jeanne had never been to Grand Pré, and since I was anxious to return there after many years to visit Benjamin, whom I hadn't seen since before my marriage, we decided to join them.

Little Isabelle, who was now ten, insisted on coming with us. She had been visiting with us and spending time with her new niece, who had been born to us the previous January. The baby was now five months old and Isabelle was absolutely enraptured with her. Her most important reason for wishing to sail with us was the wish to see Benjamin again. She was seven the last time she saw him, but her memory of him was still strong. Over time, her imagination had transformed Benjamin into a handsome prince.

Our journey to Grand Pré was a pleasant one. I was surprised, though, by a significant change that greeted us on our arrival in Annapolis Basin. The number of vessels at anchor there far exceeded what I had seen in any of my earlier visits; indeed, it seemed to be almost double. The explanation for that change lay with the arrival of Governor Philipps. He had endeavoured to establish peaceful relations with the neigbouring Natives and with the French and, as a result, prosperous trading now abounded.

Ships arrived from all parts of the continent, the West Indies, and Western Europe, prepared to trade their goods. Although the Mi'kmaqs in Acadia had not been friendly with the English, the presence of the new governor relaxed their antipathy and trade in furs increased. Beaver pelts were highly prized by the Europeans, and the felt hat business was thriving amongst the gentry across the ocean.

The day we sailed through the gut into the great bay, the water was unusually calm. Our schooner caught the incoming tide and rode a wave all the way along the coastline. We passed the North Mountain, which was covered with the fresh green of summer. As we passed Cape Blomidon, I regaled Jeanne and Isabelle with Mi'kmaq stories of the Great Spirit Glooscap.

"The Mi'kmaq say that Glooscap was the first human being on earth and that he had magical powers. His home is said to be on top of that mountain." I pointed in the direction of Blomidon. "There is a story that two men came to the mighty Glooscap and asked him for the use of his canoe so they could travel on the Great Sea. Glooscap agreed to their request and told them to go to the shore of the bay where they would find his canoe. When they arrived at the shore, they could not find his canoe. They returned to Glooscap, told him they had not found his canoe, and asked him where they could find it. He returned with them to the shore and pointed to an island off the coast.

"'There is my canoe,' he said, referring to the island. 'Go there and sail away as you please.'

"The men were startled by his answer but they followed his instructions. Once on the island, they realized that this was indeed Glooscap's canoe and they sailed magically away, experiencing many wondrous adventures on the Great Sea. Can you imagine that, Isabelle?"

Isabelle stared at Blomidon for a moment and looked quizzically at me. "Did the canoe ever return?" she asked. She wore a mischievous smile.

Confounded, I hardly knew what to answer. "You will have to climb the mountain some day and ask Glooscap in person!"

"Piau, it is only a legend. Legends exist to teach us lessons."

"Aren't you a clever girl! And what lesson do you think is being taught here?"

She paused momentarily. "Do not loan your canoe to strangers. They may not return it!"

Isabelle's reply made us all laugh. Her bold and saucy answer was a perfect reflection of her personality — forthright, with no nonsense but with a good sense of fun.

Amused and entertained, Jeanne sat quietly with the baby while Isabelle continued to pepper me with questions.

"Madame Belliveau says Benjamin lives in the grandest house in all Acadia. Is that true, Piau?"

"I have not seen all the houses in Acadia, but Benjamin's certainly must be one of the most magnificent!"

"Does he live there alone?"

"No, he has two younger sisters who live with him."

"Do you think Benjamin will remember me, Piau?"

"Of course he will. You are unforgettable," I assured her.

"I believe when I become a woman I will marry Benjamin. I certainly do not want any other woman to marry him. Perhaps I will have to tell him, so he can wait for me to grow up. If he did marry someone else, my life would be ruined!"

She spoke with such earnestness that I was forced to contain my urge to laugh. I knew from experience that one does not trifle with a young girl's fantasy.

It was time to change the subject. We were entering the basin at Minas and the summer sun was beginning to slowly sink in the western sky. The light it cast upon the valley was a deep orange — the fields of grain and corn were bathing in its warmth.

"We are nearing Grand Pré." I could feel the excitement rising in me as we approached the community I knew so well from my youth. This was the first time I had seen it in summer. I marvelled at its beauty and at the abundance I saw everywhere. "As you can see, it is a paradise here. It is like the Garden of Eden. Is it not beautiful?"

A light breeze from the northeast filled the sails of our schooner as we tacked into the harbour at Grand Pré. A lone figure strolled hurriedly along the length of the wharf. I could tell by the familiar movements it was Benjamin. Tears welled up in me and it was at that point I realized how much I had missed him and how many memories were caught up in this place. As he grabbed the rope to tie the vessel to its mooring, he smiled and greeted us with such magnanimity that we immediately felt welcome.

"*Bienvenue à Grand Pré!*" he cried. "I have been looking forward to your visit for weeks. Piau, Charles, Marguerite, Jeanne, and — oh my goodness, can this be Isabelle? You have grown into a beautiful young lady." Isabelle began to blush.

Once on the dock I embraced Benjamin, and we held one another for a delayed moment. He, too, had tears in his eyes. We began to laugh as he greeted the others with hugs and kisses.

Isabelle's boldness disappeared once she saw Benjamin. He had changed in his looks. He was a young man now, and he was even more handsome; she felt the distance in their ages more than she had two years before. So, as we gathered our things from the boat, she occupied herself by carrying the baby to the wagon to ease her awkwardness.

Two girls stood at the stone gate as we rode up to the Manor House. One girl appeared to be close to adulthood, the other Isabelle's age. These I knew to be Benjamin's sisters, Marie Josephe and Elizabeth.

Both I had known since birth. In fact, little Elizabeth was the child for which Isabelle LeBlanc gave her life. She resembled her mother in every detail. Memories of Isabelle's death came flooding back to me. Then, as quickly as they had materialized, they disappeared.

We had left Charles and Marguerite at the pier where her father was to pick them up. Four of us, including the baby, greeted Benjamin's sisters and made certain Isabelle was comfortable meeting the young ladies. Isabelle relaxed once she had found someone her own age.

Jeanne allowed the two younger girls to play with the baby. Jeanne was in awe of the Great Room in the Manor House. She had never seen a library of books before. She walked up to the bookcases and felt the leather bindings on the volumes with her fingertips. I shared with her the feelings I had when I first glimpsed this haven of literature. Benjamin had continued the collection since Uncle's death, and the library was more impressive than it had been when I was a boy. I recognized this as an opportunity to entertain the household in the evenings with stories from these shelves.

Seeing Jeanne's wonderment, Benjamin pointed to his new acquisitions. "I acquired these twelve volumes from a friend in Louisbourg. These are the *Fables of La Fontaine*. Grandfather had one volume when we were young, but when my friend Denys Bouchard visited me recently on his annual trading trip, he delivered this set of volumes as a gift. I can't tell you how pleased and grateful I was to receive them. Each time he visits Grand Pré he stays here for several days. He is a most congenial companion and a lover of literature. They are written in French and I believe they would be entertaining listening for us all. I hope, Piau, you accept the challenge of reading them to us."

Of course I was more than happy to do so. Reading aloud gave me great pleasure, a warm reminder of those winter nights in this very house when I had read for Uncle, Aunt Marie-Marguerite, Isabelle, and Benjamin.

Each evening I read several of La Fontaine's fables. I began with the first, "The Ant and the Grasshopper." With each fable read, we tried to guess the moral of the story. Once we had agreed on the moral, we would write it down. The ones we wrote down on that visit I have memorized and can recall to this day. My favourite and most poignant is "A person often meets his destiny on the road he took to avoid it."

And so it has been for me.

Chapter 14

Not only had the number of ships in the basin increased, so, too, had the number of people living on its shore. What had changed most about Grand Pré, I noticed, was the size of its population. When I was a boy living with Uncle during those cold winters, the community amounted to no more than a couple hundred inhabitants. Our ride to the Manor House, however, revealed that the surrounding districts now held triple that number. I understood why people came to the Minas area. It offered not only fertile soil and a warmer climate than most of the rest of Acadia but also independence and peace. These benefits would, over time, cause a certain amount of complacency in its population. Indeed, taking these precious circumstances for granted was to make the people particularly vulnerable at Grand Pré when they experienced times of hardship in the 1740s and '50s.

The Acadian summer of 1729, however, was blissful. Benjamin gave us daily tours of his growing domain with walks through his massive orchards of pear and apple trees and through miles of wheat fields dancing in the sea breezes. We strolled nearby sandy shorelines where we could walk barefoot on the hot sand and cool our feet in the chilly basin. And for the first time in a very long time, no one uttered a word about the English at Annapolis. Not having to give them a second thought was a rare blessing.

During the second week of our stay at Grand Pré, Benjamin held a family gathering at the Manor House. Besides his two sisters, Benjamin had a younger brother, Désiré, who had always lived with his father, René, and eight half-brothers and -sisters, children of his father and his second wife,

Marguerite Thebeau. The day was filled with games for the young children, plenty of fresh vegetables and sweets to eat, and singing and dancing for all.

I sang as many ancient songs as I could remember — the children were both a willing audience and receptive learners of those they did not already know. Benjamin and his family praised my singing and remarked on its full-bodied and rich sound.

"Your singing voice, Piau, is miraculous," Benjamin opined enthusiastically. "The sweetness of your singing is enough to make the angels weep!" I basked in the praise and laughed.

René was pleased to preside over the proceedings as patriarch, observing his numerous offspring as they played and entertained one another. He sat in the yard like a monarch on a throne. We had carried out one of Uncle Pierre's large tapestry armchairs so he could enjoy his family in comfort.

I now had the opportunity to spend time with René. In the past six years we had no more than a passing relationship — in fact, we rarely saw one another. My connection with René was more in the past than the present.

"It pleases me, Piau, to see you grown up and starting a family. Jeanne is lovely, and the baby is an angel. I should know about angels, I have many!" René laughed his familiar laugh.

Observing his eldest son amusing himself with his younger siblings, he continued, "It has been my son Benjamin's good fortune to have inherited your Uncle Pierre's estate. He may be young but he is a brilliant manager of this land. Already the people of this community look on him with the greatest respect, and they rely on him to help solve their problems. Benjamin and I work side by side to ensure Grand Pré prospers for the benefit of all."

"It is true what you say, René," I remarked. "The prosperity of your community is evident everywhere you look. I have never in my life seen such abundance. The people of Minas are truly blessed in their independence and peaceful existence."

René pondered my response momentarily and then asked, "Piau, have you ever considered moving to Grand Pré or perhaps Gaudet Village? The valley around our village is very fertile and you would have more opportunity to expand your holdings there. Melanson Village is a very special place, don't get me wrong. But it is situated in the most perilous position on Annapolis Basin. Through the years, the first attacks by our enemies have been at Melanson Village. It may be one of the ancient sites of Acadia, but who knows what the future may bring? The only reason it is safe at all is our enemies' fear of your grandmother, Madame Marie!"

We both began to laugh uproariously. René had impeccable timing. He tempered every serious discussion with humour. In the end, though, his infinite desire to strike a balance and to conciliate in all situations was to lead to his ultimate disillusionment and ruin.

I responded to his question. "We have given it some thought. If Lieutenant-Governor Armstrong returns, I believe we will be forced to move to Gaudet Village. He has his eye on me." Then I proceeded to relate the full details of Armstrong's unwelcome attendance at our wedding.

I could see the rage welling up in René as I spoke. As I completed my story, he began to rant. "That man is vile! Can you imagine him using those bullying tactics on such a solemn occasion? Men like Armstrong rule by instilling fear. I only wish I had been there to witness your grandmother putting him in his place. That would have been rich. She is indeed a human juggernaut! A force of nature! Brava, Madame Marie."

His rage disappeared as quickly as it had arisen. Neither of us wished to give Armstrong any further thought. Should he enter our lives again, we would deal with him at that time.

On the first day of July Charles informed us that we would be sailing with the tide the next day. The winds were favourable. The following day we reached the schooner, having said our goodbyes to Benjamin's family. His sisters were genuinely sad to see Isabelle leave. They had enjoyed her company. Isabelle brought a good deal of vivacity to their normally settled existence. With regard to Benjamin, Isabelle had contented herself with treating him as an older brother, realizing this was the appropriate relationship to pursue for the time being. However, when Benjamin kissed her goodbye at the pier, her heart skipped a beat, I am certain.

Benjamin embraced me and promised to make his annual visit to Annapolis at harvest time. We all had tears in our eyes as we left, even Jeanne.

As we set sail from Grand Pré, it was Jeanne who lamented, "I'm sincerely sorry to leave this place. There's such a feeling of contentment and joy to be found in Benjamin's world. He is an extraordinary young man.

Everyone wishes to be the best they can be in his presence. I recognize the depth of feeling you share with one another. You speak in half sentences when you are together, so complete is your understanding. This place has clearly nurtured an extraordinary bond between you. It is a gift that God has granted you both. We should make this an annual visit."

Jeanne's appreciation of Benjamin pleased me immensely. It made me love her even more.

Chapter 15

There was a year overlap between Philipps's arrival at Annapolis and Armstrong's departure for England. We heard from Prudent Robichaud, who had been appointed to the council by Governor Philipps, that there was a battle royal going on at the fort between Major Cosby, Philipps's brother-in-law, and Lieutenant-Governor Armstrong. They now held the same rank in the colony, and to add to their already existing antipathy, Cosby was designated president of the Governor's Council. For once, the uproar was confined to the fort and its regiments. Acadians on either side of the river could do nothing but look on with amusement and relief that we were not involved in the controversy. Of course, Cosby was certainly our favourite.

Our friend Prudent Robichaud was also quick to describe an altercation between Mangeant and Major Cosby out in the public square. Cosby rebuked Mangeant in front of the regiment and the townspeople, and came close to striking him. Armstrong intervened and complained to the governor. Later, Governor Philipps confided in Robichaud, who was now president of the Acadian Council, that he had written to the Duke of Newcastle in England describing Mangeant as a man of very bad character, who had inappropriately been granted the power to advise the lieutenant-governor. He further wrote, with some vehemence, that Mangeant "would make an excellent Minister to an arbitrary Prince!" Armstrong and Mangeant did finally set sail for Britain, and an easiness descended upon the entire colony.

Governor Philipps began to set things right at Annapolis by recalling Father Breslay from the wilderness where he had been exiled to live with the Native peoples. Breslay was extremely popular with the Acadians on the upper and lower river. He was permitted to reopen the Chapelle St. Laurent, thus enabling the residents of Belle Isle, Paradise, and Gaudet Village to worship and receive the sacraments without travelling miles downriver to Annapolis.

One of his first duties was to officiate at the marriage of Jean to Jeanne's sister Madeleine. They had finally overcome their reserve in order to commit themselves to a life together. Their union was a true love match. The father of the bride, Bernard Gaudet, rejoiced, describing the marriage as an act of divine intervention. His declaration was accompanied, of course, with his customary full-bodied laugh.

More good news came from Grand Pré in the winter of 1730. Alexandre Bourg, who was the husband of Uncle Pierre's daughter Marguerite, was appointed attorney to His Majesty, responsible for Minas, Pisiquit, Cobequid, and Chignecto. These were all the regions situated on the Bay of Fundy and the Avon River. Alexandre was known for his intelligence, his sense of justice, and, most of all, his incorruptibility. This appointment made him responsible for overseeing and regulating land transfers, which meant seeing that no land was seized except where necessary and wills were properly probated.

As one could imagine, René and Benjamin were ecstatic with their family member Alexandre's selection. Having one of their own working on their behalf was comforting for the French-speaking people living on the Fundy shores.

So much was Governor Philipps respected and trusted, he managed to persuade hundreds of Acadians to take the oath of allegiance within a year. There was never any discussion of the fact that the clause about taking up arms in times of war was missing. He nevertheless played up his success in his letters to Britain and New England, boasting that he had been able to accomplish what no other governor had been able to achieve with the king's Acadian subjects.

Just as we were beginning to relax after two years of benevolent governance at Annapolis, the unexpected happened. From the fields and orchards of Melanson Village we observed a ship bearing the Union Jack sailing past Goat Island. At the time, we were unaware whom that ship was carrying. It was not long, however, before the unwelcome news spread to both sides of the river and beyond.

Armstrong and Mangeant returned to Annapolis in the summer of 1731, triumphant. The former had been able to convince the Board of Trade in London that Philipps was mismanaging the colony; the board consequently ordered the governor to return to London to answer for his misdeeds. In addition, Mangeant somehow had manoeuvred a royal pardon from the king of France while he was away, and his murder charges had been dismissed. The fates had, for the time being, ruled in their favour.

So began the next chapter of Armstrong's arbitrary rule in Acadia. Once again we would be forced to return to our sidestepping existence under his governance. Little did I understand at the time that Armstrong's return would usher in the beginning of the dark time in my life, a time that would continue to worsen until I, my family, and my community were almost devastated.

One of the first communities to be affected by the happenings at Annapolis was Grand Pré. Before too long, Alexandre Bourg was informed that his position as attorney was to be reduced to deputy, and his duties were to be confined to collecting rents. Shockingly, it was François Mangeant who replaced him. This news sent shivers through the people of Minas. They had lived in peace for a generation, free from the daily dictates of the governor and his council. Now Armstrong's favourite was coming to live in their midst, forcing them to become a watched people.

Benjamin and René were visiting Annapolis on business when the lieutenant-governor sailed into Annapolis Basin. They had arrived early in July for the baptism of our second child, Jeanne, born in April. René's properties in the lower town were now completed and were being rented to some of the English residents. Before they sailed back to Grand Pré in early August, all had been put into place. Mangeant would be arriving before summer's end. It would be up to René to carry the discouraging news to Alexandre and the Acadians at Minas.

I warned Benjamin and his father, expressing my deep concern. "Having Mangeant live among you, without any restraints on his power, is a great calamity for the community of Grand Pré. Armstrong and the favourite share the same evil spirit and you will have a spy in your midst. Neither man has any scruples, but at least the governor must work within the law. Despite what the king of France says, Mangeant is a convicted murderer and an evil presence in the colony. His intelligence and ability to connive makes him doubly dangerous outside the control of his master, Armstrong."

"Do you not believe he can be outwitted, Piau? Perhaps he is vain enough to be manipulated by flattery," suggested René.

Benjamin pondered in silence.

"Benjamin, what are your thoughts on the matter?" asked his father.

There was a long pause. Benjamin then spoke. "There is little we can do about this situation. It is a *fait accompli*. We must brace ourselves for his arrival and make our neighbours aware of the truth about Monsieur Mangeant. Only knowledge of your enemy, and that is exactly how we should view him, can prevent him from destroying the existence we have treasured for over sixty years. Deference and compliance, if only feigned, are the only solution."

Governor Philipps departed the colony, as he had been ordered to do by his superiors in London. Although he continued to bear the title of governor of Acadia for another eighteen years, he never again returned to Annapolis. His brother-in-law, Major Cosby, who held the title of lieutenant-governor alongside Armstrong, refused to serve under his adversary. He threatened to leave Annapolis with his family and move to Boston, but somehow that transfer never occurred. Armstrong became acting governor and president of the council, relieving Cosby of his former position. Cosby continued to promote goodwill with the Acadians and never ceased to be a sharp thorn in the side of Armstrong.

Chapter 16

Mangeant! Mangeant! Mangeant! The sound of his name pierces my soul like a sword made from the finest steel. The mere remembrance of that vile name resurrects many dark and powerful emotions. He was the man who materialized out of the mist like some spectre destined to bring pestilence to the land and grief to its inhabitants. He must have been an agent of the Fallen Angel himself.

Much of what took place at Grand Pré after Mangeant's arrival there was related to me by others — René, Alexandre, and, most distressingly, by Benjamin. I say most distressingly because from the time Mangeant settled at Minas, it was my cousin Benjamin he targeted. I can only imagine how Mangeant viewed Benjamin, a young man of twenty-two with every gift that God can bestow on a single human being, a man also possessed with exalted standing in the community. He lived in a grand house, with all the power and privilege it conveyed on him, as master of Uncle Pierre's estate. The lofty position that Benjamin held was an affront to Mangeant, a challenge to his sense of entitlement and authority. And any challenge to the favourite's authority at Grand Pré had to be corrected. Mangeant came to see Benjamin's very existence as opposition, and over time he relentlessly set out to eliminate it.

Mangeant's first visit to Grand Pré was merely a reconnaissance. He arrived with a coterie of the governor's militiamen by sea and called upon Alexandre Bourg, the acting magistrate. He received no formal welcome in the community. This was his intention. He had chosen to arrive without any forewarning. Most interpreted this as his desire to intimidate the residents of the village. He succeeded in his own mind, but Benjamin had already prepared his neighbours in advance of Mangeant's arrival. He had described the favourite in great detail, and the community had mapped out strategies for surviving his arbitrary behaviour when he came to dwell among them.

Alexandre, as acting magistrate, felt obliged to give Mangeant a tour of the greater Grand Pré community, describing its farms, orchards, and produce. The favourite was introduced to few of the inhabitants of these farms, for he showed little interest in those who worked the land. He was, however, decidedly interested in visiting the Manor House. Meeting its master was worthy of his future position as magistrate. Benjamin's formal introduction to the new magistrate marked the beginning of a complex and antagonistic relationship that was to last for the next six years. Only one of the two men would survive the encounter.

Mangeant examined the exterior of the Manor House as though it was his own possession. Before knocking on the front door, he felt the masonry on the front of the building. He removed the glove on his left hand to feel the texture of the stone. According to Alexandre, Mangeant gave the impression of someone examining the work of a master sculptor. He did not utter a word but exhibited an air of appreciation.

Mangeant then moved aside and gave way to Alexandre, who, at that point, realized that he must be the one to announce their arrival. Before they could declare their presence with a knock, however, the great door opened ceremoniously. Benjamin stood tall in the entrance, wearing a scarlet waistcoat that he had inherited from his grandfather. Despite his youth, he looked every bit the English country gentleman. Alexandre was somewhat shocked by Benjamin's appearance. He was expecting his nephew to be in his usual casual dress. But the master of this house was elegant in his lord-of-the-manor attire. This, combined with his handsome face and figure, created such an impression that both visitors remained speechless for a long moment.

"Welcome to Grand Pré, sir," Benjamin declared in perfect English, directing this courtesy at Mangeant alone.

He turned to Alexandre. "Good day, Uncle. It is an auspicious day for you both to be touring the domains of Grand Pré. The weather is glorious and our valley's bounty is more than evident today." Then, facing the other, he continued, "Monsieur Mangeant, I presume. Our community has been anxiously awaiting your arrival. Please enter, gentlemen."

Benjamin had taken control of the situation, and Alexandre was certain that this made Mangeant doubt the genuineness of his welcome. However, he showed no outward sign of this.

"*Vous êtes très gentil, monsieur,*" the favourite emphatically responded in French. "*Est-ce que nous pouvons parler français?*"

"We have always spoken English in this household, monsieur. My grandfather, who was the lord of this manor, was an English gentleman, born and raised in Yorkshire. He was almost an adult when he arrived in Acadia. We have always spoken French to our neighbours in the community, but within these walls English is the preferred language. I trust your English is excellent."

"It is indeed, sir. I accept the rules of your home, with pleasure." He revealed no sign of annoyance, but Benjamin could see a distinct twitching in Mangeant's left hand.

Benjamin led his visitors into the Great Room, where his sisters stood in anticipation of their introduction to Mangeant. Alexandre greeted his young nieces with a kiss on both cheeks. Marie Josephe and Elizabeth were both formally dressed for the occasion. Elizabeth in particular looked stunning in a pale blue summer frock. Benjamin's younger sister was a radiant and beautiful young woman of fourteen. This fact was not lost on Mangeant. He gazed intently at the striking adolescent with a connoisseur's eye and gave her a polite nod.

"May I introduce my sisters, Marie Josephe and Elizabeth?"

The two young ladies curtsied in unison, exhibiting an elegance and dignity that were rare in the colony.

"I am charmed," Mangeant stated curtly.

The favourite perused the room, fixing his gaze on the library of books that lined the walls from floor to ceiling.

"Monsieur, I have rarely seen such a fine collection. These must have been acquired over many years."

"Indeed, sir, many date back to Grandfather's years in England. I have managed to continue to obtain volumes through trade. I have business connections, both in New England and Louisbourg, who provide the latest in literature from both England and France. I view the books as my treasury."

"Quite right, Monsieur LeBlanc." Mangeant paused momentarily then resumed: "You say you conduct trade with the French at Louisbourg? That is curious. Do you have close contacts with the French at Île Royale?"

Benjamin was aware that Mangeant was engaging in a subtle form of interrogation, hoping to unsettle his host.

"In these times of peace, I find it profitable to have commerce with anyone who is willing to trade goods. Exchange provides commodities, which are more valuable than pounds sterling, don't you think?"

"Yes, monsieur, as long as that is all that is traded."

Mangeant's implication could not have been misunderstood by anyone in the room, but Benjamin decided to change the subject, not permitting the comment to take on a life of its own.

After escorting Mangeant and Alexandre to the high-backed chairs situated in front of the grand hearth, Benjamin directed his sisters to fetch a bottle of their finest claret and serve it to the guests.

"Be seated, gentlemen."

Mangeant, Alexandre, and Benjamin spent the better part of an hour sipping their wine and discussing the community of Grand Pré and its many virtues. Throughout their lengthy discourse, Benjamin never lost sight of the fact that he was conversing with the enemy. It was obvious that Mangeant was equally aware that my cousin was the only person at Grand Pré who was likely to block his way at every turn. Their first meeting had a forced cordiality about it, but there was no doubt where each opponent stood.

Mangeant sailed the following day with the promise of returning with his family within the month. He had laid plans to build a home at Grand Pré on a favoured piece of land close to the home of Alexandre Bourg. He just had to find those that were willing to execute its construction in such a way that it met his high standards. Few in the community admitted to having the expertise to build such a structure. Most of the farmhouses were of a relatively simple construction. His would have to at least surpass these, given his future position at Minas.

As it turned out, Mangeant was forced to choose his construction crew from Annapolis, with considerable assistance from the militia. It was difficult enough to collect a group of skilled hands to complete the fortress, let alone manage a house at Minas. The militiamen agreed to work on Mangeant's project under considerable duress. Lieutenant-Governor Armstrong insisted on it. He would have overseen the project himself if he had been willing to leave Annapolis for a time. But this was not an option, for he believed he must remain at the garrison to keep control of the ever-precarious political situation there. Armstrong was unable to trust Major Cosby long enough to venture anywhere beyond the town.

In the end, the lieutenant-governor reluctantly agreed to pay the Gaudet brothers a large sum to supervise the beam construction along with some masonry work. Although Benjamin was the most skilled mason in Acadia, he failed to volunteer his services, even for pay. He kept his distance and forever played his part as master of his domains at Grand Pré.

I, on the other hand, did not share his scruples. I was in need of the money. Armstrong was paying well. Besides, working on the construction of Mangeant's house allowed me to spend time with Benjamin, since I was able to stay at the Manor House for the duration of the build. My father-in-law, Bernard, and his brother Denys were welcomed guests as well. It turned out to be a merry time indeed, with plenty of laughter and goodwill.

The building site was a jovial place, with little direction required of the Acadian workers. Bernard was a competent contractor, skilled in the ways of construction. Even those men from the militia who were living in makeshift tents on the building site put their complete trust in "Monsieur Gaudet." The women of the community kept our stomachs filled, and their generosity knew no bounds. Some evenings there were social gatherings with music and dancing. These were occasions for Bernard to entertain his colleagues with amusing stories and humorous banter. Instinctively, he realized that boosting the spirits of the workers made for a better and more productive workplace.

This was all possible because the master of this new edifice remained in Annapolis, confident that his future residence would be completed before the autumn. I believe he did not picture himself inhabiting anyone else's home, even for a brief time. Perhaps he thought it would compromise his mission at Minas. He was probably correct in that assumption.

Once Mangeant's new home was finished, the construction crew made their way home. Bernard, Denys, and the militiamen sailed to Annapolis, satisfied that they had managed to complete a fine home, worthy of

Armstrong's favourite. After being paid, the Gaudet brothers travelled to Melanson Village to visit Jeanne and the children. I remained behind at Grand Pré for a time, not willing to give up Benjamin's stimulating company and the warmth of the Manor House. We would follow later in Benjamin's vessel to attend the harvest festival at Melanson Village.

One late summer evening I asked Benjamin to describe his firsthand impressions of Monsieur Mangeant. He was decidedly frank in his observations of the favourite.

"A man who reveals nothing of the workings of his soul, when he feels the least significant personal revelation could condemn him in the eyes of the world, he is the most brilliant of actors, the most powerful of dissemblers. Mangeant is such a man. Every comment he made in my presence was laced with sweetness, but in reality it was laden with innuendo and accusations. Even my sisters commented that standing in the same room as the favourite caused their blood to freeze in the dead of a hot summer's day. I am finding it difficult to imagine having such a man in our presence on a permanent basis."

"I appreciate your fears, Cousin. At least in my village we have the luxury of distance from the aggravating politics of Annapolis. In the privacy of our community, we possess a certain freedom of speech and behaviour. But having a spy in your midst, the freedom is removed and one is forced to live in a world of whispers and silence."

"Poor Uncle Alexandre has been madly perusing all his legal documents to make certain everything is in its proper order. He fears for the protection of the rights of the people in the community. If all is not nailed down on paper, understandings of ownership, tenancy, and inheritances could be manipulated and changed in favour of those who govern us at Annapolis. Uncle is even able to imagine Mangeant himself gaining a personal advantage if all the legal documents are not secured."

"That is admirable of Alexandre. His kindness and concern for his neighbours is touching. I regret that he will soon be reduced to being the collector of taxes. He is such a proud man."

"Unfortunately, it is a cross he must bear. And he will bear it with dignity."

Chapter 17

While sailing home to Melanson Village on a balmy early autumn day, Benjamin and I expelled Mangeant from our thoughts. Instead, we recalled with relish all the good times we had shared as young children growing up in the glow of Uncle Pierre, Isabelle, René, and Grandmama. Some of these loved ones were still with us, but those who were not guided us in every step we took. We were young men with promising lives ahead of us. Why should anyone interfere with our happiness? Life was filled with challenges, but as far as we were concerned, none were insurmountable. Our vessel was close-hauled into the west wind and we were invincible.

We arrived home safely to discover that Isabelle was visiting Jeanne and the children. She was at that stage between childhood and womanhood where there were still flashes of the little girl wrapped in a woman's body. She did not possess a conventional beauty, but the energy she exuded from within certainly made up for any lack in her features. She had the gift for attracting attention when she entered a room.

On seeing Benjamin for the first time in many long months, the light in her bright eyes intensified. This was not lost on my cousin, although it was evident he still treated her like a child. Her persuasions, however, soon rectified this. She was absolutely effervescent during those first few days after our arrival.

"Don't you think Isabelle is becoming a woman right before our eyes, Benjamin?" I declared during the first day home.

Isabelle appeared delighted with my comment. Why is it that girls always want to be treated like adults, even at a young age?

"This is true, Cousin. I don't believe I would have recognized her. She has matured dramatically."

This brought out the flirtatiousness in Isabelle. "This is hardly surprising, Piau. I will soon be fifteen, after all," she responded with a touch of playfulness.

"And how are your darling sisters, Benjamin? I do have fond memories of them from when I stayed with you at Grand Pré. I would love to see them again. They were such engaging company. I am sure they are now beautiful young women. I do envy their extraordinary virtues." The formality in her speech was another sign of her desire to be treated like a woman.

"They would be highly complimented by your extravagant praise, Isabelle. Because they are my sisters, I must say I have to agree with you."

"Beauty seems to run in the family," Jeanne interjected.

"That is no surprise to me," added my mother. "There was no greater beauty than their mother, Isabelle. I see so much of her reflected in Benjamin and his sisters."

"That is true, Mama. Perhaps next spring Isabelle might join us on our annual visit to Grand Pré?"

"That would be splendid!" Isabelle replied enthusiastically. "How will I manage to survive the long winter? Spring seems like such a long time away."

"From one who has experienced an infinite number of winters and springs, believe me, the time will fly all too quickly, my dear," interrupted my grandmother. "Time passes slowly only for the young!"

We all began to chuckle. Grandmama's comments always inspired this reaction in us. Although she sometimes exerted her matriarchal powers with great bombast, most of what she uttered was intended to make us laugh.

"Only after I give birth," Jeanne said in a matter-of-fact manner.

We all sat there, not certain we had heard her correctly.

"Is that true, Jeanne?" I immediately crossed the room and kissed her on the forehead.

Isabelle began to clap her hands with excitement.

"Oh, how I do love children!" she said, almost singing the words.

Benjamin was very attentive to Isabelle throughout his stay with us. Together they played with my daughters and filled their days with games of all sorts.

One evening he surprised us with a new book written by a Reverend Doctor Swift, which he had acquired from an English sea captain that year. It was the strange story of a man named Gulliver. He read it aloud in English for those of us who understood and translated into French for Jeanne and Isabelle. We all marvelled at the fantastic tale of Gulliver as he travelled through the land of the Lilliputians and Giants. We were a captive audience.

"According to my Irish friend, Captain Andrew Tyrone, who presented the book to me, the stories have a more significant meaning than they appear on the surface. They are what are known as satire. They are similar to Molière's plays, which make fun of people's foibles and expose our tendency as humans to pretend to be what we are not. Mr. Swift is not only making fun of people's tendency to be hypocritical, but he secretly attacks the English government as well. He did not claim to be its author until recently. It was published anonymously for fear he might be arrested or thrown in jail."

This caught Grandmama's immediate attention.

"That is so like the two-faced English to throw a writer in jail for speaking his mind. Even if its meaning is hidden, the French would have at least enjoyed the humour in the stories."

We all laughed and continued our listening.

Chapter 18

In the month of June 1734, as promised, we boarded Charles's schooner bound for Grand Pré. Jeanne, the two little girls, our newborn, Madeleine, and Isabelle, newly arrived from Gaudet Village, set sail with my brother and sister-in-law to visit our relatives there. During the voyage, Isabelle had her hands full managing her energetic little nieces. Carefree as we may have felt as our vessel hugged the shoreline of the great Bay of Fundy, little did we imagine the complicated situation in which we were to be embroiled not long after our arrival.

It was impossibly beautiful in the valley at Minas. The contrast of rich vegetation and sprouting wheat fields with our struggling efforts at Annapolis made us wonder why we persisted at Melanson Village. But our compensation was a harmonious family compound with ancient apple orchards and reclaimed grain fields that provided us with all we needed to maintain a prosperous existence. We had the added advantage of selling an abundance of produce to the garrison at Annapolis.

All seemed at peace at Grand Pré. We were informed, not long after our arrival, that Mangeant and his family had settled into their new home and had passed the winter quietly. The favourite had neither antagonized members of the community nor did he fraternize with its inhabitants. He attended mass at the chapel, insisting that a front pew be reserved for his family. There were no objections to this honour. It allowed the parishioners to observe them unnoticed. Madame Mangeant was a timid woman; her fine clothes could not conceal her Acadian roots. Louise, the fifteen-year-old daughter, was pretty but not imposing. They were the first to depart the church every Sunday and rarely remained behind to socialize with the other parishioners. The distance between the Mangeants and the inhabitants of Grand Pré seemed natural; no one complained that the favourite and his family were haughty and unfriendly. However, most accepted that this was merely the honeymoon period.

The situation changed dramatically the first Sunday after we arrived.

Benjamin and his family shared the front row across the aisle from the Mangeants in the chapel. As usual, the magistrate and his family entered the church moments before the mass began. But the Mangeants' entrance on that day was different from other days, for trailing behind them as they paraded up the centre aisle was a tall, strikingly handsome young gentleman wearing the uniform of a British officer. We were later to discover that this was Samuel Mangeant, the eighteen-year-old son of the favourite. How he had changed since that day the Mangeants sailed into the harbour at Annapolis seven years ago. In the early years of their stay, I had noticed him occasionally at mass, but he disappeared soon after. We learned that he had been sent off to England to attend a prestigious military school, probably at Armstrong's expense. And here he was, resplendent in the king's army uniform for all to admire.

It did not escape anyone's notice that Samuel Mangeant glanced across the aisle on several occasions. It fired the imagination of those behind them that he may have been impressed by the three beautiful young women seated opposite him. The three young ladies in question were themselves noticed stealing glances at the handsome young man who had unexpectedly descended upon them.

At least this is how the parishioners imagined it.

It was perhaps for this reason that when we left the church Mangeant and his family were waiting to meet us. The favourite spotted me almost right away. He seemed surprised to see me in this setting and in the company of the LeBlanc family. Before engaging in any formal greetings, he directed a question in my direction.

"Why, Monsieur Belliveau, I'm surprised to see you here at Grand Pré. I was not aware you had connections to this community."

"Monsieur Mangeant, I believe everyone in Acadia has some connection with this place," I responded promptly. "Benjamin LeBlanc and his family are my kinfolk. I spent the winters of my childhood at the Manor House with my uncle Sieur Pierre Laverdure. I consider this my second home."

"Indeed." He gave me a curious and assessing look then turned away, affording me little more than a dismissive nod.

"Monsieur LeBlanc, my son, Samuel, has requested that I introduce him to your family. He is recently returned from England, where he has completed his officer training. Perhaps you could do the honours."

Benjamin seemed quite aware that Mangeant had granted him the honour of introducing his family because the favourite was unable to recall any of their names himself. With the most formal but friendly demeanour he could muster, Benjamin obliged.

"May I introduce Pierre Belliveau, my cousin, with whom you are already acquainted? And these are my sisters, Marie Josephe and Elizabeth. This other charming young lady is Monsieur Belliveau's sister-in-law Isabelle Gaudet, from Gaudet Village. Her father, Bernard Gaudet, supervised the construction of your new home. She is a regular guest in our house."

The young women curtsied in turn, directing their gestures at the young man.

Mangeant's son gave a sharp and formal bow. "I am honoured to make your acquaintance."

It was lost on no one that the young officer had a distinct English accent.

"Perhaps, Monsieur LeBlanc, you would allow me the honour of calling on you at the Manor House sometime soon."

Benjamin noticed the smiles on the faces of the young ladies.

"Indeed, sir. Any time you choose. We are at your disposal. And so, we must bid you adieu."

It was obvious that Benjamin purposefully claimed the advantage by being the first to dismiss the present company.

Mangeant's stern look exposed his displeasure.

"*Au revoir, mesdames et messieurs.*" His reply was a curt response to what Mangeant considered my cousin's presumptuous farewell. Speaking French was his way of changing the rules of the game.

For the time being, the rules of behaviour were still recognizable. They were certainly not lost on Benjamin, who disguised his understanding of them with his congenial smile. I was always cognizant of my cousin's iron will. This was evidence.

True to his word, Lieutenant Samuel Mangeant presented himself at our front gate two days later. Benjamin was away from the Manor House on local business and the rest of us were busying ourselves within the confines of the stone enclosure. Isabelle was playing with the little girls as was her custom, my two cousins were tending to their flower garden, and Jeanne was holding the baby in her arms, contentedly perched on an ornate chair made from birch limbs. I was unaware of young Mangeant's arrival as I hoed diligently in the vegetable garden at the rear of the house.

Announcing his arrival, the two sisters politely welcomed and escorted the young lieutenant through the front gate. As he strolled into the garden, he was introduced to Jeanne, who had been absent from the chapel two days earlier. My wife's serenity calmed the adolescent fervour that descended on the young ladies of the household in the presence of their handsome visitor so there was no embarrassment.

Jeanne spoke in French. "You are welcome, monsieur. Come into the house where we can relax and enjoy some refreshments." The young ladies followed the gentleman like puppies chasing after their mother.

Inside it was cool, and the cozy atmosphere of the Great Room made everyone relax.

"Please call me Samuel. There is no need for formalities amongst friends." He immediately put them at their ease.

Benjamin's sisters looked at one another with a look that signalled that each thought Samuel did not possess his father's arrogant ways. This was a relief for both of them.

His glances at the library suggested that he was as impressed as most guests were when they saw Benjamin's book collection. "I have rarely seen such a fine collection of books. Perhaps at the homes of my fellow officers in England, but this could compete with most I have seen anywhere."

Although Elizabeth was the younger of the two sisters, she was bold enough to speak first. "Our brother treasures these volumes. Should you wish to borrow any, I am certain Benjamin would gladly approve the loan. They are written in both English and French."

"I am afraid my French is a bit rusty, but those in English I can manage quite well, thank you."

Elizabeth guided Samuel to the bookshelves as a pretext for being alone with him. Marie Josephe looked on amused but watchful. Jeanne and Isabelle were unaware of what the two were saying because they were conversing in English. Samuel was basking in the attention he was receiving from the beautiful young woman.

Jeanne could sense that the attention Elizabeth was bestowing on the stranger might be construed as inappropriate. The only person who was in a position to interfere was Marie Josephe, and she seemed to be enjoying their flirtation.

Samuel randomly chose two books and set them aside in order to sit in one of the large chairs. Jeanne served him a cool cup of dandelion wine. The others joined him. After a few sips, the colour rose into his cheeks, which the girls later remarked enhanced his good looks. Oh, to have that much power over a room filled with beautiful women! Even Jeanne was charmed by the young visitor.

Marie Josephe was the first to speak.

"How long will you remain at Grand Pré, Samuel?"

"Only for the summer, and then I must take up my military post in the New England Regiment. My parents were hoping I would be stationed at Annapolis, but my services were required elsewhere. Lieutenant-Governor Armstrong recommended that I join the Boston garrison because it would be an excellent first step in my army career."

Out of politeness, Samuel repeated his answer in French to include Jeanne and Isabelle in the conversation. For the remainder of his visit, he conversed in French, describing his life in England and how different it was from the colonies. He confided that he preferred the peace and beauty of the New World. Jeanne thought it charming of him to say so. It certainly made a favourable impression on all the ladies present.

After a pleasant stay, Samuel rose from his chair and bid them all adieu, promising to return another day. It was only later that I discovered I had missed his visit.

Chapter 19

Benjamin was circumspect when he was informed of young Mangeant's visit. He listened patiently as his sisters enthusiastically related the details. Isabelle was more measured in her observations of Samuel. She, of course, was comparing the lieutenant to Benjamin. And on that score there was no comparison. Jeanne and I looked for any signs of disapproval in Benjamin's reaction to their stories, but there were none. Could it have been he sensed that the son was not the father? I knew better. My cousin was not one to wear his heart on his sleeve. Despite his sensibilities, he was a cautious man and infinitely guarded with those he could not read easily.

However, he did not object to the young man's visits. They seemed to brighten the mood of the household. He confided to me that he had some concerns about the special attention Samuel was affording his sister Elizabeth. He was certain she was totally smitten with the young officer. Given that he would be leaving in a few months and therefore no intimate relationship could be permitted between the two, it was wise to intervene, even if it only meant closely chaperoning the couple. The guarantee in all this was the young man was joining his regiment in Boston at summer's end.

Before we could discover the outcome of the story between Elizabeth and Lieutenant Samuel Mangeant, we returned to our life at Melanson Village. The denouement of the story was revealed later in the summer, though, by René when he arrived at Annapolis to collect his rent from his tenants in the lower town. He seemed to want to blame himself for not knowing what was happening in what he called the romantic affair of his daughter Elizabeth and Mangeant's son.

"Can you believe I was totally ignorant of their affair? Benjamin had kept me uninformed. My brood has grown so large I barely have time to remember who they all are. I blame myself. And Mangeant was so enraged by the relationship, declaring Elizabeth totally unsuitable for his son. Can you imagine? He denigrated the Acadian people, saying there was not a single Acadian girl worthy of his young offspring. Such a match, he ranted, would ruin his son's career in the British army. It pains me to even recount the story. My goodness, what a disaster!"

"Calm yourself, René," I interjected. "Surely it could not have been that serious."

He continued. "Apparently their relationship progressed innocently enough, always within the watchful eyes of Marie Josephe, Benjamin, and Madame Thibideau, the housekeeper. However, what was not known was that when they were together they were passing each other secret love notes. And not just a few. It was later revealed that Elizabeth was secretly escaping the Manor House after everyone had gone to bed. Can you envision such a thing? I don't know how she managed such a ruse.

"Well, I can say now that her reputation is ruined and Samuel Mangeant survives this affair with only a strong rebuke; he gets the chance for a fresh start in New England, free of scandal, and his honour remains intact. He has had his way with my daughter, and he is permitted to shirk his responsibility in this sordid business. Shame on him! Shame on me!"

"Perhaps Elizabeth should come and stay with us until this whole affair has blown over," suggested my grandmother sympathetically. "Time heals all, even scandal. And I have witnessed plenty of those in my lifetime. Reputations are always rehabilitated."

"You are so kind and understanding, Madame Marie. Perhaps this is a solution to our problem. God knows, Elizabeth deserves the same chance for forgiveness as the cad with whom she cavorted!"

"It's settled, then," my mother chimed in. "We will find ways to help her forget this young gentleman, and her poor broken heart will heal in no time."

"So be it. I will return to Grand Pré this very day, and my daughter and I will sail back to Melanson Village in time for the harvest. Thank you all for your support. I will not forget your kindness, I assure you."

And so it was that Elizabeth LeBlanc came to live with us. She could barely be faulted for her actions. One cannot always control the workings of the heart, especially a fifteen-year-old one. Samuel Mangeant appeared to be an honourable young man, albeit self-possessed. Truth be told, Elizabeth lacked a proper role model growing up without her mother. And Samuel had no role model at all, at least not in his father. Who can say for certain whether their love was pure or not? In any case, their paths would cross again under far worse circumstances.

Nothing could prepare us for what we saw when Elizabeth arrived at Melanson Village with René and her brother Benjamin. She was so thin and frail she could barely step out of her father's boat without assistance. She looked as if something had drawn the spirit from her body. My family was immediately aware of the magnitude of the task ahead. It would not be easy to cure Elizabeth of her broken heart.

My mother was the first to embrace her, kissing her on both cheeks. She expressed no words of comfort, knowing that words could not alleviate the poor girl's sorrow. The scene resembled a funeral, not a welcome, but we were determined as a family to resurrect this girl's life from the ashes.

The news of her affair with Samuel Mangeant had not followed Elizabeth to Annapolis. Her shame was unknown outside our immediate circle, which gave her some comfort. So, too, did knowing she was in the warm embrace of a loving and forgiving family. The story of her relationship with the favourite's son soon evaporated into the autumn air. The evidence of it, however, could not be so easily erased. One could see it in her mournful eyes and in her feeble body. Two days into her stay with us, she developed a fever and was forced to take to her bed. Benjamin and René were extremely concerned for her well-being, but all that could be accomplished was done by the women of the household. Around-the-clock nursing could not halt or lessen the burning inside her body and soul.

Benjamin refused to leave her side until the fever had subsided. It did not. Jeanne suggested that a priest be called. Charles sailed to Annapolis for Father Breslay that same day. Once the priest had administered the last rites, my grandmother demanded that everyone leave the sickroom. We reluctantly followed her orders. She remained with Elizabeth overnight in the annex, with no one else permitted to enter. All we could do was pray. Few of us were able to sleep during the night, so we kept a vigil. How infinite those hours seem when one is waiting for death to call!

Early the following morning, the door to the annex slowly opened. Grandmama entered the main room of the Manor House looking frightfully exhausted. The room was filled with expectant faces.

She uttered only one sentence. "The fever has broken."

We all heaved a sigh of relief. Grandmama made her way tentatively to the large chair in front of the fireplace and collapsed into it. She did not speak a single word for the rest of the day. What took place behind that closed door in our home that night remains a mystery. No one ever questioned my grandmother's special healing powers. They seemed to grow ever stronger as she aged.

Elizabeth remained with us for the winter. Her health improved but she never again regained the radiance and innocence of her youth. The beauty she once possessed was eclipsed by the sorrow in her soul. In the spring, she returned to Grand Pré and the life she had always known. Regrettably, she never married.

Chapter 20

The next year, 1736, saw the birth of our fourth daughter, Theotiste, and the commemoration of my grandmother's ninetieth birthday. Both were joyous celebrations. The coincidence of these events was that the new child was to grow up inheriting more of Grandmama's characteristics than any other.

Soon after this celebration, however, we were quickly plunged into a time of mourning. The summer of 1737 witnessed the old woman's passing. My grandmother, Madame Marie Dugas Melanson, had been the matriarch of the Melanson clan for over seventy years and was the last of her generation to survive in Acadia. She had been among the first to be born in the French colony and had lived to experience most of its early history. Although I grieved when Grandmama died, I was comforted by the fact that I had held on to her as long as possible. She passed on to me her strong sense of survival, her uncompromising will to live. And it has always been my belief that one may cease to breathe but one never ceases to exist. So it has been for my grandmother.

My grandmother's funeral was the largest event ever organized at Annapolis. Over a thousand mourners attended the mass for Grandmama, coming from all over Acadia. The mourners included English settlers from the town, Major Cosby and his regiment, and the lieutenant-governor's militiamen. Armstrong himself graced us with his presence at the memorial held at Chapelle St. Jean Baptiste. There were those who imagined that Armstrong had come to show his respect for a formidable adversary. I believe he jumped at the opportunity to demonstrate his superior position amongst so many colonists, many of whom had never seen him before.

There was an unusual feeling of unity, a harmony of spirit, that existed that day we laid my grandmother to rest. Never had there been such an occasion when French and English alike came together to celebrate the life of a respected member of their community. Unfortunately, there would never be another.

Life is a balancing act between joy and sadness. If one lives from moment to moment, one is merely tolerating what has been and what is likely to happen. Survival, however, requires a memory of both the good times and bad to propel one safely onward. Anticipation is foreseeing what lies ahead. Living in the moment has been a struggle for me throughout my existence. Being able to anticipate what is likely to occur, on the other hand, has ensured my survival and that of many of those I have loved. The one thing I did not foresee, however, was Benjamin's death.

The dreadful news arrived in the early summer of 1739. Charles and his wife had been visiting his wife's parents, as was their custom. We had chosen not to make our annual trip to visit Benjamin because Jeanne was close to giving birth to our daughter Agnes. Every year, for the past ten years, we had sailed to Grand Pré, but not that year. Why had fate manipulated the course of events so I was unable to be there to prevent what I later came to realize was preventable? His death at the age of twenty-eight was an inconceivable, devastating tragedy. My cousin had had such a promising life ahead of him. I was paralyzed by a grief that was beyond my endurance.

Isabelle had arrived earlier in the summer to assist Jeanne in caring for the children. This also was the first summer she had not visited Benjamin. They had become very close over the years, and she showed she was willing to wait until he decided that they were destined to be together. However strong their relationship had become since she had decided to marry him when she was still a girl, Benjamin always treated her like a younger sister. Her patience knew no bounds, and she was prepared to accept any affection he was willing to send in her direction.

Isabelle descended into anguish on hearing the terrible news. Jeanne and Mother, despite having to deal with their own sadness, were compelled to enforce some control over Isabelle's hysteria. Her wailing was heart-wrenching as it echoed across the settlement, alerting all the Melansons that tragedy was in the air.

I remember nothing of the trip from Annapolis to Grand Pré. We set sail the day the dreadful news arrived. Charles didn't ask what course of action I was about to take; he was in complete control of the situation for my sake. He knew how profound my relationship with Benjamin had been, that we had been closer than brothers. Mother often said we shared the same spirit. She was correct. Half of me died the day I was told of Benjamin's death. That part of me has never been reawakened.

I found the entire community at Minas in a state of shock. Curiously, no one spoke of the cause of his death. Endless condolences were offered to the family, but no one inquired why Benjamin was no longer with us. His body had already been laid to rest in the churchyard following a hurried funeral.

Elizabeth and Marie Josephe were distraught. They were unwilling to discuss any events surrounding Benjamin's untimely death. A veil of mystery and fear descended upon the Manor House and the community. In our community deaths were treated as a normal part of life. This was different.

René, as expected, wallowed in remorse. He regretted that he had never been a good father to Benjamin. Selfishness was his excuse. I wondered how this man, who had exhibited so much promise when he was young, had become so deluded and self-centred. It was futile to seek René's assistance in trying to investigate his son's death. I became the lone searcher for answers.

Benjamin's sisters insisted I stay in their brother's private quarters. They thought Benjamin would have wanted that. I intuitively believed their offer had a greater meaning than they stated, and gladly accepted. That evening, I entered into Benjamin's world with an immense sadness but with an expectation I might find some clues to my cousin's untimely death.

As I scrutinized the room, I felt that Benjamin's spirit had not yet departed this sanctuary, this private place once occupied by Uncle Pierre. It was obvious nothing had been moved. Books and papers were lying about the room. I noticed the ancestral Bible in an honoured place on the table beside the large bed. On Benjamin's work desk were papers of various kinds that gave evidence of his business and trade dealings. On closer inspection, however, I noticed that one drawer, below the desktop, was slightly ajar. It beckoned to me to open it. As I gently pulled on its handle the drawer opened wide, revealing a leather-bound volume. It was well worn, and I could see no lettering on its cover. I peered at it, wondering what mysteries it held. I was not prepared for what I was to discover within its pages. This was Benjamin's private journal.

Chapter 21

I sat on the bed and began to thumb through Benjamin's journal. The winter entries were routine and filled with personal observations about dealings he had with his neighbours. He regularly mentioned his concerns about Elizabeth's dark moods and monitored her good days and bad. With the change of seasons, however, the tone in his writing dramatically changed — not to one of hope, which is customary when spring arrives, but to one of darkness and foreboding. I began to read attentively.

JOURNAL OF BENJAMIN LEBLANC, 1739

April 11, 1739
Today I met with a delegation of farmers who are at their wits' end over Mangeant's persistent bad treatment. They allege that the magistrate is questioning their ownership of their farms based on the lack of proper documentation. He has told them that this jeopardizes their children's right to inherit. It angers me to think that a proof is necessary. Most of these families have worked this land for generations. They say he uses condescending and aggressive language with them on his regular visits to their farms. They feel helpless because he invariably reinforces his position of power by emphasizing his close relationship with Lieutenant-Governor Armstrong, a man they only know by reputation. Although Uncle Alexandre is officially

the tax collector, the favourite has taken that on as well. Furthermore, the farmers sense they are being watched at all times, and this fills them with unease. I emphasized to them that Mangeant is a fear monger, and that if they stand their ground without causing offence there is little he can do to retaliate without a justifiable reason. They, however, have always looked to me for counsel and, as they see it, protection. Therefore, I shall do my duty and discuss the situation with the magistrate.

April 12, 1739

I visited Mangeant today at his home. Madame Mangeant was very gracious and offered me tea while I waited for her husband. She spoke only a few words of welcome in French and left me alone. I glanced around their Great Room and noticed there was evidence of comfort and style in this house that Bernard Gaudet built. It was decorated in the English style, which was not surprising. The Mangeants had lived at the Annapolis garrison for many years and were exposed to more things British in that time than anything French or Acadian. I realized that the Manor House was, in stark contrast, decorated in the style of the old French regime. For the first time it dawned on me that I had not changed a single thing at the Manor House since Grandfather died, except for the addition of a considerable number of volumes to the book collection.

Mangeant kept me waiting for a long period, perhaps to give him the advantage in this ongoing power game he is playing with me. He appeared in the doorway of his study wearing an English waistcoat. I was not invited to join him in his private quarters. He joined me in the Great Room, and after engaging in simple courtesies, he sat on the chair opposite me with a look of anticipation and false politeness.

I wasted no time in expressing my concerns about his treatment of my Acadian neighbours, hoping he might consider tempering his behaviour in order to keep the peace.

He remained silent as I spoke, but I was aware that the blood was slowly bringing colour to his cheeks. I sensed that the changing demeanour was evidence of a controlled rage. He stiffened in his chair, and his boots rigidly came together in an "at attention" stance.

At the end of my plea, there was a brief silence. Suddenly he began to bellow his disapproval. He chastised me for presuming to give him advice, stating he was living in Grand Pré as an official representative of the British governor at Annapolis.

He declared that having shoddy legal documents or none whatsoever was absolutely unacceptable. He accused the Acadians of being a horde of half-witted labourers who required direction, and that they had been living too long under no governance at all. He announced it was high time they learned to act like His Majesty's loyal subjects, of which he implied they had shown little evidence to date. He assured me he had the full confidence of Lieutenant-Governor Armstrong himself, and that despite the position I inherited from my grandfather, a title he insisted was an obsolete one from the French regime, I did not have the right to make recommendations to him.

With a threatening tone, he warned me that should I persist in attacking him either in private or in public, there would be severe consequences.

That is when I abruptly rose from my chair. I stared at Mangeant in disbelief. Bowing politely and uttering not a word, I stood my ground defiantly. There was no doubt we both understood that from that moment the rules of the game had dramatically changed. We were now dire enemies. I sensed this would be our last direct encounter. From that point on I was committed to the idea that all my resistance would now be underground. I was more determined than ever to oppose him at every turn, not out of anger or spitefulness but out of a desire to help the poor, mistreated people of Grand Pré. I let myself out and walked triumphantly home.

April 23, 1739

I met with several of the farmers at my father's house today. There is always a crowd there, with the legions of half-brothers and -sisters roaming around, engaged in any number of activities. Several more people on the property went unnoticed. We have found it prudent not to meet at the Manor House. It is too conspicuous. Subterfuge and canniness are necessary when planning strategies. My father and I have been working with Uncle Alexandre, trying to straighten out the myriad legal documents that had been left to languish in his home. I stressed the importance of having things in order so Mangeant could not find fault with the wills, deeds, and tenancy agreements. Involving the farmers in this effort eases their fear of Mangeant. It seems to give them hope and peace of mind.

April 25, 1739

Mangeant struck François Babin in public today, claiming he had been insolent to him. Thank goodness François did not strike him back. I dare say that would have created a catastrophe. When François related the story to me, he was still filled with a fury I had never seen in him before. He said he was paid up in his taxes and Mangeant declared he was not. François had not thought to ask the favourite for written proof when he had paid what was due in March.

I told François he was not to pay another penny. I would make up the difference this time, but this was a good lesson. Everyone who pays his taxes in future must request written proof of payment. We would spread the news throughout the community of Minas. I told François to send one of his children to Mangeant with the sum I had provided. Payment with no respect was the best line of resistance.

François's ten-year-old son delivered the sum to Mangeant relaying a message from his father that a written proof of payment was required. The boy returned to us looking white as a ghost. He said Mangeant had been enraged but provided what they required. We thanked the boy for being so brave.

We both agreed this was a cruel deed to inflict on a young boy but it was a wise lesson learned.

May 1, 1739

I crossed paths with Mangeant today while returning from my father's house. It was a beautiful spring day and I decided to walk rather than travel by wagon. On seeing him approach, I was determined to be cordial without stopping to converse. As he approached me, I noticed a determination in his gait. As we grew closer, he surprised me by thrusting himself in my direction so our bodies bumped with such a force that I was nearly knocked down.

He shouted at me for all those who were close to hear. "Do not trifle with me, young lord. I am aware of the game you are playing and you will not get away with it.

"Continue and I warn you, I am perfectly capable of making your life miserable. If you push me too far, it could be far worse!"

I informed him that it was he who had just assaulted me and that there were witnesses present to attest to that truth. I stood out of his way and proceeded along the road as if no altercation had occurred. I must say I was sorely vexed, but I was compelled to practise what I had been preaching to the farmers in the community — to engage in passive resistance. This encounter was evidence that the strategy we had adopted was working. Perhaps Mangeant will temper his behaviour in future and we can all live together in harmony. I pray I am not deluded.

May 25, 1739

Yesterday, Mangeant sailed for Annapolis on official business, with the lieutenant-governor, no doubt. He will invariably lodge formal complaints against the members of the Minas community, and me in particular. He believes I am surreptitiously undermining him. Let us hope he does not find a sympathetic ear.

Otherwise, we are living in a splendid and intoxicating world of pink and perfume for as far as our eyes can see and our noses can smell. Thousands of apple trees have burst into glorious bloom. I am organizing an apple blossom festival at Grand Pré, so hundreds of farming families from Minas and Pisiquit can celebrate their survival of another winter and the promise of an abundant crop in the coming summer. Everyone arrives in three days' time. I have personally invited Madame Mangeant, the two babies she has borne since her arrival at Grand Pré, and her daughter Louise. She seemed touched by my gesture. I believe she is as happy as the rest of us to get a reprieve from her husband's presence.

May 28, 1739

It is very late as I sit here, remembering a marvellous day of games, dancing, singing, and an abundance of food and sweets made from maple syrup. I believe every human being in Minas and Pisiquit was present. They were decked in their finest apparel, and the women's crisp white bonnets dotted the landscape as if to complement the puffy pink blossoms on the thousands of apple trees. Hundreds of wooden shoes kept a steady rhythm, while violins and mouth harps played ancient and merry melodies. Today the people of our community felt the ease of the carefree life they had enjoyed for over a hundred years, with nothing and no one disturbing the flow of their happiness.

June 4, 1739

Mangeant has returned. The ten days he was away were blissful ones. I am certain he has returned with a message from the lieutenant-governor directing us onto the path of righteousness! Poor Madame Mangeant — she has the misfortune of living with him.

June 10, 1739
The favourite has been home a week and no proclamation. Perhaps the lieutenant-governor advised him to be
less heavy-handed in his dealings with us "simple-minded"
Acadians. It is only a matter of time. The devil will raise his
head again, I am certain.

June 11, 1739
Today Elizabeth seemed much better. She is enjoying her
garden again, and her appetite is returning. I do love to see
her in a merrier mood. These warm beautiful days are perhaps the elixir she needs to improve her health and lift her
up from her melancholia. It saddens me that Piau will not
visit us this summer. Another baby is on the way. Perhaps I
will visit Melanson Village in late July.

Reading the final words of this entry of the journal, I began to weep
uncontrollably. Benjamin had never lived to visit us at Melanson Village. I
lay on his bed and surrendered to my grief.

Chapter 22

The following day I strolled through the village and ventured out into the countryside. I walked all the way to René's farm to relieve myself of the gloom I felt staying in the Manor House. It was clear that even Benjamin's death could not quell the enthusiasm of his half-siblings, for they played and worked in the yard as I arrived. They were laughing and shouting at the top of their lungs, even though Benjamin was barely cold in his grave. I stared at them, marvelling at their number and their actions. There was a herd of them, their ages ranging from three to eighteen. All I could think of was René's lack of restraint. He was a loving man, but the sheer number of children he had sired offended me because they were alive and Benjamin was not.

I secretly blamed René for not watching over Benjamin when he knew full well that there was bad blood between Mangeant and his son. Although I could not be certain, I felt to the core of my being that Mangeant's evil hand was in play the day Benjamin died. I needed explanations, however, so I was willing to swallow my contempt in order to find answers to my nagging questions.

When I met René at the front door I could see that he wasn't overjoyed to see me. He greeted me warmly but it was far from genuine. "Piau, you look very tired. I realize everything must seem unreal to you — Benjamin being no longer with us, I mean."

He began to look agitated and tears appeared in his eyes. It was then that I decided this would be just a social visit. The interrogation I had planned now seemed inappropriate and I was in the presence of a genuinely grieving man. My questions would only deepen the guilt he was already finding unbearable. We sat in the garden drinking apple cider and observing the frenzied activity of the children. These were the living, and Benjamin was no longer among them.

After we had been seated for some time, I made my apologies and said that I had promised to drop in on Charles's in-laws, the Grangers. As I left, I noticed the look of relief on René's face.

I did not visit the Grangers. Instead, I made my way to the churchyard to Benjamin's gravesite. The freshly piled earth and the temporary white cross gave me no comfort. Benjamin was not there in the graveyard. I felt his presence more in the words of his journal, so I returned to the Manor House and found solace in my cousin's private quarters. There I continued to read where I had left off the night before.

June 15, 1739

The summer solstice is a week away, but the heat has arrived early. This would normally be a blessing. An early crop is a favourable omen and something we all hope for. However, each day I find the heat oppressive as if the fates were willing my discomfort and sucking every drop of sweat from my body. Mangeant follows my every move, and like a spider he waits for the opportunity to pounce and inject his venom into my soul.

I am certain he was not pleased that we had managed to organize a celebration in his absence. At Sunday mass, Madame Mangeant secretly directed a smile in my direction out of the watchful eye of her husband. His demeanour, on the other hand, was antagonistic. He commented to the priest within my hearing that the community had enjoyed a spring festival in his absence. Was he to think this was intentional?

He glanced at me for only a moment, but it was enough time to direct a menacing grin in my direction. It was then that I recalled the story of the ship's captain who had been the victim of Mangeant's sword. The thought of it sent a chill through my body. Will I be his next target? I have to stop having these thoughts. They are paralyzing me and I am unable to escape their poison. Perhaps Elizabeth's melancholia is contagious. I must sleep. It is only then that my spirit feels free.

June 21, 1739

Today was the first day of summer and the entire community gathered at dusk to light a great bonfire on the beach. The sun set behind us as we enjoyed its pink reflection in the clouds over Minas Basin. It was a massive gathering of all the people of the valley. It is an annual event that for me evokes happy memories of days past, of my mother's warmth as we sat on the sandy beach when I was a very young boy, of Grandfather sitting in his birch limb chair acting like the King of the Solstice, and of my friends and me splashing our bare feet in the cold basin water until we had no feeling in them at all. All these recollections have filled me with joy. Thank you, Lord.

June 25, 1739

What makes a man victimize others? Is there some satisfaction one receives from causing others anguish? Obviously! Alexandre arrived here today in a frantic state. Mangeant had arrived at his house early in the day and confiscated all the legal documents remaining in his possession. He accused Uncle of being an incompetent old fool, and advised him that he need not bother himself with official matters from this day forward. He said he could not for the life of him understand how anyone could have entrusted important legal and tax concerns to Uncle when he was notary. Uncle is a very proud man and known throughout the community and beyond as a man of extreme good humour. To see him that distraught was so disheartening. I joined him in a healthy glass of dandelion wine and tried my best to quell his anxiety.

June 27, 1739

I decided to throw caution to the wind and invite all the
men of the valley to the Manor House today. Mangeant
was not included. I masked the gathering as a social event.
The assembly was held inside despite the heat. This way
those who attended could express their grievances and
not fear reprisals. Alexandre and my father were the first
to voice their displeasure with the situation at Grand Pré.
Everyone agreed that someone had to volunteer to make
formal complaints to the lieutenant-governor regarding
Mangeant's arbitrary treatment of the members of the
Minas community. There was not a single individual who
had not had at least one unfortunate encounter with the
magistrate. It turned out I was the man chosen to represent
them. How to achieve the task was left to me. I decided
that I would sail to Annapolis and lodge a formal com-
plaint to Lieutenant-Governor Armstrong on behalf of the
people of Minas.

July 1, 1739

Mangeant noticed today that I was preparing my schooner
for a voyage at sea. This was not my usual time of year to
visit Annapolis or anywhere else, and he seemed to linger
at some distance wondering why I was preparing to sail
from Grand Pré at the beginning of summer. Visitors were
often expected — Piau and his family arrived for a stay
every year — but this was a particularly busy time of year
for landowners in the valley and if anyone at Minas left the
community by sea, everyone noticed. Some discretion is
required on my part but it is difficult to hide one's comings
and goings to and from the harbour. I have postponed my
sailing for several days so as not to draw attention to my
unexpected departure.

Mangeant is aware of my every move and he hovers
like a bird of prey, ready to strike should I decide to leave
unexpectedly by boat.

July 4, 1739

A bit of good luck arrived today by ship. Captain Andrew Tyrone sailed into the basin with things to trade. It was early for a trading visit, because we had little to trade save last year's apples and fresh strawberries. He was en route to Dublin and decided to sail up the Bay of Fundy to avoid a nasty storm that was brewing in the Atlantic. He felt it was an opportunity to visit the Manor House and deliver a collection of the latest volumes he had brought from Britain.

With the arrival of Tyrone, I have devised a plan to escape Grand Pré without Mangeant noticing that I have left. I will entertain Tyrone for several days, sleep on my schooner the night before his departure for England, hop on his ship before dusk, and have him drop me off at Annapolis on his way to his ocean voyage. Thus, I will safely set about my mission to meet with the lieutenant-governor. The fates have been kind in having Captain Tyrone arrive just in time for my rescue.

July 7, 1739

I have enjoyed Tyrone's visit immensely and we were able to relax in the sun today and enjoy a taste of the rum he had brought from the Indies. He had many a tale of his far-flung travels to tell me, and they were a fine accompaniment to the drinks I concocted with his strong spirits. I revealed to him my plan of escape, with a complete explanation of the situation and why it was necessary for me to leave in the dead of night. He was more than willing to assist me but seemed gravely concerned for my well-being, having heard the story of Mangeant's obsession where I am concerned. I will soon be off to my schooner for a good night's sleep and I predict I will have a safe voyage tomorrow beginning before dawn.

These were the final words Benjamin wrote in his journal.

Chapter 23

What an odd place to discontinue your journal entries, Benjamin. Did you actually sleep aboard your boat that night? Why did you not leave with Tyrone the following morning? Where were you found dead? How? Why? By whom?

There were too many unanswered questions and I had used up my patience with Elizabeth, Marie Josephe, and René stepping around the details of Benjamin's death and not delivering even the simplest piece of information. If he died as a result of foul play, as I suspected he had, then it was high time someone investigated the entire affair. What was everyone afraid of? Whom was everyone afraid of? If it was Mangeant, then something had to be said and now!

I got no sleep that night; I was waiting for my two cousins in the Great Room first thing in the morning. I lost no time in confronting the ladies, beginning with Marie Josephe. She was the elder sister and the one less wounded by life.

"Cousin, I have spent the better part of the last three days reading your brother's journal. Did you not know Benjamin kept one?"

I stopped for a moment to assess the ladies' grim looks. They obviously had not known of its existence. Neither spoke.

"I discovered his journal several days ago and have read all the entries for this year. And what I have found is extremely disturbing. I demand answers, here and now!"

Elizabeth was the first to speak.

"What is it you wish to know, Piau?"

"To start with, I want to know how Benjamin died. I need to hear the details, now."

The two sisters glanced uncertainly at one another.

"You are aware of a certain sea captain named Andrew Tyrone?" asked Elizabeth tentatively.

"Yes, Benjamin's last journal entries describe Tyrone's visit to Grand Pré."

Elizabeth answered with caution. "Yes, well, it was he who discovered Benjamin the morning he was to leave for England. Strangely, it was on our brother's vessel that Tyrone found him. Someone had inflicted numerous sword wounds on Benjamin's chest."

She began to sob uncontrollably.

I looked at Marie Josephe, entreating her to continue the story. She reluctantly obliged.

"Yes, Tyrone placed Benjamin's lifeless body into his dory and rowed to the wharf. He lifted it onto the plankway and marched down the main road of the village to the Manor House. When we opened the front door Tyrone stood there distraught, with Benjamin in his arms. I do not remember much after that. It seems like some unbelievable nightmare. Why would Benjamin be on his boat during the night?"

I explained to them in considerable detail the story their brother had related in his journal and his plan to visit Armstrong at Annapolis. They were confused and dismayed, but the story presented only one possibility for all of us, that Mangeant had murdered Benjamin in cold blood.

"How could he have hated Benjamin enough to kill him?" asked Marie Josephe. "Our brother was loved by everyone!"

I remarked that that was precisely why Mangeant detested Benjamin.

Elizabeth interjected, "It was Mangeant who suggested that Tyrone was the likely suspect. He was suspicious that the captain had sailed away too hastily after delivering Benjamin's corpse. Mangeant speculated that Tyrone's speedy departure was powerful evidence of his guilt. He even suggested that perhaps Benjamin had taken his own life.

"Mangeant thought this a possibility. Few believed either of his theories. After all, how does someone stab oneself to death? Most of us guessed at the truth. But no one was prepared to accuse anyone. It was as if the world had decided to permit Benjamin to vanish from our lives. Nothing could possibly return him to us. Better leave him to heaven."

"The warning signs were there but no one had knowledge of them. They were privately stored in the pages of Benjamin's journal," I replied. "I have to say that a large degree of discretion is required in investigating this treacherous act. I intend on discussing the case with Lieutenant-Governor Armstrong in person, completing the task Benjamin started a week ago. You are to relay this to no one, not even your father. I will notify Charles that I wish to sail immediately, and we will leave on the next tide. Damn that accursed man!"

Chapter 24

The evening I arrived back at Melanson Village, my fifth daughter, Agnes, was born. She was an angel from the beginning and she still is. After living among the bereaved for ten days, the joy surrounding her birth was all the more poignant to me. Babies arrive, I am certain, to ease the grief of losing our loved ones.

Jeanne was extremely happy that I had been present at Agnes's birth. I chose not to unload the discoveries of the past week on her or anyone else. That would have to wait. I possessed the journal and that was all I required to proceed in my quest for justice. I was optimistic that I would achieve satisfaction, but from whom? Could I expect Armstrong to pursue a murder investigation that conceivably implicated his closest friend and confidant? I felt it prudent to allow some time to pass before I approached the lieutenant-governor with my evidence.

In time, I mustered the courage to relate the complete story of Benjamin's murder to Jeanne and my mother. They were horrified and saddened that someone as exemplary as he should experience such a tragic end. When I finally filled in all the gruesome details, neither of them wished to discuss it any further. They loved Benjamin deeply, and even imagining his horrendous final moments was too painful for them.

As far as the community at large was concerned, I merely explained that it was a sudden illness and left it at that. Nothing in how I delivered the news about Benjamin revealed that I was secretly fuming inside with a combination of rage, sorrow, and vengeance. Revenge and justice were my best friends. I was embracing both in the late summer of 1739.

I chose to wait until the autumn to present my case to Lieutenant-Governor Armstrong. Charles and I floated into the harbour on the day of the autumnal equinox. My heart was beating furiously as I ventured up from the lower town to the fort. I had not contacted the lieutenant-governor, not wishing to alert him of my mission in advance. I encountered Major Cosby as I passed the garrison. He greeted me warmly.

"Monsieur Belliveau, I was saddened to hear of the death of your cousin Benjamin LeBlanc. He was a fine fellow, and so young. He was highly regarded in his community at Grand Pré, was he not? I hope he did not suffer in his final days. Captain Tyrone delivered the news of his death as he passed by Annapolis en route to the Atlantic. He met with the lieutenant-governor privately for several hours. I was not privy to their conversation, so I am not aware of the details of your cousin's death."

"You are kind to express your sympathy. I wonder if you might grant me a favour. It is necessary for me to meet with the lieutenant-governor to discuss my cousin's death. Would you be able to arrange for me to see Lieutenant-Governor Armstrong on short notice?"

Major Cosby exhibited a curious look and responded promptly. "I would be happy to do so. The urgency of your request suggests to me that you suspect foul play. Is that so?" I could tell he was fishing for information.

It was not the appropriate time to elaborate on the matter so I made my apologies and promised to discuss the entire affair after I had met with the lieutenant-governor.

He appeared to understand and left me momentarily to seek the audience I had requested. He returned after a short time.

"His Excellency has granted you an audience. You may proceed to the lieutenant-governor's quarters at the garrison. I look forward to our next meeting, Monsieur Belliveau."

I thanked him and bid him good day.

Armstrong sat in a large leather chair beside a small fireplace. The room was panelled and painted a mint green. Painted walls were a rare sight in the colony. Above the mantel hung several swords — one above the next, all different. There was a writing desk piled neatly with papers, with several ink pens sitting upright in their bottles. There was a crispness in the decor. There were no paintings on the panelled walls. There were no signs of loved ones, no souvenirs of places the lieutenant-governor had visited.

The lieutenant-governor himself was in complete contrast to the tidiness of the room. He was not wearing a uniform, and his apparel showed no sign of his position at Annapolis. Seeing him for the first time in an informal setting was a shock. He appeared to have taken little care in his dress, and he had a beleaguered expression on his face.

"So, young Belliveau, we meet again. You and I have a long history, do we not? From a very early age you have shown yourself to be a bold and cheeky fellow. That being said, I had the misfortune of encountering your now deceased grandmother, Madame Marie, on a few occasions, and I recognize such impertinence to be a family inheritance. I must say, though, I respect pluck in a person. Please sit."

I sat opposite him in a straight wooden chair and felt rather more comfortable in his presence than I had anticipated. There was something about the man that was different, something almost humane. Something I had not witnessed in him before. This was, of course, the first time I had been alone with him in private.

"So, what brings you to the garrison, monsieur?"

"Excellency, I have come to discuss the death of my cousin Benjamin LeBlanc of Grand Pré."

"Indeed. I did hear of his passing. Allow me to express my condolences to you and your family. He was a highly respected young man in his community."

"He was much loved, sir."

I had Armstrong's full attention, but the expression on his tired face did not alter.

"Was his death sudden, or did he suffer a lengthy illness?"

"His death was decidedly sudden and he was in perfect health when he died. It is my belief, Excellency, that he was murdered."

"I see." The lieutenant-governor uttered these words without any change in his demeanour. I recognized that this was not news to him.

Before continuing, I reached for the bag I had carried into the interview and slowly drew out Benjamin's journal.

"This is my cousin's journal. The entries here were all written this year. The spring entries tell a story of bad blood between François Mangeant and Benjamin. My cousin even expressed his fear that Monsieur Mangeant might possibly end his life."

I began to relate all the details of Benjamin's secret community meetings and Mangeant's antagonistic treatment of him. The lieutenant-governor asked to see the journal. I complied, passing it to him with great care. He fingered through its pages in a cursory way then closed it firmly in his hands.

"And what is it you believe this journal suggests, monsieur?"

"Forgive my boldness, Excellency, but I believe it suggests that Mangeant murdered Benjamin LeBlanc."

"That is a bold accusation, monsieur. Monsieur LeBlanc could not possibly have described his own death in his journal."

Armstrong scrutinized me carefully, but his expression never changed.

"No, certainly not, but it describes in detail the events leading up to that evening he when received four fatal wounds from the blade of a sword."

"And did you inspect these sword wounds yourself?"

"No, sir, I was not in Grand Pré at the time of the death, but his wounds were described to me by his sisters and his father, René LeBlanc."

"So, this information is second-hand knowledge?"

"Yes, sir."

"If there were no witnesses to the so-called murder, then any accusations against Monsieur Mangeant are purely circumstantial. That being said, I will peruse LeBlanc's journal and discuss its comments with Monsieur Mangeant himself."

"Would it be presumptuous of me, Excellency, to ask from whom you received the news of my cousin's death?"

"It is indeed presumptuous, Monsieur Belliveau. The lieutenant-governor always has his sources when someone of note dies in his colony."

It was at that moment I realized I must drop the cannonball.

"Could that source have been Captain Andrew Tyrone? After all, he was the person who found Monsieur LeBlanc."

There was still no alteration in his facial expression.

"And what makes you believe this Captain Tyrone would have relayed this information to me?"

"I have been told this very day that the day following Benjamin's death Captain Tyrone sailed into the harbour at Annapolis and met with you for a length of time."

For the first time since the audience began I noticed a subtle hint of agitation in his features.

"Where did you acquire this information, monsieur?"

"Major Cosby told me that your Excellency met with Captain Tyrone when he visited the garrison on his way home to England in July."

"That is true, but what makes you believe he discussed your cousin's death with me?"

"It is highly likely that he would have done so, given the fact that he was the person who found my cousin's body. It seems inconceivable to me that he would not have related such an event to the governor of the colony. Benjamin was a very influential person at Grand Pré."

I felt my heart begin to beat faster with every word uttered.

"Again, sir, that is merely your personal opinion. There are many things I could have discussed with the captain. I have traded with Tyrone often. Let me put this question to you, Monsieur Belliveau. Did it occur to you that Tyrone himself may have had an altercation with your cousin? There is as much evidence to suggest that Tyrone murdered your cousin as Monsieur Mangeant. After all, Tyrone was the one to find LeBlanc aboard his own vessel."

The final sentence stopped me in my tracks. I had not mentioned that Benjamin was found on his own boat. I now felt I was on shaky ground.

"What motive would Tyrone have had for killing my cousin? To my knowledge their relationship was a good one."

"Who really knows what relationship one person has with another? I will say to you now, monsieur, that you have a very weak case against Monsieur Mangeant. However, I will read your cousin's journal and then meet with Mangeant to confirm your cousin's observations. Then I will speak to you. I can see you are shaken by Benjamin LeBlanc's death. I say to you there is a possibility he took his own life. Has that not occurred to you?"

"It never has, sir. I am certain he was murdered, and all I wish is that justice is done."

"Time will tell, then. Thank you for bringing this matter to my attention. I will return the journal to you after I have thoroughly given it my full attention. Good day, Monsieur Belliveau. It was a pleasure to see you again."

Having been dismissed, I left the garrison in a dejected state. The meeting with Armstrong was a necessary step if I was to obtain justice in Benjamin's murder, but it did not appear to have brought me nearer my goal.

I never saw Lieutenant-Governor Armstrong again.

The events that occurred at Annapolis over the next two months are not easy to describe, because I did not return to the town again until the following spring. I gave the lieutenant-governor time to digest the evidence I had given to him but I received no response. I was to discover there was a reason for his silence.

Early snows in December kept us close to home, so any news from the town eluded us. However, on a walking visit to Annapolis to trade with the English merchants, Charles received momentous news. On his return home, I was the first person he visited. He informed me Lieutenant-Governor Armstrong was dead. There were few details, but the rumour was he had committed suicide.

Apparently, he had been found in his quarters after having inflicted five sword wounds on his chest. The sword was found by his side on the bed.

The word was that the lieutenant-governor was despondent and experiencing severe attacks of melancholia. I thought of how ironic this was. The last time I spoke to him he had suggested the possibility of Benjamin ending his life in the exact same manner. The death was being investigated. What if he, like Benjamin, had been murdered in his bed? I don't know why, but the news saddened me more than I would have expected.

We did not attend the funeral service.

When finally I sailed into Annapolis in the spring of 1740, I met Colonel Cosby by chance. He told me he had completed the inquiry into Armstrong's death and it had been designated a suicide. Furthermore, he wished for me to follow him to his quarters at the garrison. I did, and he produced Benjamin's journal, saying he thought I would wish to have my cousin's property. It had been found in the lieutenant-governor's rooms at the fort. He also informed me, knowing I would be interested, that Mangeant had resigned his post at Grand Pré.

"Do you believe François Mangeant murdered your cousin, Monsieur Belliveau?"

I was taken off guard by his question but chose to be forthright.

"I am certain of it, Colonel."

"I share your belief. Unfortunately, there is no real evidence that can connect Mangeant to Benjamin LeBlanc's death."

"What about Benjamin's diary?" I asked in desperation.

"I read the journal after I found it beside the lieutenant-governor's bed and there appear to be a large number of pages missing. So, I am afraid you may be compelled to give up on your quest for justice and leave that to the Almighty. Divine justice is the most powerful justice of all. If Mangeant killed Benjamin LeBlanc, then he will roast in the fires of hell, which is where I predict he is destined in any case. That should be comfort enough for you, monsieur. Good day."

I walked to the harbour with Benjamin's journal under my arm and remained huddled on Charles's schooner for the entire day until he returned in the early evening. Sailing back to the village, I held the book to my breast, feeling that somehow I was embracing Benjamin's spirit.

PART 3:

THE FRENCH MENACE

Chapter 25

The five years following Armstrong's death proved to be a short reprieve from the usual anxieties we had experienced under his governorship. Colonel Cosby acted as lieutenant-governor for a short time, but despite his kindness to the Acadian community he never quite managed to achieve quietude at the fort. His sudden death in 1742 ended the unrest that had existed at the garrison for decades. One of the officers, Major Paul Mascarene, who had been stationed at Annapolis Royal for many years, replaced him as lieutenant-governor, and things settled down among the English considerably.

In 1742 Jeanne and I welcomed another daughter into the world. We named her Rosalie. She was our sixth daughter. My home had become a girlish domain, but I continued to treasure it as always. I was the recipient of my family's attention and love.

Isabelle continued to visit Benjamin's sisters at Grand Pré following his death. It was obvious she was tenaciously holding on to his memory. However, in time she met a first cousin of Benjamin, Joseph LeBlanc, son of René's brother Jacques LeBlanc, and they married in Annapolis at Chapelle St. Jean Baptiste in the summer of 1742. We held the wedding feast at Melanson Village, and it gave us great joy to witness Isabelle moving on with her life. She was more radiant than I had ever seen her, although I detected a tiny glint of melancholy in her beautiful eyes. She moved to Grand Pré to live with her husband's family.

Throughout this period of peace, there were nevertheless rumblings of war from afar. Across the ocean in Europe, they called it the War of the Austrian Succession, but its name was just a name to us. We imagined that succession meant something to do with monarchs, but which ones none of us knew. We were not even aware which Louis sat on the throne of France. Nor did we care. We were loyal subjects of King George II, although we had never even seen a portrait of this ruler. As for Austria, it might have been some imaginary place.

We Acadians were French-speaking and French in culture, but the menace from France that arrived in Acadia in 1744 was almost our undoing. It led to a series of calamitous events that the English governors for the next decade were not soon to forget. France's determination to regain control of Acadia was to cause us no end of grief. Without consulting us, our mother country, France, was as responsible for the destruction of Acadia ten years later as the British were in carrying it out.

With the risk of war between England and France looming on the horizon, Lieutenant-Governor Mascarene began to panic. He was more than aware that the fortifications at Annapolis Royal were incomplete, insufficient, and in frightful condition. He sought assistance from Boston, requesting engineers and a military construction crew to build new ramparts and walls. Soon the Acadian community was asked to supply timber specialists, masons, and carpenters. This was our opportunity to acquire pounds sterling. Bernard and Denys sailed down the river to be supervisors on the site of the new fortress. Working together was like old times.

By mid-May 1744, after Mascarene informed us that Britain was at war with France, news arrived at Annapolis Royal that the French had attacked Canso, the other important British settlement in Acadia, and left it in ruins. This made our construction efforts all that more crucial in the eyes of the British settlers living in the town. Many of them had already packed their wives and children onto ships and sent them to New England, a place of greater safety. Most decided to stay, however. They desperately wanted a safe haven at the fort to retreat to should the French forces attack Annapolis.

On the work site, there was much discussion among the Acadians about our precarious position, wedged somewhere between the British who governed us and the French-Mi'kmaq alliance. Bernard, as usual, led the outspoken charge. "Our problem is, we cannot live alongside the British and the Mi'kmaq at the same time. The two are natural enemies and we are allied to both. Where does that put us? I will tell you where that puts us, between a rock and a hard place! And the French are taking advantage of our dilemma, insisting we follow them. Remaining neutral in this world, which is in our nature as Acadians, is made almost impossible by both sides of this conflict."

"As difficult as it may seem," I interjected, "we have no choice but to stay the course of neutrality, for it is the only path we can follow. Otherwise, we are forced to choose sides and that would be perilous."

"Therefore, if the French attack Port Royal tomorrow, we jump aboard our vessels and sail upriver to safety. Let the British defend the fortress."

"The French have not arrived yet, Bernard. Meanwhile, it is our job to make this fort impregnable." With this comment, I began to sing a cheerful tune to lift the spirits of the labourers.

It was in the beginning of July 1744 that we heard the cannon fire coming from the fort. We heard repeated shots and at times we recognized distant musket fire as well. We questioned who it might be. Considering no ships had passed by us at Melanson Village, we concluded it was not the French.

Indeed, it was not the French who arrived at Annapolis Royal that day, it was the Mi'kmaq. They must have portaged through the woods from Grand Pré and canoed downriver to the fort.

By late evening we were witnessing the clear night sky illuminated by the fire of the burning town. It was so alarming we thought we could feel its heat from our village. Our entire community watched anxiously from the water's edge. We hoped we would be spared the fate of our Acadian neighbours at Annapolis. We had always been on good terms with the Mi'kmaq, but our neutrality toward the British was a thorn in the side of that relationship.

The next day or two were relatively quiet save for a few distant gunshots. But on day three we spotted a large ship looming on the horizon of Annapolis Basin. Was it French or British? The answer to this question would have a major impact on our future. I am hesitant to admit it, but we were actually relieved to discover it was a British warship bearing the name *Prince of Orange*. It was trailed by another vessel carrying at least a hundred soldiers. This British ship had arrived to protect Annapolis; a French vessel would have meant the destruction of both the fort and our way of life. Despite our relief on that day, this would be the last time we supported the British in our hearts and minds.

After several days had passed, Charles and I decided to sail into Annapolis to survey the damage done by the Mi'kmaq. It was worse than we had imagined. Most of the town was in ruins. We heard from our Acadian friends that much of the damage was created by the soldiers themselves, wishing to deprive the Mi'kmaqs of a place from which to launch their attacks on the fort. The New England volunteers had even destroyed the church and the priest's residence despite Mascarene's orders to spare them. The church still symbolized the French regime and the support the Natives gave to the French Catholics. The New Englanders were Protestant, and destruction was the price of war.

We had heard that the lieutenant-governor promised to compensate the English subjects and merchants for their losses. The Acadians' losses were also great, but no compensation was promised them. The principal loss to both the English and the Acadians was their livestock, destroyed by the Mi'kmaq warriors. We promised our Acadian friends that we would assist them by donating the fruits of our breeding stock so they could begin rebuilding their herds of sheep and cattle. We knew they would have done the same for us.

Chapter 26

It was a summer of struggle and coercion. Struggle to distance ourselves from something that was threatening but never quite there. The Mi'kmaq were menacing spectres flying through the trees along the Annapolis River, there but not there. The coercion came from the French, who arrived in the dying days of summer, demanding of us things we could not spare but dared not withhold. We neither resisted nor did we assist. The only payment we received was the services of Father Le Loutre, who accompanied the French and Native forces. As a conduit to God he gave us spiritual sustenance; as an enemy he represented everything Armstrong had always feared and detested in the French Catholic clergy. We were, as always, conflicted.

Bernard and Denys delivered the alarming news in late August that the French and Native forces were camped at Belle Isle, the largest Acadian community on the river, awaiting an opportunity to attack the fort from a position upriver. From merely a sail by, Bernard estimated the soldiers and warriors to be three hundred strong. He did not stop to investigate. He and his brother were on their way downriver to continue their work on the fort. They spent their evenings with us at Melanson Village.

Work on the fort's ramparts was not an easy task. Torrential rains made the work extremely difficult, but the workers persevered. I had completed my work as mason earlier in the month, but the weather would have made my work impossible in any case.

In early September we heard the first sounds of cannon and musket fire from Annapolis Royal. Bernard and Denys had wisely decided to remain at Melanson Village while the battle was raging in the town. The fighting continued every evening as the sun went down and kept us awake through the night. It ended only in the early hours of the following morning. The barrage of gunfire persisted for days, leaving us ignorant of who had the upper hand in the siege of the fort. An unexpected coincidence was to bring us closer to the French-Mi'kmaq forces.

On the third or fourth day a large contingent of French army officers appeared above the apple orchards at Melanson Village. Their arrival did not surprise us. They were visiting all the neighbouring farms searching for supplies and assistance. They generally received the former but seldom the latter.

They marched down the main road into the village, stopping at the Manor House. I was waiting at the front gate as they presented themselves in military formation. The commander stepped forward. He and I stood face to face. I remained straight and defiant as he approached me.

He was the first to speak.

"Piau, it has been a very long time."

I gazed at the commander, searching for some memory of the familiar face.

"François? Can it be you?"

Without a moment's hesitation, we embraced warmly, letting the years of separation wash over us.

"Gentlemen, this man was my best friend when I was very young growing up in Port Royal. We are finally reunited after thirty years."

Smiles crossed the faces of his fellow officers. This was François Duvivier, my childhood friend, whom I had not seen since he left with his parents for Louisbourg in 1713. His father had been a French officer at Port Royal and his mother was Marie Muis d'Entremont, the niece of Uncle Pierre's wife, Marie-Marguerite. Benjamin and François were cousins.

"I see the Melansons have multiplied. The village has grown into a town. I do not suppose Madame Marie is still alive?"

"François, you are kind to remember my grandmother. You only missed her by a few years."

"She was a remarkable woman, one I could never forget. She was one of the great matriarchs of Acadia."

By this time, everyone in the Manor House had ventured into the front garden to investigate the officer I had embraced so readily. My mother recognized François immediately and approached him with no trepidation.

"Welcome home, François. I did not believe I would ever see you again after you left us thirty years ago. I would have known it was you despite the passage of time. You have grown to be a handsome and distinguished gentleman."

François lifted my mother's hand and kissed it.

François was introduced to Jeanne and my seven daughters and we entered the Manor House to reacquaint ourselves.

My mother offered François some dandelion wine and cheese.

"Piau, do you remember scaling the walls of the fortress when we were children? I cannot believe my father allowed us to do such dangerous things. I suppose he knew we were well supervised by the guards manning the fortress. It was a fortress then. Now it is barely defendable. The British have left it in deplorable condition."

Despite our ancient history, I was aware that François was fishing for information. Because I was involved in the recent construction, I decided to agree with him and not reveal any information that would suggest that there were strengths in what we had recently completed. I was certain this was not the first time he had attempted to extract sensitive information from the Acadian farmers. He was intelligent enough to sense my reticence.

"But I suppose you are no different than the other Acadians in this colony, determined to preserve your neutrality. That is admirable, Piau, but I think it is worth considering that Acadia, or Nova Scotia, as the British call it, might conceivably return to the French."

"Perhaps you are right, François, but we have been under British rule for most of my lifetime, and despite recognizing that those that govern us could turn against us at any time — we are French, after all — we have survived by remaining neutral. And survival is what we seek."

"I notice that the British have destroyed your place of worship. That is a strange way of seeking your support or even neutrality in this war. Remember, they are Protestant and therefore opposed to the Catholic faith. I do not understand how you can even be neutral in this conflict when you are being deprived of the mass and the blessed sacraments. Well, I am willing to provide what the English will not, with no strings attached. Father Le Loutre will say mass at Melanson Village this coming Sunday and he will be willing to conduct baptisms, marriages, and other sacraments that have been delayed because of your loss of the parish church."

"For that, François, I bless you," said my mother with genuine gratitude in her voice.

That night he slept in the annex as our guest.

True to his word, Captain François Duvivier did return on Sunday with Father Le Loutre, the Jesuit who came to celebrate the promised mass and administer the sacraments. We were familiar with Le Loutre. He had been our pastor during Father Breslay's banishment. Little did Lieutenant-Governor Armstrong suspect that Le Loutre was far more dangerous and conspiratorial than the exiled Breslay.

The French commander and the priest arrived with the same officer escort that had visited Melanson Village earlier in the week. After celebrating the mass, Le Loutre baptized our latest arrival, Felicity, whose name did match her character. She was to be my shining light throughout our life in exile.

I believe François found a peaceful haven in our old familiar community. My mother treated him no differently than she had years before when we were children dangling from the trees in the apple orchard. She had been a close friend of his mother, Marie, when they were girls. The one virtue of being neutral was that it allowed friendship to exist within the atmosphere of war. Anger had no place to hide in our village; therefore, it found no sanctuary there.

The mood was festive. Every baptism was a celebration, a reason to rejoice in the beginning of a new life. François's presence made the passage of time vanish. We were momentarily living in the past, the French past. Our conversations were of remembering, pleasant and comforting for both of us. The war did not exist in that world.

François brought a surprise gift with him. He arrived with six bottles of fine French wine to share on this special occasion.

"You may ask from what source this vintage claret came," he said with a mischievous smile.

"Perhaps it was from the king of France?" I questioned.

"The donor might surprise you, Piau. Guess."

"You have me at a disadvantage, François. But judging from that cheeky grin it must have come from somewhere unexpected."

"Indeed! It was from Governor Mascarene himself! Such a gift is hardly what one would expect from the commander-in-chief of the English garrison.

The shocked look on your face makes my bringing these bottles worth every taste." He began to laugh heartily. The sound of his laughter brought back floods of childhood memories.

"I merely sent a letter to him demanding the surrender of the fortress based on the imminent arrival of French warships in the bay. He included a basket of fruit, sugar, and various other treats. Perhaps that was his way of saying he was going to deliver a sweet capitulation."

We both chuckled.

"I know nothing about matters of war and diplomacy but to me that sounds highly peculiar."

"Well, I must say it proves that he is a gentleman. And, of course, war is a gentlemanly affair."

"I leave these things to the English and the French to work out. I am Acadian, and as an Acadian I am free of all such considerations."

"That may be true now, Piau. I don't claim to be a prophet, but some day, if we do not prevail in our enterprise, you will be abandoned by these English of yours; trust me, they are a brutal people. They will throw you out of your beloved Acadia and scatter your people to the eight winds. They were threatening to do that when I was nine years old living in Port Royal. My father made the proper decision to move us to Île Royale. We have enjoyed an excellent life at Louisbourg and we have prospered there."

I pondered what he said, but I refused to believe that such a thing could possibly happen to my people.

"We have been living in Acadia for a century and we have watched Port Royal fall back and forth between the French and the British. But regardless of who governs us, we prevail. No matter which king we pledge our allegiance to, we still refuse to fight our brothers."

"I admire your determination and your optimism, Piau, but I believe this time we will drive the English from this land forever, for such is our destiny."

"If you are correct, François, then we will see one another far more often." I raised my glass of wine to his.

"To your good health!"

"To friendship and peace!"

François and I never saw one another again after that day. He had re-entered my life only for a brief, blessed moment.

Chapter 27

The French troops persisted in barraging the fort with gunfire, but the capitulation Duvivier was seeking never came to pass. A French ship did arrive in mid-September from Louisbourg with a small contingent of soldiers, and a face-to-face battle ensued, but the British refused to give in. We learned later that no French warships were being dispatched to Annapolis to assist Duvivier and his French-Mi'kmaq alliance.

By the end of September we watched from Melanson Village as two ships flying British flags sailed by Goat Island heading for the harbour. They appeared to be filled with hundreds of troops. We heard later that one Captain John Gorham of New England had arrived to assist Mascarene and his militia to rout the French and the Mi'kmaq and drive them into the wilderness. British troops raged through the woods as far as our village and beyond, pursuing the Natives. We heard gunfire all around us for days. The courageous Governor Mascarene had managed to hold on to Annapolis Royal with the assistance of Gorham's Rangers, and their enemies had been compelled to retreat.

I could imagine François's humiliation. I also recalled his prophecy. The dark future that he had predicted should the British triumph did seem to be coming to pass. Gorham was not conciliatory like Mascarene; he was very mistrustful of the Acadians and convinced that they were complicit with the French. He read a proclamation from the New England governor, William Shirley, directing the British at the garrison and those living in the town to cease trading and associating with the Acadians until further notice. No Acadians were permitted in the lower town after dark. These edicts were delivered and read in person by assigned officers to all the Acadians from Gaudet Village and Belle Isle to Annapolis and beyond. We Acadians were forced into a state of isolation and confined to our communities.

By November three more ships arrived from New England carrying additional orders from Governor Shirley. These vessels were directed to transport Gorham's Rangers to Minas immediately to scour the settlements for traitors — particularly Grand Pré, where the French had camped — and to burn their homes and barns, and take hostages to guarantee the loyalty of the French-speaking colonists.

Later, we were told by some of our neighbours that Mascarene had convinced Gorham and the ships' captains not to sail to Minas until the spring, advising them it was too late in the season to manage the treacherous winter gales of the Bay of Fundy. We realized that the governor was doing us a supreme favour, sparing the Acadians any further grief and, in so doing, ensuring our continued loyalty. It was his only means of circumventing his superiors' orders. This was a relief to those of us who had cherished family members like Isabelle and others living at Grand Pré. Perhaps hostilities would cool over the winter months.

Mascarene's efforts were successful. The ships returned to Boston soon after. The vessels were in full sail by the time they passed our shores. We sat at the water's edge, shivering in the chilly autumn air while the thought they were leaving at last warmed our spirits. Our loved ones at Grand Pré were safe for the time being.

The four years that followed were little more than a nightmare. So many ships from both sides of the war sailed in and out of the bay that we stopped noticing which flags were flying from their masts. In the spring of 1745 warships under the command of French lieutenant Marin set anchor between Melanson Village and Goat Island. Marin had chosen our settlement to provide horses, canoes, and flour to those on board the French vessels, threatening that if we resisted the Native warriors who accompanied them would burn our homes to the ground. We had no choice but to comply. Handing over our horses was a huge blow to our community, which relied on the animals to plough our fields and bring in the harvest.

The war at Annapolis Royal raged on for the next three years. We Acadians were in a state of panic most days, always prepared for invasion. The Acadian communities became isolated from one another. River travel was too dangerous to attempt, so we could not visit our families upriver. We became prisoners of our own lives, our communities islands of solitude, surrounded by the threatening sounds of cannon and musket fire.

Through all the chaos and uncertainty, one event brightened our existence in the dying days of the war. It was the birth of our first boy child. We called him Joseph — he was later known as Jospiau. He was an oasis of joy in an otherwise ominous world. His early life was to be blessed with seven years of peace following the Treaty of Aix-la-Chapelle in 1748. These formative years shaped his character and cultivated an inner strength that produced in him an ability to withstand the tragedies he was to experience as he became a man.

Chapter 28

Change is inevitable, but forced change is tyrannical. As peaceful as the 1750s began, by mid-decade my people's lives were turned upside down and altered forever. It was I who felt responsible for guiding those willing to be led to a place of greater safety. The choices I was compelled to make were not always clear, but the possibilities were far more numerous than the British were willing to allow. Those who chose to follow me and my family were not spared hardships, but they were able to make choices of the will. Those who remained docile in the face of an enemy they did not expect paid dearly for their unwillingness to resist. I do not judge my compatriots at Grand Pré. They were ambushed by a force that held them hostage. I was determined that this would not happen to those I loved.

The change we chose in the summer of 1751 was the result of considerable personal loss. A contagion passed over Gaudet Village like the plagues of ancient Egypt. Within days of one another, Bernard and Jeanne Gaudet succumbed to the disease. The fever descended and Jeanne's parents were suddenly lost to eternity. The illness reached Melanson Village within the month and claimed my brother Charles's wife. Jeanne and I had remained at Melanson Village to watch over Mama, but now we believed it was time to choose our time of exodus and settle at Gaudet Village. Charles moved in with my mother in the old Manor House. The decision to leave would prove to be a prudent one, allowing us to sustain our freedom in the coming years when others suffered an unwanted exile.

We were not alone. Jean and Madeleine followed us as well, hoping to seek the same peace we knew was more achievable upriver. Even though we

had received the news a few years earlier that a new capital had been chosen
for Nova Scotia, called Halifax and located in Chebuctou Bay, we still believed
that creating a greater distance between the British at Annapolis and ourselves
was a sound idea, with the threat of expulsion permeating the air we breathed.

The most encouraging news we heard was that the new lieutenant-
governor in Halifax, Cornwallis, had, after some persuasion, agreed to a qualified oath of allegiance. Some had thought he would be pressing a harder line,
having no previous exposure to the Acadian people. The Acadian delegates
seemed pleased with themselves in being so successful in their negotiations.

Dealing with the Acadians was the least of the lieutenant-governor's
worries. He was plagued by raids from the Mi'kmaq, who were terrorizing his new settlement in Chebuctou Bay, so he was more conciliatory
in his relations with the Acadians. He did not wish to alienate the king's
French-speaking subjects in the colony. Lieutenant-Governor Cornwallis's
successor would not uphold this policy. Cornwallis's departure from Nova
Scotia in 1752 was the beginning of the end for all of us living in Acadia.

Leaving Melanson Village was a monumental step for me. For Jeanne,
returning home to Gaudet Village was a natural thing, as expected. Although
I had always moved freely between Port Royal, Gaudet Village, and Grand
Pré, leaving the spirits of my ancestors behind at Melanson Village was a
profound event. For the children, it was a new adventure. They had visited
their grandparents at Gaudet Village annually and the change was easy for
them. I now realize that you carry the spiritual bones of your forebears with
you no matter where you go. And so it has been with me.

René arrived from Grand Pré just before our departure. Elizabeth accompanied him on his sail along the Fundy shore. She remained his maiden daughter, caring for her aging father at the Manor House. His numerous other children
had grown, married, and begun their own families and lives. She seemed content to fill her existence with his needs. Although her beauty had faded long
ago, she had a timelessness about her, changing little from year to year.

Elizabeth brought a going-away gift for me. She carried it in a large
leather sack and delivered it to me on the first night of her visit. When she
presented it her eyes welled up with tears.

"Benjamin would wish you to have what I have here inside this satchel. He treasured it and I remember on your visits to Grand Pré that you gave it considerable attention as well. Do not open it now. The memory of Benjamin is too strongly associated with its contents. Perhaps you should wait until your first evening at Gaudet Village and have it revealed then. It will serve as a special welcome to your new life upriver."

I kissed Elizabeth's hand and responded gratefully.

"I am pleased to receive this mysterious gift and I am certain I will cherish it because of your thoughtfulness and in memory of our beloved Benjamin. I sincerely thank you, Elizabeth."

We embraced. I noticed tears in René's eyes as well. He quickly recovered and began to speak. "I wonder why you are moving to Gaudet Village, Piau. It is an unusual move for someone at your stage of life. Things have settled considerably since the capital was transferred to Halifax. Melanson Village has been your family home for your entire life and is the place of your forebears. I would not contemplate leaving Grand Pré for any reason now. All things considered, as a notary in the employ of the British, I have been treated quite well."

I was unwilling to debate with René. He had always been a deluded man, hopeful, seldom seeing things the way they were or how they were likely to be. With age this had only increased. Some would say he was filled with optimism; I would describe him as misguided. Such men as René die bewildered, disenchanted, and crippled by disappointment.

"We have been planning our move to Gaudet Village for years, René. The soil is more fertile there and far less exposed to the elements. The climate is warmer as well. Furthermore, I have grown tired of the hundreds of vessels that have sailed past us to and from the Atlantic over the years. We never knew whether they were friend or foe. My family has lived a life of constant anxiety here overlooking the bay."

"I understand that what you say is true. But the traffic of ships has diminished since the new capital was established at Halifax. And to return to my previous point, what is lacking in the soil here is more than compensated by what the sea provides. You have access to the bounty of St. Mary's Bay. The upper river is unable to produce the fish catches of the bay."

"You are wrong in that, René. The Gaudets have been fishing the great Bay of Fundy for generations without sailing down the river to

St. Mary's Bay. They have forged a path through the woods over the North Mountain, which they take to their fishing vessels hidden in the woods at St. Croix Cove. This has forever been unknown to the British at Annapolis. My father-in-law, Bernard, insisted that he and his kin would not have felt secure without a convenient escape to the sea. The path over the mountain provides this for his community."

René and Elizabeth remained with us until our day of leaving. We loaded three fishing boats with all the things we would need at Gaudet Village. Jean and I carried Grandfather's trunk filled with muskets down to the water's edge, where over a hundred family members, young and old, gathered to bid us adieu. We gently placed the trunk in the final vessel. Charles was there but he had decided not to accompany us on this occasion. He was emotional about our leaving, as if he sensed prophetically that our lives were about to direct us on separate paths, ones that would take us on journeys that would divide us forever.

Our eldest daughter, Marguerite, remained with her husband and three children at the Manor House, but the remainder of my brood set sail with us. As our boats floated far from the shore, the sound of children singing echoed across the rippling waves.

> *Il y a longtemps que je t'aime,*
> *Jamais je ne t'oublierai.*

The sweetness of the children's song of farewell caught the light summer breeze of the bay, directing its warmth into our sails and powering our gliding vessels to their final destination upriver.

The last image I have of that time is of my mother standing alone on the shore after the crowd had dispersed. She waved and remained fixed on the spot until our vessels were out of sight. I had lived forty-nine years with this amazing woman, and now she was disappearing from my life. If she had only come with us, how completely happy I would have been. Her destiny was to be similar to that of most of the Acadians who remained near Annapolis.

Chapter 29

We were filled with melancholy, as we all had left family and friends at the shore of the village. At the same time, arriving at our destination and sensing a new beginning filled us with an excitement that caused the sadness to dissipate and a supreme happiness to descend.

Bernard and Jeanne Gaudet's home was just as they had left it. Neither had had time to contemplate their end, both having succumbed to the fever within days of one another. Both Jean's family and mine crowded into the large, timbered farmhouse, and despite the number of young ones there seemed to be space for everyone. We decided to remain together for at least the first winter and concentrate our efforts on planting and expanding the crops being raised. Charles would transport our livestock in one of his larger vessels over the summer months.

On the first evening, having comfortably settled into the Gaudet homestead, my children insisted on my opening the satchel that Cousin Elizabeth had given me. They all stood around expectant and enjoying the moment that this gift provided. I had guessed what the gift was before opening it, but I wished the sharing to be the source of a common joy.

My great-grandfather's King James Bible sat on the table before us after I had removed it ceremoniously from the leather bag.

"What is the book, Father?" asked Theotiste, the curious one.

"Remember the Bible stories I have been telling you since you were old enough to listen? Well, it is from this very book that I learned them. This is the King James Version of the Holy Bible. What makes this particular volume so precious, besides the fact it reveals God's presence among us, is that it was brought to Acadia by your great-great-grandparents from England."

"I thought we were French," declared Felicity.

"We are, but your great-great-grandmother Priscilla was English, and her husband was a French Huguenot. They shared the same religion as the English at the fort. We all believe in the same Creator, but we French practise the Catholic faith."

Only the older children were able to comprehend the difference between Catholic and Protestant. The younger ones were left to ponder this as we all began to peruse the illustrations in the Bible. Each picture told a story. I revealed each one fully in French so all could appreciate its beauty and the lesson each story conveyed. This would be an evening ritual we continued, even during our years of exile and captivity.

That first summer at Gaudet Village was blissful. Despite the absence of Bernard's humour and his bigger-than-life presence, we all felt freer than we ever had. There were no ominous ships passing by our home, no soldiers, and no English. It was like enveloping ourselves in a peaceful and loving cocoon, weaving a soft silky protective cover around us and basking in the summer sun, not allowing anything sinister from the outside world to penetrate our seclusion and happiness.

After the livestock had been safely delivered by Charles, we sailed down-river with our fishing boats, out through the gut into the Bay of Fundy, and along the coast to St. Croix Cove. There we drew our vessels into the woods, adding ours to the eight *chaloupes* already hidden. That numbered ten fishing boats to be used in the bay for fishing or a sudden escape. We later returned home, descending the North Mountain by foot along the path much worn by years of use. In the autumn, Charles returned to Gaudet Village to transport us to Annapolis to pick up the new fishing vessel he had built for Jean and me for the purpose of general river transportation.

Ludivine was the first baby born to us after moving to Gaudet Village. She would always symbolize the freedom we felt at the time of her birth. She entered the world at a time of serenity, and she would forever remind us of that all-too-brief period in our lives Jeanne and I began to lose count of the number of children in our house. We were all so busy with our new life upriver that one more child just added to the joy we felt.

All was quiet in the spring and early summer of 1755. As I remember it now, it was almost too peaceful. We would later recognize that this was the calm before the storm. Having a distant capital in Chebuctou lured us into a sense of false security. The threats of an impending war in Europe were not part of our consciousness, nor did we anticipate the horrendous effects the war would have on all our lives.

It was the sound of Native moccasins on the forest floor that alerted us to the dangers descending upon the Acadian settlements throughout the colony and beyond. It was not unusual to have the Mi'kmaq in our midst. We had been allies and co-inhabitants of the land for nearly one hundred and fifty years. Many of the Natives were fluent in French from continuous exposure to us and through friendly trade. We had always relied on them for the knowledge they possessed of the wilderness. They had taught us how to survive when Mother Nature chose to be unpredictable and brutal. They had always honoured their alliance with the French-speaking peoples of the New World, but the presence of the English and the Acadian decision to remain neutral had tested their patience. They understood only friendship and antipathy. There was no middle ground in their lexicon. Now, however, they were arriving at Gaudet Village to warn us of the English danger and prove to us that we had been foolhardy for ever trusting the British. The story they told of the fate of our friends and kin at Grand Pré filled our hearts with sadness, fear, and disbelief.

The warriors told of the British soldiers arriving at Minas by sea without any warning and imprisoning the Acadian men in the church of St. Charles, the stone church built by Uncle Pierre. The women and children were herded like cattle, with little time to gather their belongings, and placed on ships. The Natives heard their fearful cries from their lookout in the woods.

Their vivid descriptions froze the blood in our veins as we listened in disbelief, unable to imagine that such a thing could be done to our friends and relatives.

The Acadian men held captive in the church were paraded through the streets at gunpoint and placed on ships waiting in the bay. We were told of the homes and barns being set ablaze and the livestock confiscated. The warriors, having witnessed the terror, raced through the woodland prepared to warn every Acadian community in the valley. The final piece of information was that the British leader was someone we all knew well, Captain Winslow.

"It is hardly believable," I responded, "that Captain Winslow would undertake such a heinous operation. We all knew him to be a fair and honest officer at Annapolis for the many years he lived among us, and as one who treated us with considerable respect. I cannot imagine he could act with such treachery!"

The abrupt arrival of the Native warriors awakened Jeanne from her calm composure. The threat that her baby sister, Isabelle, was facing in Grand Pré changed something in her. She leapt into action, insisting we leave our home as soon as possible.

The children were alarmed to see their mother in such a frenzy.

"I cannot imagine what Isabelle is suffering at this moment or where she is being taken. And that I am unable to help her. That is the duty of the oldest, to protect the youngest of the family. What if she dies at sea in the stinking belly of some overcrowded ship? God help her and keep her safe!"

With those words she ran from the house into the garden. The youngest children began to cry uncontrollably, while we tried to control our emotions in front of the children. From this point, however, we all knew that we had to be prepared to make a move that would alter our lives forever. We later understood that we were the lucky ones and that it was up to us to perpetuate that good fortune through our survival.

Days later, four young men appeared from the woodland carrying muskets and panting vigorously. They wore panic on their faces. The leader I recognized immediately. It was my twenty-year-old nephew and namesake, Pierre, son of my brother Charles. His three huge companions were not familiar to us. These three handsome giants were Bonaventure, who was called Bouon, Charles, known as Charlitte, and Joseph, known as Coujeau, LeBlanc. Their sudden presence made quite the impression on my oldest daughters, whose faces exhibited both wonderment and excitement. Once in our midst, they decided to join our group for the journey ahead. They provided the physical strength we needed to manage our survival. Without it, I believe we would have all perished that first winter in exile.

Young Pierre was bursting with stories from Annapolis.

"We could tell in late August that something ominous was blowing in the wind. The number of British ships sailing into Annapolis was astonishing. Major Handfield and the now Colonel Winslow seemed to be up to something. They demanded that all men and boys report to the authorities and surrender their muskets and other weapons voluntarily. We knew we would be also surrendering our rights with the firearms, so most of us took to the woods still armed.

"Many returned to their homes, but the LeBlancs and I, we preferred to avoid capture in the woods. We have been wandering the countryside for several weeks. One Acadian man we met said he was returning to Annapolis because he had heard that Handfield had promised to treat the Acadians of Annapolis mercifully. The major was able to convince them to return by declaring that his mother-in-law was Acadian and his wife had many Acadian relatives and friends. We were not so confident in his promises so we continued our flight. Can you imagine luring people back by using your Acadian mother-in-law as bait? It is shameful!"

Jeanne was the first to respond. "You were wise, Pierre, to come here. And the timing has never been more auspicious. We are planning our escape from this land and the sooner we depart the better it will be for all of us. But first we must feed you. Come into the house. I have a rabbit stew cooking in the hearth."

The four young men were overjoyed at the prospect of a home-cooked meal.

"Aunt, you are more than kind. The thought of a warm meal is beyond anything we have imagined this past month. *Merci!*"

And so it was that my nephew Pierre and the LeBlanc brothers became adjuncts to our family and fellow travellers in exile.

Chapter 30

The day of departure arrived. Grandfather's trunk was emptied of its contents. The arms were distributed among the men and I burned all the Melanson family papers in the fireplace. With this act, I felt, the shame that Grandfather had brought upon us by conspiring with the British was disappearing like smoke up the chimney. The heavy burden I had carried since I first read those traitorous letters years before was finally lifted from my shoulders and I now felt strangely forgiving of Charles Melanson. My grandmother would have approved.

It was difficult to slaughter the livestock, but we knew we could not travel through the woods with the animals and we were not magnanimous enough to leave them for the British. The cattle and sheep were sacrificed ceremoniously, Jeanne remarked, just as the priests of the temple had in ancient Jerusalem. We would never again return to our homes. The wool had already been carded and the meat would survive our travels now that the weather was becoming cold. Some could be cured and stored.

Everyone was equipped with a strapped pack filled with lightweight essentials. Each person was responsible for one heavier item: the men and boys carried the firearms and tools, the women and girls cooking utensils and smaller iron pots. The days were getting cooler, so we were able to replace our wooden shoes with moccasins and wear our winter furs, which would keep us warm during the freezing winter days and nights to come.

I explained to our new compatriots how we planned to follow the trail to the Fundy coast using the path established by the Gaudet community over the years, and I told them of the boats hidden in the woods. They were astonished by our foresight.

"How could you have anticipated that you would have to use this trail as an escape route?" asked young Pierre.

"Through the years, the path was used as a shortcut to the sea," replied Jeanne. "Although the authorities at Annapolis encouraged the Acadians along the river to sail to St. Mary's Bay to fish, so they could keep a watchful eye on our comings and goings, the inhabitants of Gaudet Village felt that by creating a trail over the North Mountain they would have easier and closer access to the Bay of Fundy. It has been extremely useful."

"And you must understand, Pierre," I interjected, "that those of us born under French rule have always feared the possibility of being thrown off our land and shipped out of here to parts unknown. I was born under the cloud of war, so I have never felt entirely secure in where I live or in the permanency of my life in Acadia. We have always pondered our escape."

"My father certainly felt that way," Jeanne added. "He and my uncle Denys spent several years in Île Royale doing construction, testing the waters to see whether they wished to move to French territory permanently. They used this mountain trail to secretly leave Gaudet Village and board a French vessel near St. Croix Cove."

"Why did they return?" asked Pierre.

"My father and his brother were fearless men who seldom worried about the future. They both loved adventure. They had gone to Louisbourg as adventurers, seeking the excitement one gets from exploring new places and believing there was money to be made. However, they always intended to return home. My father referred to Gaudet Village as the home of his ancestors. And let us not forget the skills they cultivated in the construction of the fortress at Louisbourg. They returned with money in their pockets and the ability to construct beams that kept them busy for years working for the British at Annapolis. Through it all, they used the North Mountain pass."

"Escape is not a luxury we have enjoyed living in Melanson Village. Almost every day since my birth I have seen the British ships sail by, never knowing why they were arriving or why they were leaving. The French invasion when I was ten years old frightened me so much I still have nightmares about it. Now that the deportation of Acadians has begun, I fear for the safety of my father, my grandmother, and all my relatives at Melanson

Village. I worry, not knowing what their fate will be. And having heard the horrendous stories you have related about the sad people of Grand Pré, I wonder whether I will ever see my father and grandmother again."

"Rest assured, young Pierre, if anyone is capable of surviving it is your father. He is very much like his deceased father, Jean Belliveau, willing to take on the entire British army if necessary to protect his family. Rest easy on that account."

My comments seemed to change the mood as we prepared to start our journey.

"You are so right about my father!"

My nephew began to laugh heartily as we all paraded out of the village for the last time. Our collective determination did not allow for tears. We all realized we were unlikely to return.

Jeanne took the lead as more than a hundred relatives and friends headed in the direction of the forest. We all looked upon our departure as a celebration of life. We knew we were carrying the spiritual bones of the Gaudet ancestors with us; they seemed to lighten our load as we ascended the North Mountain.

Jeanne raised her voice as we entered the woodland. "Let us begin our great mountain adventure. Perhaps we will come upon a burning bush!"

As we disappeared into the forest, the angelic voices of our children rose in song above the canopy of the trees, a song that echoed through the valley and enriched the vivid red and gold leaves in the autumn sun.

> *Trois beaux canards s'en vont baignant,*
> *En roulant ma boule.*
> *Le fils du roi s'en va chassant,*
> *Rouli, roulant ma boule roulant.*
> *En roulant, ma boule roulant*
> *En roulant, ma boule,*
> *En roulant, ma boule roulant*
> *En roulant ma boule.*

Our group reached St. Croix Cove before nightfall and we set up camp. The fires were lit and the evening was surprisingly balmy along the Bay of Fundy the first night in exile. We were buoyed up by our new adventure and a celebratory mood. The young danced in the moonlight to the sound of fiddles and mouth harps. The food was excellent and we shared a sense of relief that we were out of the reach of the British.

The following day we heard a persistent crackling of brush on the forest floor. The entire group seemed to freeze on the spot, not knowing whether it was the British following our path. We knew, however, that the British preferred to travel not by land but by sea. Relief arrived in the form of a band of Mi'kmaq. Their leader informed us that they were there to serve as our guardians in the wilderness, having pursued us over the mountain in order to help us build wigwams. These would keep us warm and comfortable during the upcoming winter months.

Both the men and women participated in the construction of the wigwams. First the Natives showed us how. Five large spruce poles were tied together at the top with split spruce roots, and then the poles were spread out at the bottom. A moosewood hoop was tied under the poles at the top where shorter poles were lashed to the moosewood hoop to make a frame for the birchbark sheets. The Mi'kmaq warriors placed the wide sheets on top of the frame, beginning at the bottom and overlapping them as they moved up the pole frame.

An opening was left at the top for the smoke from the fire to escape. The Natives provided deerskins for the doors to help retain the heat from the fire. They produced the first couple of wigwams and then assisted us in building ten more. Each wigwam was large enough to house twelve to fifteen people. To this day, I could construct one by myself in half a day. The knowledge imparted to us by the Mi'kmaq at St. Croix Cove on how to erect these temporary homes was to be our salvation during the next five years of our exile.

The Mi'kmaq remained with us for more than a week, hunting with the men for deer, partridge, and rabbit, and helping the women smoke the meat we had brought from the farm. We ate the fish we caught in the weirs and nets along the shoreline. The boats collected the catch daily, and despite the variable weather we managed to extract a great abundance of things from the sea. Spiritually, we were at one with the Native warriors; they were our lifeline. Knowing they were there in the wilderness, out of sight but nearby, filled us with a confidence we would not have felt on our own.

Over the next six weeks we watched in horror from our sheltered position in the cove as prison ship after prison ship, flying the British ensign, passed by us in the Bay of Fundy on its way to who knows where. We could only imagine our relatives and friends from Grand Pré, Pisiquit, Cobequid, and Chignecto all forced to lie like a catch of fish below the decks with barely room to move or breathe. We felt the humiliation they must be experiencing at the hands of the British. This was our payment for fifty years of neutrality, fifty years of providing for their needs, and fifty years of compliance, never once rising up in rebellion.

Were we not a peaceful people? For every Englishman in Acadia, there were a hundred of us. We could have overpowered them at any time over the years of British rule. The Native people would have supported us and the French would have assisted us in turn. After years of peaceful coexistence, the English were now our enemy. Our neutrality evaporated with the mists rising over the great bay. It was replaced by an antipathy that would last a lifetime.

Jeanne was looking out at the bay one day when she spied a ship sailing southward. "To think I may be this close to Isabelle," Jeanne declared, with a mixture of desperation and melancholy in her voice. "I can feel her pain. It is heartbreaking to think I will never see her again!"

"René and Elizabeth would likely be with her," I lamented. "How disillusioned René must be, the final blow to a life where he believed he was so favoured by the British authorities. Think of the promise and brilliance he showed as a young man. In the end, he turned out to be a perfect fool. A tragedy!"

"You are being very harsh with the man you once so admired," Jeanne admonished. "All of us have our weaknesses. His was that he believed in his dreams. Dreams are just that, things we long for or imagine but that are not real."

"May they all find peace in exile."

"Amen."

Chapter 31

Throughout November, Acadian families who had escaped the British from the lower river area followed our path to the bay. We now numbered forty-eight families, over three hundred strong. By the beginning of December we realized that with these numbers of fugitives it would not be long before the British followed our trail and descended upon us unexpectedly. The heads of the families decided we should board our vessels and sail up the coast to a place of greater safety. The number of British ships passing had decreased to only a few every several weeks, so we felt confident that we could settle in a cove that would protect us from both the weather and the British.

Our day of departure was unseasonably warm and the Bay of Fundy was as calm as it ever was, given the variable winds and high tides of December. We did not need to travel far. We understood that a cove with no access to the Annapolis River or to the forest passage to Grand Pré would be our wisest bet. We pulled our *chaloupes* onto the rocky beach. We no longer feared being spotted by the enemy because traffic on the bay had ceased for the winter. While the decline in the number of ships passing put us at ease, it also made us aware that our friends and relatives in all the communities along the Bay of Fundy had already been exported to parts unknown, scattered by the winds of fate.

On our arrival, we constructed a grand cross to celebrate our freedom and the beginning of our journey to the Promised Land, wherever that might be. After we had carefully erected the cross at a rising above the sea, I recited from the Bible I kept in the satchel I carried with me and translated into French from the Book of Exodus.

"Keep this day in remembrance, the day you came out of Egypt, from the house of slavery, for it was by sheer power that the Lord brought you out of it. And so, in this same month when the Lord brings you to the land of Canaan, the land he swore to your fathers he would give you, a land where milk and honey flow, you are to hold this service."

All present appreciated the significance of the words spoken by Moses in this passage from Holy Scripture. His words gave us the strength we needed to continue our uncertain and perilous journey.

Jospiau was deeply moved by the translation of the Scripture I chose. Anything recited from this holy book he sensed seemed to hold great gravity and importance. He gave me a quizzical look.

"Papa, are you Moses? Are you leading us to the Promised Land? Where is the Promised Land, Papa?"

"Jospiau, my son, I would never presume to compare myself to the great prophet Moses. But every group needs a leader, and if the Lord has chosen me to inspire this group of Acadians to carry on until we find a land where we can again settle in peace and freedom, then so be it."

"I believe he has, Papa, I truly believe he has!"

Jeanne smiled as she stood and prayed. She whispered, "Our eight-year-old son possesses wisdom beyond his years, Piau."

"He does indeed, Jeanne."

I, too, was impressed by Jospiau's remarks, but they also filled me with trepidation, not knowing whether I was equal to the task of leading this large assemblage of Acadian families. It was one thing to be the patriarch of a family of ten, but there were forty-eight families in this group, and to convince the heads of every one that we should do this or do that was a daunting task. There were many decisions to be made on our journey; to assume that all would agree to act as one was too much to expect. It was not long before I had to put my misgivings to the test.

That inner voice that spoke to me and enabled me to imagine what was likely to happen in any situation told me that although we were no longer exposed to an imminent threat from the British, an even greater one would come from exposure to the winter cold. This was a place that eventually would ravage us, no matter how secure our wigwams made us feel. If we stayed here, the treacherous winds would become our enemy and we would likely perish.

At a gathering of all the husbands and wives, I suggested that it would be prudent to make our way back to St. Mary's Bay, where the conditions were less harsh, to tough out the winter there.

"St. Mary's Bay is far kinder to those who wish to endure the winter open to the elements. The shelters we construct will be better protected, and we will have better access to an abundance of wildlife in the forests if we camp at sea level. The North Mountain will be a barrier to the winds that endanger our survival."

One of the senior family heads was quick to object.

"We trust your judgment in most things, Monsieur Belliveau, but the temperate weather may persist. It may be better to establish a more secure village here, to live out the winter knowing that in the spring we can sail across the bay to freedom. Many of us are exhausted. After travelling all this distance to reach this place, finally we may be free of the terror the British soldiers have inflicted on our people."

Another patriarch added his voice: "Why would we wish to return to St. Mary's Bay when we all know that a settlement on its shore will be that much closer to Annapolis? The British are certain to spot our encampment."

I responded with authority.

"My knowledge of St. Mary's Bay and its shipping traffic come from almost fifty years living on its shores and witnessing hundreds of ships that have sailed into Annapolis. I know the times of year when British and French vessels arrive and depart from the bay. Between December and April ships rarely sail into Annapolis Harbour. With all due respect to most of you who have grown up on the upper river, I grew up outside Annapolis and I know the ways of the British. They would not expect us to hide out so close. We would be wise to opt for a more sheltered spot to make camp for the winter, and make our escape to the far side of the Bay of Fundy at the first sign of spring. As our friends the Mi'kmaq say, the Great Spirit Glooscap is very unhappy in the cold of winter and he demonstrates his displeasure by causing the Great Bay to release its fury. Do you wish to endure such an ordeal?"

"We are willing to take our chances," replied an elder spokesman for those who opposed my recommendation.

The younger Acadians seemed to see the wisdom in my proposal. Perhaps it appealed to their sense of adventure. The LeBlanc brothers agreed to follow my lead because they were smitten with my daughters. How easily swayed is youth! Jean and my nephew Pierre, having been raised at Melanson Village, also saw the wisdom in what I was suggesting.

After much discussion and many heated arguments, I recommended we put it to a vote. People voted along family lines. The families of Gaudet Village and many more adventurous souls in the group were willing to follow my lead. Of the three hundred and fifty Acadians who had come to the place we now called French Cross, half decided to remain there for the winter. The rest of us were prepared to sail to the eastern shore of St. Mary's Bay. And so we had sealed our fate, and those staying behind had sealed theirs. Spring would reveal which group had made the right decision.

Chapter 32

Our spirits were lifted on the day of our departure — December 8, as I remember. The bay remained calm, with a cool breeze and a light dusting of snow. As we set sail, following the tide south, we sang songs to keep ourselves merry and to negate any thoughts that we may have made an imprudent decision.

There was no evidence of the British, only a pod of whales sounding loud alarms as they exhaled into the crisp air. Our six vessels floated all day until we reached Petit Passage, a gut that divides the large peninsula the British called The Neck. On entering St. Mary's Bay we could feel the warmer winds coming off the land from the east. The bay lay still as we glided safely across the calm water, stopping only when we spied an island close to the coast. I remembered landing on this small patch of land years before on fishing trips when I was growing up. I felt it was providence that had led us here, and it was providence that would provide shelter for our families during the winter.

There was a wondrous sense of relief when we finally settled on our little island retreat, resolved to construct a safe haven that would help us face the coming winter days and nights. We pulled our boats ashore upon a sandy beach. For our camp we chose the shoreline between the island and the mainland so we would be protected from the southwest and northwest winds.

After an evening of sleeping under makeshift shelters of spruce boughs, we set about copying the lessons taught to us by our friends the Mi'kmaq, erecting pole frames and covering them with birchbark. These wigwams were even finer and larger than the ones we had built at French Cross. Along with the heat created by a central fire, ten human bodies in each shelter provided the necessary warmth. These would be our homes for the next three months. We all felt proud that we had journeyed this far under a light cloud of freedom and goodwill.

As the colder weather descended upon us at Yuletide, we were able to cross the icy channel to the mainland on snowshoes to hunt for rabbits and deer. Great-Grandfather's muskets were essential to our survival. We had carried his musket collection with us to the island in the large wooden chest it had been stored in for almost a century and reverenced it much as the Israelites had the Ark of the Covenant. I regretted not leaving a few of the muskets with the families we had left behind at French Cross, but they had managed to keep a few of their weapons when they fled the British. In my own way, I begrudged them such a luxury, since it was they who had stubbornly insisted on remaining in that perilous place.

The women stored the root vegetables we had carried with us from Gaudet Village in straw bags buried in the cold ground. Buried deep enough, they did not freeze, and sparingly they were rationed out to add to stews. To celebrate Christmas, we shot partridges and roasted them slowly over an open fire in each wigwam. The air was redolent with the aroma of game swirling about the winter night, enveloping us in a miasma of delicious scents. With these heavenly odours rose our songs celebrating the birth of the saviour.

Il était le divin enfant …

We shared homemade gifts, and we thanked our Creator for delivering us to this sacred place.

Our exuberance was soon replaced by a frozen layer of fierce reality when the January snows and bitter winds descended upon us. January and February, when the days are short and the nights are infinite, seem to be the longest of months.

Despondency set in as food became scarce and sunlight scarcer. I remembered the tales told me when I was still a child about the great Champlain settling at Port Royal. Faced with surviving the brutal winter, he created the Order of Good Cheer to lift the spirits of the settlers during the long dark season. I set out to emulate him by organizing evening entertainments and encouraging the inhabitants of each wigwam to be responsible for an evening of fun and games. We discovered, though, that during the long sieges of inclement weather our people were confined to their own quarters.

As the weeks passed poor health became a concern. Not even Native remedies were a cure for the illnesses of the body and spirit.

Jean and his wife, not having children, decided to live out the winter in a smaller wigwam of their own. Neither was strong, and when both fell ill they seemed to lose their will to live. One early morning, before gathering my daily collection of firewood, I checked in on them. I noticed there was no smoke rising from their shelter. This filled me with a feeling of sudden fear.

Looking into their wigwam, I saw that they were lying wrapped together under a fur blanket, still and at peace. I gasped as I felt their frigid and lifeless bodies with my reluctant hands. Standing motionless and staring at these two fragile souls no longer with us, I began to weep. Their presence on this earth had always been tenuous. In life, both had been shy and waiflike. They adored one another and now they had escaped into eternity. The loss of my brother only strengthened my resolve to live, regardless of the challenges placed before me by nature.

I stormed out of the tent, threatening the wind and the snow, my feet breaking through the crusty surface of the forest. I ran through the birches and brush, across the icy channel, slipping and falling, slipping and falling, until I reached the ice floes on the beach. I raised my arms into the air, challenging the fates.

I shouted toward the bay, defying anyone or anything to vanquish me.

"Try to destroy me! I challenge you to destroy me and my family. You will not succeed. You may block my path, but I will not be defeated. I will prevail. We will prevail!"

Having shouted until I could yell no more, I fell on my knees and asked God for forgiveness. I lay on my stomach, stretched out on the beach, exhausted and contrite.

Lying there on the ice floe, having lost track of time, I suddenly felt small hands on my back. Was this my guardian angel? Then a young voice pierced through my sorrow.

"What is the matter, Papa?"

Awakened from my agony, I recognized my eight-year-old son's voice.

"Why are you lying here, Papa?" Young Joseph began to shake me.

"I am fine, Jospiau," I assured him. "I have just had a terrible shock. Your uncle and aunt — I don't know how to tell you this. Your uncle and aunt are dead."

"I know. Mama found them in their wigwam. She says they are now in heaven."

I rose to my feet and placed my hands securely on the boy's small shoulders.

"Indeed they are, my son. But I promise you, Jospiau, that we are not going to die. We have everything to live for, and you must grow up and have children of your own some day. You must prosper. If you do not, then the British have won."

"I will, Papa, I promise I will. The British will not win. Let's go home. I am hungry."

I grasped his hand and we walked home together, more sure-footed and filled with confidence.

That same day we buried Jean and my sister-in-law Madeleine — the first of many graves dug that first winter in exile. Fortunately, my children remained healthy and robust, proof of the strength and defiance of their parents.

That first winter in exile taught us many lessons of survival: how to ration our food, how to retrieve our musket balls, how to fish through the ice, how to keep the fires burning at all times, how to resist the melancholy brought on by a lack of sun, how to maintain our good health, and, most important of all, how to work as a group. Avoiding loneliness was essential to our survival.

Although we often lost track of time, certain signs in nature filled us with hope. Despite the snow, we began noticing the trailing arbutus on the forest floor peeking out through the white icy crust, reminding us that spring was close at hand. Much like the Native people, we collected bouquets of the tiny spring flower to fill our wigwams with the intoxicating smell of its tiny blossoms.

There were days when Jospiau and I returned home with little game. On these occasions we tried to make up for this lack by bringing a full array of trailing arbutus. My son made a ceremony of presenting the tiny blossoms to his mother. Jeanne never showed her disappointment on these occasions. She would smile and remark that she would have to find a way to cook the trailing arbutus, since that was the catch of the day. Jospiau was a clever boy and caught the significance of his mother's humorous remark. He would assure her that the next day we would hunt and return with double the catch. Many days he kept his promise.

Although we managed to maintain our supply of buckshot, our gunpowder reserves were depleted. We became more and more dependent on fish and snared rabbits. Our only antidote to scurvy was the bark tea that the Natives had taught us to drink when vegetables and berries were no longer available.

As April approached, the survivors in our group — there were many, despite the many deaths — began to plan our journey to the north side of the Bay of Fundy. We asked ourselves if we should return to French Cross to discover the fate of the companions we had left behind. After a lengthy discussion, we unanimously agreed it would be prudent to sail directly across the great bay to the St. John River. There, it would not be long before we re-established contact with our fellow Acadian exiles.

We chose a calm day in April to cross St. Mary's Bay, retracing our path through Petit Passage directly across from our island retreat, which the members of our group had begun calling Île à Piau. They named it in my honour, insisting I was the person responsible for saving their lives. I was flattered, but I knew they had survived through sheer strength and courage on their part. I only helped them realize this in themselves.

When we reached the Bay of Fundy, the winds and tidal currents were stronger than we had anticipated. However, the winds were in our favour. With strong southeast winds, we were able to cross the bay safely despite the high waves. Everyone aboard the vessels was soaked to the bone by the time we neared the St. John River, and many were suffering from seasickness. Sight of land, however, gave us some comfort that soon we would be sailing up the river to the Acadian villages on its shore.

As our *chaloupes* drifted near the mouth of the river, we noticed ships moored at its entrance. They were bearing the Union Jack. Our sailing vessels were forced to veer right and follow the coastline to the northeast to avoid the British. Again the southeast winds and the inflowing tides whisked us along the bay, and we continued looking for a new home, hugging the shoreline as best we could. It was not long before we were sailing into Shepody Bay.

Our boats floated on the tide as we entered the great estuary which, from that time on, would play an integral part of our lives. The Natives called it the Petitcodiac. Entering the river, we felt the powerful surge of the tidal bore driving the current swiftly over the bright red mud. The children let out cries of glee as they felt the exhilaration of the waves carrying us along with no effort on our part. The force of the water was so strong we were compelled to lower our sails.

Before evening, we found ourselves within sight of an Acadian refugee camp. This filled us with excitement, knowing there were others who had escaped the expulsion. As our vessels drew closer, however, we beheld hundreds of skeleton-like figures moving so slowly they could have been the walking dead. Perceiving our boats floating in the direction of their camp, the refugees began to line up along the embankment, staring at us as if they were witnessing a flotilla of ghost ships.

Our exuberance soon turned to horror. We had experienced the same winter, but these Acadians wore a look of starvation and desperation.

As we cast anchor, a family of children made their way through the crowd. They possessed a liveliness that was lacking in the others standing above us. Suddenly the children were jumping up and down and shouting things we were unable to hear from the river. In time they became audible.

"Uncle Piau, Felicity, Rose, Jospiau!" shouted the young people on the shore. I recognized the oldest boy. It was the seventeen-year-old grandson of my brother Charles. A woman with a beaming smile joined the group. She, too, began waving. It was Madeleine, Charles's daughter, standing beside her husband, Grand Pierre Boudrot. Unlike the others, they appeared to be in good health and spirits.

Our boats rose with the tide. My niece Madeleine and her family remained fixed in place until we were almost level with the shore. Then each of us jumped into the wet red mud, little caring that when we dried off we would resemble clay figures.

Madeleine was the first to speak as she helped Jeanne and the girls onto the embankment. "This is a very happy day. God has spared you all. Never in my wildest dreams did I imagine I would see you again. Is my brother Pierre with you?"

As she uttered those words, Pierre and the three LeBlanc brothers climbed the muddy bank, slipping and sliding as they ascended. Once Madeleine spotted her brother, she placed her hands over her mouth and began to cry. Her tears were tears of joy. Her baby brother was alive and here with her. They embraced as everyone on the bank shared in the emotional reunion. For many of the refugees this joyful event had temporarily awakened them from their horrible dream.

"Maddie, you are alive and well. Thank God. Is Papa with you?"

"No, but he is alive and healthy and on his way to Quebec with Grandmama and others from our vessel. Grand Pierre and I decided that the journey to Quebec was too taxing for the children. They have been through an ordeal and we felt we would manage better if we found a community along the Fundy coast to travel with. Governor Vaudreuil of Quebec has ordered that we all travel to Restigouche and the Miramichi to be out of the way of the British. England and France are now at war in Europe, so the British here are hunting down Acadians and shooting them like wild animals. For the time being, we are safe here. We are far enough from Fort Beauséjour for us to relax for the time being.

"Come, and once you are settled I will relate the story of our escape from the British. It is a story you will not believe. And Papa was its hero."

The children embraced one another and began running around the camp, overjoyed to be reunited with their cousins.

I stopped and pondered the fate of my brother Charles and my mother. They were safe and sound at Quebec. This I thanked God for. On the other hand, I was painfully aware that our paths might never cross again, and that filled me with a profound sorrow.

As we walked through the camp I was appalled by the conditions. There were several wigwams, but they were poorly constructed, and most of the people were living in makeshift fir shelters. I asked myself how such a resourceful people came to be so destitute when all Acadians were educated in the ways of the wilderness. We had lived among the Natives for over a hundred years and were skilled in their ways of survival. Then it became apparent to me. There were no muskets anywhere to use for hunting. I was reminded that although we no longer had gunpowder, for the greater part of the winter we had had working firearms. All that was needed to improve the conditions of this camp was to acquire ammunition for our hunting muskets and to instill a little hope in their miserable lives here in the wilderness.

I realized it was up to me to develop a plan. But first we knew we must construct our living quarters.

Constructing the wigwams at this point was easy for us. We were now highly experienced in the task. Many of the refugees watched us carefully so they could emulate what we had learned from the Mi'kmaq. They seemed to look upon us as their saviours. Time would prove them right.

Chapter 33

Having completed our construction, we settled into an evening of storytelling around the campfire. The principal tale that unfolded that night was that of the His Majesty's Ship *Pembroke* and the part my fierce and indomitable brother, Charles, had played in the incredible story of its capture.

Charles had always been my hero growing up, but the story we were told that evening under the April stars of how he managed to outwit the British and gain control of the HMS *Pembroke* filled even me with wonder.

That evening we sat around the fire to hear the tale. All the children were there to listen, too. It was particularly important for Madeleine's family to relive the story in the presence of their cousins; it was their story as well. Charles's grandchildren sat enthralled as Madeleine and Grand Pierre told the tale: Charles, aged seventeen; Hilaire, thirteen; Isaie, ten; Jean, six; and baby Pierre-David, one. They were joined by my children: Madeleine, aged twenty-six; Jeanne, twenty-four; Theotiste, nineteen; Agnes, sixteen; Rosalie, thirteen; Felicity, eleven; Jospiau, eight; and Ludivine, four.

Grand Pierre began, "I was at the shipyards with my father-in-law, Charles, when the *Pembroke* arrived in the harbour in early December. All the other British vessels that had collected the Acadian families for deportation had left for the Thirteen Colonies and destinations unknown.

"Prudent Robichaud came to us and informed us that he had spoken to Colonel Handfield at the fort. Handfield promised him special consideration because of his many years serving as justice of the peace and his other services to the Crown, and in respect of his eighty-six years. Prudent was relating these things to us when the captain of the *Pembroke* approached us at the wharf. He had just come from Handfield, who had directed him to the shipyards in search of Charles Belliveau, shipbuilder.

"'Which of you is Charles Belliveau?' he bellowed.

"I knew my father-in-law well and I wondered what his reaction would be to the captain's aggressive tone.

"'I am he, and what business do you have with me?' spoke Charles, addressing the captain in perfect English.

"'I have come to demand that you construct a centre mast for my ship, the HMS *Pembroke*. Our mast is broken and we are in need of a new one. Do you have white pine logs here in your shipyard?'

"'I do indeed, and if you ask me politely, as a gentleman should, I might just agree to do your bidding.'

"'Monsieur, you are a cheeky and insolent fellow. I command you to do as I ask.'

"'And if I do not, sir, will you shoot me on the spot? If you do, you will never sail out of Annapolis on the *Pembroke*, because I am the only qualified shipbuilder still living here. I believe I have you at a disadvantage, Captain.'

"The veins in the captain's neck began to engorge and his face went red with rage. Silence followed. We could see the captain working this over in his mind. Old Prudent stood there, smiling and leaning on his cane, enjoying the heated discourse.

"The captain's tone changed to a more conciliatory one. 'Sir, would you kindly agree to build a new mast for one of His Majesty's ships?'

"Charles paused to indicate he was in control of the situation.

"'I will do the job, Captain, for His Majesty and for pay.'

"'Agreed, monsieur.'

"We set about stripping the pine log as Prudent sat himself down on another log, holding himself erect with his cane.

"'It is my belief that those of us who remain may perhaps be permitted to stay in the colony,' the old man mused.

"'And what gives you that impression, Prudent?' Charles asked. 'The inhabitants of Melanson Village are the last Acadians remaining. Why would the British leave us in peace? It is beyond logic.'

"'First of all, I and my family have held a privileged status here at Annapolis for many years. I think perhaps we will be spared.'

"'That may be true, but I hardly think that those of us who are living at Melanson Village will be permitted to stay. Even though the *Pembroke* is a provision ship, there is still room for all of those who remain here.'

"'You lack faith, Charles.'

"'No, I have just lived among the English too long to be fooled by their assumed goodwill. Never be too trusting of the British. They have only had a conciliatory attitude toward the Acadians because we outnumbered them — and of course we have been useful to them over these past fifty years. We are being useful to them at present.'

"'Time will tell.'

"Charles and I worked diligently through that day and the next until the mast was completed to Charles's satisfaction. The captain returned at the end of the following day with an entourage of soldiers. His demeanour was one of a man in full command. This filled me with misgivings. Would he pay Charles for his labour?

"'I see you have completed the job, sir. I thank you.'

"The soldiers were prepared to mount the mast and carry it to the ship's lifeboat. Charles stood defiantly in front of them, barring their way.

"'Just one moment, gentlemen. First I wish to be paid my due!'

"'You are due nothing, sir, for you are now a military prisoner.'

"Charles was holding an axe in his hands as the captain bellowed these remarks.

"'You will pay me what I am owed, sir, or I will destroy this mast before your very eyes.'

"The stunned captain paused, holding up his arm to halt the soldiers from falling upon Charles.

"'Agreed.'

"He placed his hand into his satchel and drew out pounds sterling, passing them reluctantly to Charles.

"Charles took the money and placed it into his pocket.

"'Now you must leave us be, Captain. We will be off to Melanson Village. Good day.'

"Charles and I jumped into our fishing boat and sailed home, feeling exhausted, relieved, and fearful that we had not heard the last of the captain of the *Pembroke*."

Madeleine continued the story from there. By this time, we were spellbound.

"Over the next few days we prepared for the inevitable. We packed our things in an organized way, something I have learned was a luxury that other deported Acadians did not have. More days passed and there was still nothing. Then, around December 8, we noticed the HMS *Pembroke* anchored opposite us at Goat Island. By midday the soldiers from the garrison appeared above the orchard at our village, a hundred strong. Major Handfield led the regiment down the main road of the settlement, stopping at the Manor House where Papa stood at the gate. No one else was in sight.

"We had decided that we should remain inside, away from the cold. We wore our fur coats in case we were forced to leave our homes suddenly. We did not hear Handfield's orders, but we could see Papa's demeanour. He returned to the house where we waited with Grandmama. I cannot speak the words my father uttered that day or describe how we reacted, for it is too painful. The garrison escorted us down the main road of the village to the icy shoreline with all the others of our community. There we were herded to the waterside where we were loaded into our own fishing boats at gunpoint, many weeping at the inhumanity of what was happening to us.

"As my father filed by Major Handfield with the others, he stopped short and stared into the eyes of the man with whom he had had good business dealings for the past decade. The moment was not lost on the major — there is no way to describe the look of remorse on the British officer's face, while my father's face was filled with contempt.

"The fishing vessels filled with our neighbours, cousins, and their families floated to the island, where we joined the Acadians being deported from the town and its surrounding areas. The first person we saw was Prudent Robichaud, leaning on his cane, bewildered. Here was a broken eighty-six-year-old man. We all thought that he would not likely survive the voyage into exile.

"To ensure that all were accounted for, we were obliged to sign our names in the ship's log before boarding, or make our mark if we could not read or write. Everyone, even the children, signed their names. Believing that most of us were not literate was typical of how the British viewed His Majesty's Acadian subjects. We were simple-minded farmers.

"My father was stopped in the lineup by Fontaine, the captain of the *Pembroke*.

"'Monsieur Belliveau, your mast is in place and is a very fine one. I see you are not so confident as you were the day you extorted money from me. You will certainly need the money where you are going.'

"'And where might that be, sir?' Father inquired, giving the captain an inscrutable stare.

"'It is none of your business. But since on another occasion you insisted on being treated like a gentleman, I will tell you. The *Pembroke* is bound for the Carolinas.'

"As we turned in the direction of the *Pembroke*, we witnessed a horrifying sight. Our homes and barns in Melanson Village were ablaze. The settlement our patriarchs had built a century ago was disappearing with the smoke rising above our burning homes. The spirits of our ancestors were evaporating with it.

"Everyone was transferred to the ship and ordered to climb below deck. There was little room for passengers because the *Pembroke* was a provision ship. So we were squashed in like sardines with almost no room to move, especially with the goods that we had carried on board with us. The perpetual darkness bothered the children the most. In the blackness of the cabin, the only evidence of who the person was next to you was a familiar voice. There were times I did not know which child was speaking to me! An oil lantern was provided during mealtime — it was always a joy to see the faces of my children while we ate our meals."

My seventeen-year-old grandnephew, Charles, was enthusiastic to relate the next chapter of the story.

"It was lucky for us that we were permitted time on deck to get some fresh air. It was biting cold winter air at sea, but we were able to see the light of day. Grandfather was made responsible for choosing the five or six people permitted above deck to take the air. He changed the groupings every time for variety. It lifted our spirits no end. This routine continued for over a month. But you all know my grandfather, Charles Belliveau; he was always scheming, thinking of a plan to change the situation in our favour. He was able to speak to every Acadian on board, revealing to them the plan he had devised to capture the *Pembroke*. The vessel became a ship of whispers, everyone involved in the scheme he was hatching. By early February, as we continued to sail south, every prisoner was aware of the part they were to play in the capture of the ship.

"The day chosen to put our plan in motion came. Grandfather had chosen all the groups very carefully. Each one arrived on deck creating no suspicion in the captain or his British crew. Finally, Grandfather came up into the winter air with the largest and strongest five men among the prisoners and with ten more as brawny waiting below, ready to spring on the crew when he sounded the alarm. I was fortunate to be part of that second band of warriors!

"The first five, with our assistance, found it easy to overpower the British crew by force. They were caught totally unawares. Grandfather made it his duty to bring the captain to heel. Captain Fontaine, however, was determined not to capitulate without a fight. He raised his pistol, aiming it directly at Grandpapa. He saw no fear in Grandfather's eyes, however. The captain was about to pull the trigger and fire at Grandfather point-blank. I catapulted myself at him, bringing him to the deck. The musket ball whizzed over the two of us and penetrated the chest of his first mate. The surprised officer fell into the arms of one of the women. The officer survived his wound thanks to the nursing skills of Great-Grandmama, God bless her.

"From that point on, the captors on board the HMS *Pembroke* became the prisoners. It was a glorious day for us! Two hundred and thirty-two Acadians, young and old, rose from the depths of the ship to celebrate their new-found freedom. Praise the Lord! We were free. Some were singing, some laughing, others cheering. Prudent Robichaud was carried up the stairs, jubilant for the first time in months.

"Grandpapa faced the defeated captain and declared with all the authority he had earned: 'Sir, I am now the captain of this ship!'

"Everyone cheered.

"'Take the prisoners below and chain them,' Grandpapa ordered. 'We will now turn the vessel around and head north to freedom. Man the sails.'

"And that is how we won the day aboard the HMS *Pembroke*!"

All the children around the fire clapped and cheered with excitement. It was truly a story right out of the pages of a great adventure story.

"Well told, nephew. Well told!" I exclaimed. "Such heroism. I am astounded by your story."

Jeanne entered the conversation at that point. "Do not leave us in suspense. Where did you sail from there?"

My niece's husband, Grand Pierre Boudrot, continued the fascinating tale of survival. "Being in possession of a British provision ship was like being on a boat filled with gold. There was food to last us six months, not to mention an arsenal of muskets, ammunition, and gunpowder. With such booty, we could survive for more than a year.

"And with a skilled navigator and experienced mariner at the helm, we would be able to maintain a course to safety. That mariner was Charles, now the captain of the *Pembroke*. With his skills we were able to arrive at the St. John River by the beginning of February. The first sight of land was exhilarating for us all. After many months at sea, we were more than ready to land on terra firma! Sailing into the river, we spotted the French fort on the embankment. We had kept the British flag flying at sea. Not wishing to risk being fired upon by the French, we replaced the Union Jack with a makeshift French one the women had sewn while we were at sea.

"Guns were shot from the fort, but as we floated closer, those inside the fort recognized that our clothing was not British. You can imagine how shocking it must have been to see a ship filled with over two hundred Acadians waving madly from the deck of a British cargo ship. We disembarked from the *Pembroke* with both our human cargo, British prisoners of war included, and the provisions remaining on board after our long voyage.

"Once the French officers heard the story of how your grandfather Charles Belliveau captured a British ship and sailed it into French territory, he was celebrated and treated like a dignitary. I am certain that our tale has been told at every Acadian and French settlement on the St. John River by now."

I chimed in at this point with an important question. "Why are my brother Charles and Mother not with you?"

Madeleine answered cheerfully, "Most of the Acadians decided to sail to a French settlement further upriver, for it became very unsafe at the fort.

"Britain was now at war with France. Ten days after our arrival, a British warship bearing the French colours as disguise sailed into the mouth of the river. Once the French soldiers discovered the British ruse, they set fire to the HMS *Pembroke* to prevent the English from capturing her. The cannon fire kept the British at bay until armed reinforcements reached the fort days later. The British vessel soon withdrew to the Bay of Fundy and sailed away. We moved upriver to wait out the winter.

"The majority of the Acadian refugees decided that they would remain upriver until summer, and then travel to Quebec to start a new life there. Prudent Robichaud did not survive the winter, but he died happy, having experienced his freedom before he passed on. Grandmama Belliveau remained with Charles and the others. As we said before, we decided to remain in Acadia and take our chances. Those chances have led us to this wonderful family reunion. We have made our way easily with two muskets and provisions to last us until now. However, when we arrived in this camp we became aware that not everyone was as fortunate as we have been. As you say, Piau, we must devise a plan of survival."

"I believe I have a way. And it might amuse you to know that we may reach our goal by following your example."

By this time, the LeBlanc brothers had joined us. They were interested in what I was about to suggest.

"Look at these giants sitting here among us. God must have gifted them with their Herculean strength and size for a purpose."

I knew I had the attention of the entire group.

"Look outside this group and you become aware that most of the refugees in this camp do not have the energy to carry out any plan of survival. But with these handsome titans and a brilliant plan anything is possible. What I suggest is we board a fishing vessel and sail down the Petitcodiac to Fort Beauséjour. It is now in the hands of the British. We have several muskets, but we are out of ammunition and gunpowder. These are essential for us to continue hunting — we have these starving Acadians to feed. Our only option is to try to steal some. So, Joseph, Charlitte, Bonaventure, and Pierre, are you up for a grand adventure?"

All four leapt up and shouted their approval.

"Splendid. *Stealth* and *strength* will be our watchwords."

Chapter 34

O n the day of our departure we added Cyprian Gautreau to our group, for he was a massive man and we required at least one other to achieve our objective. It was a fortuitous decision. Indeed, so successful were we that the tale of our exploits has been repeated over and over again through the years and has made its participants famous to this day. Our story is eclipsed only by the heroism of my brother Charles capturing the HMS *Pembroke*.

There were two pistols in Abraham Dugas's trunk. Ammunition and gunpowder were provided by Grand Pierre from the remnants of the arsenal pilfered from the *Pembroke*. The irony of the situation was not lost on me: our firearms were reinforced by ammunition stolen from one British ship to assist us in the takeover of another English vessel.

Our fishing vessel sailed with the tide down the mighty Petitcodiac. Its passengers were fortified by the belief that we would win the day. We entered Beaubassin early in the morning, and I conjured in my mind Jesus navigating his fishing boat in the stormy Sea of Galilee with his disciples. In our case, we were mastering a different storm.

It was not long before we noticed a schooner anchored out in the bay.

As we approached the vessel, my nephew Pierre exclaimed, "That is Father's schooner. I would recognize it anywhere. We have arrived here for a purpose. God is guiding us this day."

The boat did appear to have Charles's imprint upon it. There was no question I had sailed in this very schooner many times. Now was our chance to recapture it and benefit from its booty.

We dropped our sails one hundred yards from the schooner, and it was not long before its captain and his eight crew members appeared at the railing.

I was the first to speak, being the only one of our group fluent in English. "Good day, Captain. We request permission to come aboard."

The captain appeared to be shocked by our sudden arrival, but he smiled broadly, not attempting to disguise his look of good fortune at having six fugitive Acadians in his spider's web.

"Come aboard, gentlemen." The captain continued in his congenial manner as we climbed onto the deck of the schooner.

Once all six of us were standing on board the vessel, the captain declared, "I can now inform you what our mission is aboard this schooner. It is our duty to search for and apprehend Acadian fugitives. I declare you under arrest. You are now our prisoners."

It was at that point that I looked at Charlitte the Great and shouted, "Charge, Charlitte!"

With a massive blow, Charlitte sent the first officer to the deck. He was dead on impact. With blows equal to the first he downed two more crewmen. Bonaventure and Joseph were equally deadly in their attacks. The largest of the crew, who was an extremely powerful man, attacked Pierre and attempted to throw him overboard. Seeing his compatriot in trouble, Charlitte gave a horrifying roar, knocking the man down with the force of three men.

Cyprian and I drew our pistols and pointed them at the captain and his remaining crew members. They recognized immediately that they had lost the day. The captain capitulated easily and got down on his knees, begging us to spare him. I had only one thought at that moment, and that was the memory of my heroic father succumbing to the British when I was a year old. I could not remember his brutal murder, but I could never forget the loss.

"I beg of you, monsieur. Set me adrift in a lifeboat and I promise you I will not pursue you."

"Captain, I will deliver you the same justice as the English granted my father back in 1707. Ask God to forgive you for your sins."

The terrified captain rose and crept backward toward the railing of the schooner. A feeling of overwhelming anger overcame me as I aimed directly at the heart of my enemy and pulled the trigger. The Englishman fell backward over the side of the boat, splashing into the freezing bay. I stood motionless, mindful that justice had been done and that retribution for my father's death had been finally achieved.

Cyprian finished off the other crew members with his pistol, and Charlitte and Bonaventure threw their bodies overboard. Had any of the British crew been permitted to live that day, we would have been in serious trouble. We had eliminated the prospect of future regrets.

Chapter 35

Our arrival back at the refugee camp was greeted by hundreds of cheering Acadians. At first they saw the British flag and were filled with alarm, but once they beheld us waving vigorously from the deck of the schooner the people erupted in cheers. I am certain the sound was heard all the way to Fort Beauséjour. The boat sailing onto the shores of their encampment was a schooner of salvation. They knew it must contain a cargo of foodstuffs and ammunition. This was the moment of their deliverance, and my compatriots and I were their deliverers, just like Moses, Joshua, and Aaron from the Book of Exodus.

"Praise the Lord!" shouted the grateful Acadian refugees. If only for that moment they were able to forget their desperate state. Pierre, Cyprian, the mighty LeBlanc brothers, and I had given them hope, and this was an elixir that was as important as the provisions aboard the stolen vessel.

The story of our exploits travelled like wildfire through the camp. Even the children told the story to one another. I suddenly found myself the designated leader of the refugees on the Petitcodiac. To the refugees I became simply "Piau," a name I wore with considerable pride, for it was accompanied by a feeling of great responsibility.

More Acadians continued to appear at our camp with the morning mists of summer. One day, a lone fishing vessel, much like the one that had transported us to that place, floated with the tide to our settlement. It had only two occupants — an Acadian and a young Native boy — and their dog. Such a nearly empty fishing vessel was a rarity. I stood on the bank to watch them dock. I looked carefully at their sallow, emaciated faces, ghostly with hunger — even the dog.

I gathered my family together to form a greeting party. The face of the Acadian aboard looked slightly familiar. A feeling of horror filled me as I finally recognized the Acadian coming ashore. My cousin Pierre Melanson stood before us, his wasted form an emblem of the deaths of all those who had perished during the winter. His story would reveal the final end of those we had left behind at French Cross. The gruesome tale haunts me to this day.

"We regretted not following you, Piau," Pierre whispered, with what seemed to be his last breath, "but by that time it was too late. We were locked into an existence we were no longer able to control. The winter on the Bay of Fundy was like nothing we had ever experienced before. It possessed a fury that would not cease. Once our group lost hope, death soon followed. We lacked leadership like lost sheep. The wolf stalking us was winter, and it devoured us one by one."

Jeanne took Pierre by the hand and led him to our campfire where she had cooked a rabbit stew. She sat him down on a blanket and served him in a wooden bowl. As he ate, I joined them, having first sent the children away. I did not want them to hear the story he was about to tell. They had befriended many of the children from French Cross, and although they had become accustomed to death and suffering, they did not need to hear all the gruesome details of the early deaths of their friends.

Pierre and his Mi'kmaq friend devoured the stew, barely pausing to breathe. It was the first real meal they had eaten in some time, it was clear. Only when he was sated did Pierre continue his story of survival.

"Why did I live and the others not? Only God knows. We were fine until Christmas. We had settled in and food was still plentiful. However, after the New Year the frigid cold winds descended upon us, the dampness from the bay penetrated our bones, and soon it was impossible to remain warm. The northwest wind became our enemy. When it snowed, we were relieved, for it covered us like a blanket. But soon the mornings began to deliver to heaven those who had died in the frozen night.

"We seemed to forget all the lessons the Natives had taught us and scurvy became rampant in the camp. We ran out of ammunition and were unable to hunt. Even the rabbits refused to become trapped in our snares. Those who still had some semblance of health began to fight among them- selves, stealing food from one another like thieves. In time, starvation and typhus took hold of our group. It appeared that everyone was in a state of delirium. One by one my compatriots perished before my eyes, and when they died, we wrapped their bodies in birch bags to keep them frozen. We dragged them into the woods to keep the pestilence at bay.

"When the camp and surrounding woods became a graveyard of the entire community save myself, this Mi'kmaq boy appeared miraculously out of the woods. He has been my guardian angel ever since. I do not wish to be parted from him. Our spirits are one. He saved my life. I call him Angel."

Jeanne, moved by the sadness of his story, said to Pierre, "There is always a divine purpose when one is permitted to continue living on this earth against all odds. God has guided you to us, Pierre, and now you have no need to fear starvation. Although we too endured the cruel winter, spring is here and we have prevailed. We embrace you as a member of our family. You must leave heaven to those who are gone and join us on our journey."

"You are so kind, Jeanne. Perhaps I will be your lucky charm!"

We all smiled then, and we saw that humour in this man was a sign of his healing soul.

Chapter 36

In early summer I convinced the Acadian elders that we should abandon the refugee camp on the Petitcodiac and travel to the coast. There we could venture north to be safe from the guns of the British. It was only a matter of time before the English and New England troops at Beauséjour found their way up the river. We were aware at the time that England was at war with France in Europe, therefore we perhaps cautiously hoped the English had larger battles to fight.

Our destination was the Miramichi River, a place none of us had ever been but one that was much talked about by the Native peoples. They spoke of a sea of salmon plentiful enough to walk across. There we would be among the Malecite, who were the people of the more northerly lands. We hoped to reach the coast by the first of July. The Natives informed us it was a week's journey.

We found pathways mixed with brush, trodden down by groups travelling before us. This eased our efforts as we were loaded down with our food, ammunition, and iron cooking pots. We had been forced to leave our vessels behind.

We were aware that when we arrived at the coast other Acadian communities there would be expecting our arrival. When we reached the coast a fortnight later we found a huge group of our compatriots. Indeed, as the ocean came into view, we beheld thousands of Acadians camping at the beach. The place was called Cocagne.

The sandy beach spanned farther than the eye could see. The encampment stretched endlessly in both directions. Beyond the water's edge, fishing weirs followed the coastline for miles and the beach was filled with refugee Acadians working, playing, and enjoying the summer sun.

There was little evidence of the winter the people here must have
endured. Sun and heat warm the soul as well as the body, filling us with
energy. The Acadians on the beach when we arrived may have been thin but
they were not unhappy. This was a relief for us. We felt the safety one feels
when one is living among large congregations of like-minded people. These
were our people. Like us, they had escaped the deportation and lived to tell
a tale of survival. Many of these would reach the Promised Land with us.
None of us, however, was sure where that was.

I soon made it my business to acquaint myself with all the elders of the
camp. Daily I walked the beach, stopping by each group and discovering
from whence they came and what Acadian community they had escaped
from. Their stories of survival were similar to ours. These were the Acadians
who, like me, had had their ears to the ground during the spring and summer of 1755. Like us, they owed a great deal to the Native peoples.

Introducing myself to hundreds of compatriots made it easier for me to
influence a large number of people to continue our trek. I spread the word
that we should move on to the mouth of the Miramichi as soon as possible
for our greater safety, and I told the people that the sooner we established
permanent lodgings for the winter the better. It would give us more time
to clear the land. In a more settled camp we could co-operate to plant root
vegetables to be harvested in late fall, and we could dry berries, meat, and
fish to last the winter.

At the end of each day, having travelled the beach for miles, I returned
home with tales of those who had been forced into exile. We learned through
a few who had eluded the expulsion at Grand Pré, and there were only a few,
that Jeanne's beloved Isabelle had been placed on a ship bound for Louisiana
with her entire family.

"It is so comforting to know that Isabelle is with her family," Jeanne
said with relief. "Perhaps she will be fortunate, landing in a territory that is
friendly and kind to French speakers. Is not Louisiana a French territory?"

"That is my understanding," I answered, "and having Mama and Charles
safely delivered to Quebec also eases my mind to no end."

"Indeed."

Jeanne invariably became quiet after hearing news of loved ones. It
appeared to improve her mood considerably. She treated each piece of good
news as a gift, as we all did.

What I remember most vividly of those first summer nights at Cocagne were the miles and miles of bonfires on the beach stretching north and south, illuminating the night skies and demonstrating a hope that God would not forget where we were. We received no sign that the Lord had seen our fires, but they did attract French ships sailing along the coast from Quebec. These French vessels often moored off the shore, sending provisions by tender and keeping us abreast of the events in what was to be known as the Seven Years War. Their generosity knew no bounds, and they shared as much as they could spare to supply us with the things we were not able to provide for ourselves, particularly ammunition and gunpowder for our muskets. These we preserved for the winter game hunt, restricting our diet primarily to fish during the summer months.

After discussing our trek north with all the heads of the families along the seashore, we began our journey, beginning with those farthest up the beach. Because of the numbers of people on the move, the process of relocating took longer than we had anticipated, but we managed to reach the mouth of the great Miramichi River by mid-July. Once arrived, we all acknowledged that our new location could sustain the Acadian refugees who had made the trip. Together with the settlers who had already taken root there, we numbered in the thousands. This was one time when one could say there was safety in numbers.

The Malecite welcomed us on our arrival at the mouth of the great Miramichi River. They let us know that they would assist us in constructing our wigwams. French ships continued to arrive with messages from Governor Vaudreuil of New France, placing all the Acadians under his express protection. He sent written messages outlining the details of France's war with Britain. He declared that the British treatment of the Acadians during the 1755 deportation was beyond cruelty and a crime against decent people everywhere. He stated that French ships would create a sea blockade from Louisbourg to Quebec, preventing the British from hunting down and terrorizing any French-speaking people in the New World. For the first time in my life I felt that I was being protected by those that govern and respected by them as a human being. I was fifty years old and finally being recognized as someone who mattered in this world.

There was music, dancing, and games that summer. Our encampments were further upriver, following the habits of the Malecite who fish in the ocean in summer and move inland to seek protection from the tidal surges and winds in the winter. And so we gathered into family groups, and we cleared enough forest to have small gardens alongside our wigwams and create a more permanent existence for as long as we could manage it.

Regularly, in the summer and autumn, a priest was sent from Quebec to administer the blessed sacraments. On one of these visits my twenty-two-year-old daughter, Madeleine, married Jacques (known as Tourangeau) Amirault. This happy event was the first of its kind while we were in exile. The event was hopeful and gave us all a sense that life was continuing as it should.

Named after my mother, Madeleine was the most beautiful of my daughters. She resembled Grandmama Marie but clearly favoured my mother in temperament. There was no shortage of people to celebrate the nuptials, and a party mood spread like wildfire down the river.

"Please sing for us, Papa — something romantic," requested Madeleine.

"Am I able to refuse my beautiful married daughter anything?" I asked.

At the first notes of the song a sudden silence descended on the river. My voice echoed into the night.

> *Ah, si l'amour prenait racine,*
> *Dans mon jardin j'en planterais,*
> *J'en planterais, j'en sèmerais aux quatre coins,*
> *J'en ferais part à mes amis qui n'en ont point.*

As I continued to sing I was joined by hundreds along the river. I felt the arms of our new community wrapping around me as I stood facing my daughter and her new husband. Applause spread through the settlement like a warm breeze. That was a special moment for me during those times of trouble. Madeleine ran into my arms and kissed me.

"Thank you, Papa. That was the most wonderful gift you could possibly give me on my wedding day."

I looked over her shoulder to see her mother with a huge smile and tears in her beautiful eyes. Life seemed blissful for those brief shining moments.

The summer of 1756 was particularly pleasant and warm, with only a smattering of rain. The seasons passed, and winter moved on to summer, bringing few changes in our lives. We had become accustomed to wilderness living and we were now assured assistance from both the French and the Native peoples.

The last ship to visit our settlement was in the summer of 1758. It was sailing from Quebec to Louisbourg. The news it carried was not good. New France, particularly the city of Quebec, was plagued by a smallpox epidemic; and all the ships had been directed to Louisbourg, for it was about to be besieged by the British navy. We learned from the captain of the last vessel to stop at our camp that many of the Acadians who had travelled to Quebec from the St. John River had succumbed to the disease.

This news made us very uneasy for my relatives in Quebec. It was only during the final years in exile that their fate was confirmed by an unexpected source. Both my mother and Charles died of smallpox in 1758. After all his heroic exploits and their survival of the journey by river to Quebec, he and Mother lived only two more years.

The news from Quebec was delivered by a far greater human force than we were anticipating. In the middle of June 1760, just when we were becoming accustomed to our existence at the Miramichi, events began to unravel that would alter our life in the wilderness. Summer took us all to the mouth of the river to reap the benefits of the sea and to feel the hot sands beneath our feet. That is when we first heard the rumblings from the south.

Legions of Acadians and Mi'kmaq, fifteen hundred strong, appeared by land and by sea. Hundreds of schooners sailed into the bay, while militiamen and tribesmen swept into our communities. They told us that Quebec had fallen in October of the previous year and demanded that our men join them in their battle against the British. They gave us no warning and they expected every man in our region to decide immediately whether to join the fight or remain with our families. They told us that Father Manach, the priest who had been leader of the Acadian and Mi'kmaq militias, had made peace with the British following the fall of Quebec. The Acadian leaders, like the elusive

Beausoleil, declared that Manach and the other priests who followed his example were traitors and that there was still a chance to vanquish the British.

One of the priests who had remained loyal to the French cause informed us that he had administered the last rites to the now famous Charles Belliveau and his mother at Quebec. Despite our grief, we were comforted by the fact that neither had suffered for long. Amen!

Most of the elders understood that with the loss of Quebec an Acadian victory was impossible. Some were caught up in the excitement of the imminent battle and joined the militias, but I persuaded most of my group to wait and see. In the coming weeks we watched from the shore as flotillas of French and British warships forged their way through the choppy seas, sailing north to meet in battle at the mouth of the Restigouche River. Militias of Natives and Acadians continued to parade north through the woods to help defend the communities in Chaleur Bay.

It was through the network of communications of the Mi'kmaq, Malecite, and Algonquin tribes that we had become aware of the fall of the fortress of Louisbourg in 1758 and the capitulation of the people of New France in 1759 to the British. Beaten and wounded survivors of the Battle of Restigouche returned south to tell stories of victory against the British. However, the final page of their saga was one of defeat. The colonies in the New World were now in the hands of the British. Hearing this news, we realized that the game had abruptly changed and we were hiding out in a territory that was under British domination. The idea of living peacefully under French rule had evaporated not long after it had begun and our future suddenly became uncertain.

Chapter 37

The changes we make in life are governed by time and circumstance. After Quebec fell to the British in 1759, we found that we were again living in a time of English rule. We were again fugitives fleeing the British forces, not refugees under French protection. Changes of time and circumstance force decisions that would otherwise not be necessary. We Acadians at the Miramichi were compelled to plan our next move. Better to hasten the inevitable than run away from it. I set about to convince the elders of our settlement that our only choice was to give ourselves up to those who now governed us and finally sign the unconditional oath of allegiance.

Many were unwilling to make this move. I had learned from my experience at French Cross that it is impossible to convince everyone to make a prudent decision. Fortunately, at least half those assembled at the Miramichi saw the wisdom in my suggestion. Therefore, in the summer of 1760, after a gruelling winter with no assistance from the French and no ammunition or gunpowder for our weapons, we gathered our belongings and began to travel by foot south along the seacoast, returning by the route from which we had come four years earlier. At Cocagne we united with other fugitives who had fought at the Battle of Restigouche but had come to the same conclusion, that it was best to surrender to the British and give up our arms.

Early in summer we arrived at Fort Beauséjour, now Fort Cumberland, at what had been known to us as Beaubassin. The British received us outside the walls of the fort at gunpoint. They declared that we were prisoners of war according to the law passed by the English Parliament that no Acadians were permitted to reside in Nova Scotia. We relinquished our arms and our liberty with profound regret, for we had been the ones among our people to retain those rights the longest. As prisoners of war, however, we were assured of food and some degree of lodging. It was indeed ironic that our captivity was to be our place of greatest safety. Had those same British officers known of my complicity in stealing the schooner four years earlier and the execution of its captain and crew, I would have been executed myself. Ah, the vagaries of war!

The young commanding officer who read the declaration had a most familiar face, startlingly, a ghostly memory from the past. The resemblance was uncanny, but this officer was too young to be the man I remembered. That man would be in his seventies by now. I watched him carefully as he read the document perfectly in the King's English. Then the recollection became clear. This was Samuel Mangeant, thrown by fate back into my life. Here stood the son of Benjamin's nemesis and murderer, François Mangeant, a young man who twenty years earlier had stolen my Cousin Elizabeth's innocence, only to desert her. I stood there paralyzed, attempting to keep my anger from erupting.

Having delivered his declaration in English, he repeated it immaculately in French. This confirmed my suspicion. This was indeed Samuel Mangeant! He did not have the haughty air of his father. Perhaps his father's final banishment tempered any feeling of superiority he may have had, or it was quite possible he inherited some of the good qualities of his mother. I remember her as a refined and gentle woman.

Having completed his duty, he asked who among our large group spoke fluent English.

"Monsieur," I said, "I will speak for all the prisoners present."

Mangeant appeared puzzled.

"You have a perfect English accent, sir. Are you English?"

Ignoring the intent of his question, I remarked sarcastically, "I have been a loyal subject to His Majesty the King of Great Britain for nearly fifty years, monsieur."

Young Mangeant looked at me quizzically. I was not certain whether he noted the sarcasm, but my insolent tone was unmistakable.

Dismissing my comment, he spoke emphatically. "Since it will be you who communicates with the officers at Fort Cumberland on behalf of the Acadian prisoners, I will require your name, monsieur."

"I am known to every member of this august group of proud Acadians as Piau. Using this name will be most convenient to all concerned. It has been so long since I have been referred to by my birth names, I almost forget what they are."

"When you sign the oath of allegiance, which you will see is the unconditional oath, you will have to sign using your surname and birth name. You must at least provide the officer who administers it with your proper designation. I trust you can write your name, sir."

"That I can, monsieur. I was formally educated in both French and English. I am an Acadian, there is no doubt, but my heritage is both French and British."

"You are a bold one. Your English heritage will not be recognized here or anywhere else in His Majesty's colonies."

Did Samuel Mangeant recognize me? Perhaps, or perhaps not!

So began our captivity. The Acadians were ordered to immediately set about restoring the dikes surrounding the fort. The system built before the fall of Fort Beauséjour had been badly damaged in the battles between the British and the defending French. Fortunately for us, the foundations were still intact, so the work was not onerous. By late summer they were completely mended owing to the work of hundreds of Acadians.

Our numbers were not as numerous as they had been in exile, but they were still too great to be manageable in such a small fort. Therefore, it was decided by those in command that half our group would be transported to Fort Edward, situated at Pisquit on what they now called the Avon River, just upriver from Grand Pré.

The prospect of returning to the valley near Minas filled us with some excitement. For me, it would be close enough to consider this move a return home. Grand Pré was as much a part of me as Melanson Village and Port Royal. It would, of course, be difficult to return to a land where all the Acadian farms had been transferred to English and New England planters. Our destiny would take us to our previous lands, but we would be forced, as prisoners of war, to work the land as indentured servants, unable to reap the benefits of our labours.

It came as no surprise to me that Captain Mangeant accompanied us to Fort Edward. By the end of August we boarded ships that conveyed us by sea across the Bay of Fundy into Minas Basin and up the Avon River to our new home, or prison camp.

We entered the basin, sailing past Grand Pré as the sun was setting over the valley. Tears streamed from my eyes as I stood on the deck with six others in our group.

Mangeant sensed my nostalgia for this special place. "Piau, do you know this place, Grand Pré?"

Not wishing to share my important memories, I merely nodded.

The young man persisted. "When I was little more than a teen, I passed a most agreeable summer visiting my parents at Grand Pré. My father was the magistrate there at the time. My youngest brother, Jean Baptiste, was born there. There are few places on earth as beautiful as this valley in summer."

"I must agree with you on that point. As for me, I spent every winter here when I was a child, in the home of my great-uncle. He was responsible for my English education. He was born in Yorkshire."

"So, that is the British heritage you referred to when we first met at Fort Cumberland."

"That is so." I was reluctant to offer any more information about myself.

"You might find this odd, but I am a British officer with not a drop of English blood flowing through my veins."

"Is that so?"

"Yes, and I am at liberty and you are not."

"The state of being free is not of the body but of the soul," I said as a rebuke.

Mangeant thought for a long moment. "I suppose one does have to adopt that attitude when one is under arrest, monsieur."

There the conversation ended. This was an exchange I was certain he would not have had with one of his fellow officers.

To my surprise, as our vessel sailed closer to Pisiquit I could see in the early evening sun that, unlike Grand Pré, all the farms still retained their houses, barns, and outer buildings. I was certain that this was a unique situation, for on our travels to this place we had seen no evidence of Acadian farms being left intact. The British had burned all the Acadian villages to the ground to prevent us from returning to them and using them as a place to resist the British army. Not only were these farms intact, but there appeared to be people actively working them. How strange, we thought.

We soon came to realize that our futures would be tied up with these former Acadian lands.

Arrival at Fort Edward was routine. Captain Mangeant presented several hundred of us to the commander of the fort, Captain Jotham Gay. We were all accounted for, and the prisoner list was transferred into the hands of the commanding officer. Mangeant and Gay saluted one another and shook hands in a friendly and familiar way.

"It is good to see you again, Samuel. It has been some time since we have been in one another's presence. I trust your wife and children are happy and in good health."

"Kind of you to ask, Jotham. They were robustly healthy when I last saw them, but, of course, the war has prevented me from returning to them in Boston, my leaves have been so infrequent. I receive their news by letter when the dispatches are delivered from New England."

"Your human cargo appears to be in excellent health compared to those I have witnessed previously. They will make strong and productive workers."

"Indeed. I believe they lived quite comfortably in isolation on the Miramichi River, regular recipients of victuals, arms, and ammunition from the French at Quebec. Once they realized that Quebec had fallen to our forces they surrendered voluntarily. They have even signed the oath of allegiance to His Majesty King George III."

"Voluntary submission, you say. Well, these prisoners will provide the labour we need to build a productive English-speaking colony here."

Hearing these words, I became aware of what these plans implied. Like the Israelites in bondage in Egypt, we were destined to be a people forced to endure a life of servitude. This was something I had not anticipated; we were now indentured servants, stripped of our rights and freedoms. My hope evaporated like a morning mist. I was the only member of the group fluent enough in English to understand their intent, so I was left to suffer my own anguish in silence. The inevitable would be revealed to the rest of my family and friends in due course.

"Captain Gay, I would like to introduce you to Piau."

Mangeant motioned for me to come forward. I complied, not showing any pleasure being singled out in the group.

"This Acadian gentleman is the leader of this group. He speaks the King's English far better than either of us and has been well educated in our language."

Gay laughed as he scrutinized me carefully. "Has he indeed? And where, Monsieur Piau, did you acquire this education?"

"My grandfather was the son of a Huguenot, born and raised in Yorkshire. He and his brother came to Port Royal with his parents when the English first took possession of the colony in 1657. Both my grandfather and his brother married Acadian women. His brother, my great-uncle, took on the responsibility of my English education when I was a young child."

When I had finished, I noticed a change in Captain Mangeant. Our eyes met. It was obvious to me that his mind was stripping away the layers of the past and discovering our common history. The look I gave him was one that could no longer conceal what I knew. He knew what I knew, it was now clear, although I could not be certain if he was in possession of the complete story of Benjamin's death and his father's complicity.

"Well, Monsieur Piau, I am fortunate to find that you will be a useful liaison between my company and your people. I am certain we will get on famously. This man is truly unique, Captain Mangeant, would you not agree?"

"I agree, Captain. Quite unique." His expression never changed as he uttered those words.

The following day, Samuel Mangeant approached me while I was stoking the fire at the tent site where the soldiers had assembled sleeping quarters for the newly arrived prisoners of war. It was still summer, so these were sufficient until the colder weather arrived.

"Bonjour, Captain."

"So, Monsieur Belliveau, when were you going to reveal your true identity to me? Your great-uncle was Sieur Pierre Laverdure, the founder of Grand Pré, and your cousin was Benjamin LeBlanc." Mangeant seemed to take a degree of pleasure in finding me out.

"That is true. Elizabeth LeBlanc is my cousin as well," I responded, adding this comment to inflict a well-deserved sting on behalf of my dear exiled cousin.

"It has been more than twenty years, Piau. I was no more than a boy that summer at Grand Pré."

"I do not consider eighteen a boy, Captain. You were a young officer in His Majesty's army. You were certainly old enough to tarnish the reputation of a naive and unsuspecting young lady. She never recovered, you will be pleased to know. But, as we all do, she learned to accept her lot in life. I hope she is safe in some friendly corner of the globe."

"She is, monsieur, I assure you. I was part of the military battalion under Winslow who evacuated the Acadians from the lands of Minas Basin in 1755. I made certain that Elizabeth's father and his entire family were safely shipped to New England through the port of New York. I was captain of a ship sailing to Philadelphia and I manoeuvred to ensure that Elizabeth, her sister, and her brother Désiré were aboard my vessel. And so they were. On our arrival in Philadelphia, employment was arranged for all three in the home of a wealthy Quaker merchant. Elizabeth is governess to his children. René LeBlanc and his family were reunited with Elizabeth and her two siblings in Philadelphia. Monsieur LeBlanc has since died. I sense he was not a happy man. But those were the times, Piau. You see, sir, I am not the villain in this story."

I stood still and remained speechless. I knew, of course, that it was his father who had been the villain. The son resembled his father in appearance, not in character. François Mangeant had been a demon, but the son clearly was not. I felt ashamed of myself for unjustifiably making the wrong judgment about this man.

"I owe you an apology, Captain, and a huge debt of gratitude for all you have done to soften the blow of expulsion for my poor exiled family. Kindness from a British officer is not something any of us have experienced in a long time. So, thank you, Samuel."

"There is no need for thanks or apologies. You must believe me when I say that my intentions toward your cousin Elizabeth were honourable and that I loved her and hoped to marry her. My father would have none of it when our affair was revealed, and he banished me to New England, ordering me to concentrate on my standing in the British army and improve my fortunes with a suitable New England girl. I did marry an English girl from Boston, and we have lived a reasonably happy life with two children. You understand, however, I have been at war for the past four years, and army life allows few opportunities for one to be with one's family. Despite your captivity, I envy your being able to be with your loved ones daily."

"All I can say to you, young Mangeant, is God bless you. You cannot carry the burden of your father's crimes, nor should you. François Mangeant, wherever he may be, dead or living, will eventually be judged on the same scale as all of us. Justice comes from only one place. Believe me, my soul has been tarnished by many sins. I wish to live to be an old man so I can make proper restitution for what I have been forced to do in this ghastly war."

"Did you join the resistance at Restigouche? You can answer truthfully; I will impose no punishment. This, after all, is a time of war."

"I left that battle to the young. I have a large family to raise and I am of no use to them dead. I learned from my father's early death when I was one year old that a man has a responsibility to live and care for his children. My father died a hero, attempting to protect our home, but he was also fighting to defend French rule at Port Royal. And there lies the problem. From that time until the deportation, we attempted not to take sides, but the fates refused to allow us the luxury of neutrality. And so we are here, alive and together. And you have told your story, so I can find it in my heart to forgive you for my cousin's sadness and her brother's murder."

"Benjamin LeBlanc was murdered? I had no idea. If he was murdered, what connection do I have to this calamity? I heard from my mother in a letter she sent me at Boston that he had tragically met his end through some mysterious circumstance, but she was not aware of the details."

"I hope that is what your mother truly believed, for her own sake. Nothing will bring Benjamin back to me. I will leave the rest to the Almighty."

Mangeant the younger appeared troubled by my words, but I thought it served no purpose to share with him my theory on how Benjamin had met his untimely end. I did not discuss it with him again. Perhaps he surmised the truth.

Chapter 38

So began the next phase of our lives. We were a captive people but it was comforting initially to know that we did not have to be fugitives on the run anymore. Our years wandering through the wilderness were at an end. We never again were forced to live that nomadic existence. Freedom has its hardships and responsibilities, but many lessons were learned along the way.

Jospiau became my constant companion during those years. He was thirteen when we arrived at Fort Edward, and I took it upon myself to take him everywhere I went, even to meetings with Captains Gay and Mangeant. It was important that he begin to learn the things I had been taught by Uncle Pierre. There were different lessons learned in the wilderness, but I wished him to understand the business of those men who possessed power.

The humiliating part of our imprisonment did not come from chains, for we had the freedom of our limbs, and although we were guarded by British soldiers we could come and go as we pleased, so long as we remained within the confines of the fort and nearby lands. What caused us considerable embarrassment and sadness was that we were forced to work the farms that had formerly belonged to Acadians but were now in the possession of what they called planters from New England. We were paid a penny a day, so officially we Acadians were not considered slave labour. The pennies were no more than tokens, however, and in actuality we were indentured servants no matter how hard the British tried to conceal the fact.

"This is slavery!" I railed to Captain Gay. "And it is humiliating for us to work the land that belonged to our brother Acadians. There are people in this camp who are being forced to work the farms that were established by their own families. Such cruelty is unconscionable."

Captain Gay was taken aback by my vehemence but was quick to respond: "Piau, you must understand that work is a permissible expectation of prisoners of war. By law, no Acadian is permitted to reside in Nova Scotia, so your presence in this colony is tolerated only by the fact that you chose to voluntarily surrender yourselves. We are providing your people with food and lodging, and you enjoy our protection so long as you reside here. In point of fact, you all should have been on the British ships in 1755, when all Acadians were expelled from this colony."

"If these conditions represent our status in Nova Scotia, why were we encouraged to sign the oath of allegiance to a king who is not our king?"

"Taking the oath of allegiance was merely a formality, to prove your sincerity in accepting to be prisoners of war. It is also quite possible, once this war has come to a successful end and the English have prevailed in the Americas, that you may again enjoy the privileges of British subjects."

There was little point pursuing this matter, but there were ways I could manage the situation so that those who were being forced to labour on their former farms were placed elsewhere. To this request, Gay conceded.

Shortly after agreeing to this request, however, Gay came to me with another demand.

"The lieutenant-governor is in need of skilled labourers to continue the construction of the fortifications at the citadel in Halifax. I was told by Mangeant that you have experience as a mason and that several of the Acadians here do as well. Certainly the mighty LeBlanc brothers have the brawn. You would not have permanent residency in Halifax. Consider it temporary. You will be permitted to return here at regular intervals to visit your families."

"Captain Mangeant would be correct in that. I was trained by my great-uncle, who was a master stonemason from Yorkshire, and by my father-in-law in timber construction."

I made it a point at every opportunity to remind the two captains that I was also English. They respected my Englishness, particularly Mangeant, who did not possess one drop of English blood. This placed us on an equal footing, a position I was willing to exploit in order to ease the burden of my people.

"Why do you not teach me to speak better English, Papa?" pleaded Jospiau after attending this meeting with the two British captains at Fort

Edward. "I could not understand much of what you were saying to Captain Gay. How am I to learn if I do not comprehend English well?"

"You are right, my son. We have been so busy surviving that I neglected your English lessons. Having been an Acadian refugee for these past five years, I have barely spoken a word of English myself. I intend to reverse my negligence and begin our lessons today."

And so it was that from that day on I spoke to Jospiau in English when we were together, family time excepted. As a boy he soon absorbed the language, and his comprehension improved greatly. He would need fluency in English as a resident of this British colony.

The unexpected happened when we were preparing to transfer to Halifax for the building of the citadel. For the first time in my fifty-five years I became seriously ill. I have little memory of this critical time in my life, but I am able to describe it based on the stories I was told by Jeanne and other members of the family.

During my times of lucidity, I beheld angels administering to my needs in the form of my loving daughters Rosalie, Jeanne the younger, Felicity, Theotiste, Agnes, and, of course, my dear wife, Jeanne. The girls seemed to have the healing touch of their great-grandmother Marie, so my recovery was more likely in their hands. But Jeanne later told me that my fever had been dangerously high and that they had been certain they would lose me. Can you imagine me departing this world after surviving every possible hardship in exile? That would have been a true injustice. But these things are not determined by humans. There were times when I felt I was being drawn into the light of what must have been eternity, but as soon as I arrived at the precipice I turned away from the light and returned to the living. They say I went in and out of consciousness for several weeks. Jeanne confessed she was terrified at the prospect of losing me and that she could not imagine not having me present in her life. They all prayed constantly and attended to me every hour of every day until I rejoined them in the world of the living. Moses had survived the worst and was able to continue to lead his people on their journey to the Promised Land.

Others succumbed to the fever as well — they were afflicted with the disease but they too survived. The most surprising event was that all three of the mighty LeBlanc boys became sick simultaneously: Charlitte, Bouon, and Joseph. When they finally recovered, they not surprisingly continued their pursuit of my daughters. The herculean threesome had been openly courting Theotiste, Rosalie, and Agnes respectively for the entire time we spent in the wilderness. My daughters were not resistant to their advances; over the next two years each couple was married at Fort Edward by a visiting priest. Each commenced married life in bondage, but their marriages have lasted many years, most of them in freedom and happiness.

Chapter 39

Healthy and strong, with Jospiau by my side, accompanied by my titan sons-in-law Charlitte, Bouon, and Coujeau LeBlanc and my nephew Pierre, I made the trek across country to Halifax with a military escort, our first visit to a city. The citadel was already under construction. On our arrival at the work site, a familiar face caught my eye. It was Bastide, the engineer who in 1744 had been our architect and overseer in the restoration of the fortifications at Annapolis. He looked my way and recognized me immediately, even though I was now eighteen years older.

"As I live and breathe, if it isn't old Piau! The fates have finally decided to be kind and deliver me a skilled stonemason. Are Bernard and Denys with you? Of course not. They both would have joined the ancients! Well, well, welcome to my building site. How fortuitous!"

"This is an unexpected pleasure, Captain Bastide."

"I am compelled to correct you, Piau. I am to be appointed lieutenant-general in the autumn. And do you think that promotion will give me access to more skilled workers? Not in this God-forsaken place they call Halifax. But out of my past comes a deliverer."

I introduced Bastide to Jospiau and the rest of my group.

"These men, sir, have been trained in stonemasonry and timber construction at Fort Edward under my tutelage, especially my fifteen-year-old son here. Jospiau has inherited his talents from his great-great-uncle Pierre and his grandfather Bernard Gaudet."

"I can see he favours Bernard in his looks. I hope he has also inherited his grandfather's good nature. I have never met a man more jovial than your Gaudet grandfather, young man."

"I am afraid there is no way God could create another Bernard Gaudet. When my father-in-law died, the mould was broken, monsieur."

"So true, Piau, so true!" he laughed heartily.

As we continued our conversation, a distinguished-looking officer appeared on the ramparts, ignoring our presence and watching with considerable concentration the work being done by the labourers. Noticing our interest in this new arrival on the hill, Bastide's mood changed abruptly.

"You will be required to acquaint yourself with this gentleman, although I use that designation with considerable reservation. He is Major Frederick DesBarres, a Huguenot like me, born in France or Switzerland, although I hardly care. You will hear his tales of heroism before long and more than likely from the man himself. He won the siege of Louisbourg and Quebec single-handedly, I am told! No one remembers that I was there as well. DesBarres claims he held the dying General James Wolfe in his arms after the defeat of the French on the Plains of Abraham at Quebec. Humility is not something he aspires to. The gentleman is a shameless self-promoter. He is an adequate assistant military engineer, but I must give credit where credit is due. He is a brilliant cartographer. That is what he should be occupying his time with, not bothering himself with my efforts here!"

Bastide left little to say after his brief tirade.

"So, Piau, you and your companions will be directed to your quarters at the barracks by these soldiers and I will speak to you later on how you can best assist these poor excuses for stonemasons."

Carrying our few belongings, my group was ushered to our quarters to settle in for the evening. The following day I met DesBarres. He appeared at our barracks looking for me.

"The man named Piau, please show yourself," he commanded in perfect French. There was no formal greeting. No *bonjour*. This was a man who straightaway got right to the point.

In perfect English, with no formalities, I answered the major.

"I am he. I am fluent in English, Major, and at your service."

DesBarres gave me a quizzical look but showed no sign of affording me any more than a cursory acknowledgement.

"Bastide was correct in describing your English as remarkable for an Acadian. He and I are equally fluent in your native tongue, but as foreman of our stoneworkers your ability to speak English will simplify communication as we construct the walls of the fortress. We have both English and French labourers here."

I was somewhat shocked that I had so readily been chosen as master stonemason on this project.

"I am honoured for the trust you and Captain Bastide are placing in me. It has been many years since I have applied myself to my trade. However, skills, once acquired, last a lifetime. There are several of us who have knowledge of timber construction as well. Acadians have engaged in this skill since the building of the fortress at Louisbourg. My wife's father, Bernard Gaudet, and his brother Denys were responsible for this type of construction, both at Île Royale and Annapolis. Captain Bastide employed them on many occasions. I learned from them and I have passed my knowledge down to my companions and my son."

"Then your reputation is justified, monsieur." At that moment I was no longer just a labourer to this man. The use of "monsieur" was the first sign of respect he was affording me.

"Piau, I will give you a thorough tour of the fortifications being constructed around the citadel. As much work is being done underground as above. An entire system of bunkers will be built and subsequently covered in giant mounds of earth. Probably you have experience with such a system at Annapolis, perhaps on a smaller scale."

"Yes, Major. I am familiar with such a building scheme."

"I have a feeling, Piau, we are going to get along famously." For the first time, I was aware of a twinkle in DesBarres's eyes. A sudden smile appeared, to seal the deal.

After having been introduced to the workers, I proceeded to toil as hard as they did. Uncle Pierre always said, "model the work and others will imitate and learn from your example." I preferred not to encourage any special treatment or status among the British at the citadel, for they were, after all, still our captors and we were still their prisoners even though we were being paid a meagre stipend.

I was polite with the officers and friendly with Bastide. Soon the lieutenant-general was too preoccupied to cast his attention on me. His trust in me was sufficient for both of us. The stonemasonry spoke for itself, and Bastide was happy with our work.

"Oh, it was fate that brought you to the citadel, Piau, and my good fortune!"

I accepted his praise with a nod and a smile. Otherwise our relationship was a working one.

Major DesBarres, however, was a different matter. I found myself drawn to this young man who, despite Bastide's reservations, was a genius. His knowledge was so broad and varied that I could not prevent myself from engaging him in conversation as often as possible. Sometimes he was drawing military plans and at other times he was drafting maps of what I presumed was the coast of Nova Scotia. He often shared the map creations with me, trusting my judgment.

"This is the entire coastline of Île Royale, drawn precisely here. I have renamed the island Cape Breton." Following the coastline with his finger, DesBarres explained, "Last summer I circumnavigated the island, beginning at Louisbourg, sailing into all the bays along the coast, into an inland sea, north along the coastline, and south until I reached the Strait of Canso on the southwestern side of the island. This rugged coast is the one between the port of Canso and the fortress at Louisbourg. It was the most difficult to map. There are hundreds of inlets and islands. It almost drove me mad!" The major began to laugh as he proudly rolled up the map.

"I marvel at the work involved in creating such a map. The accuracy is spellbinding. Where did you learn such drafting skills?"

DesBarres seemed pleased that I appreciated his craftsmanship. He was clearly a vain man, but his vanity was well justified.

"I studied mathematics and science at the university in Basel, in Switzerland. Later, I moved to England, where I was taken under the wing of the Duke of Cumberland, who financed my military training at the Royal Military Academy at Woolwich. I studied cartography, drafting, and military fortifications there."

"I have never met anyone who attended a university. What exactly occurs there?"

"It is an institution where men go to study languages, history, philosophy, mathematics, and science. When you have studied any of these disciplines and have acquired a proficiency in the necessary course of studies the university grants you a degree. My degree is in science and mathematics."

"And mathematics is measurement?"

"What a clever observation, Piau. It is essentially advanced arithmetic, where you use numbers, or letters that represent numbers, to measure things, yes."

I found such a prospect fascinating. For the time being, however, I withdrew from this new knowledge to digest it later.

DesBarres's enthusiasm increased with every word he uttered. It was clear he possessed a passion for what he called cartography. "I hope to map the entire coastline of the colonies north of New England beginning next summer. How would you like to join me on one of my voyages? Do you have knowledge of the sea?"

"I hope to be with my family at Fort Edward next summer. You are kind to consider me for such an expedition. If my brother Charles were still alive, he would be the one to take. He was a master shipbuilder and mariner. I probably should not reveal this story, but he is gone and his fame has already spread throughout the colonies. He was the Acadian responsible for the seizing of the HMS *Pembroke*. Charles Belliveau, he was called."

"*That* Charles Belliveau was your brother? Incredible! As embarrassing as the seizure of the *Pembroke* was, there were many in the British navy who marvelled at your brother's heroism and skill as a mariner. Well, well! You implied earlier that he was no longer with us. Did he fall to a British musket?"

"No, something far worse. He made it safely to Quebec in 1756 with my mother in tow, only to have both of them succumb to smallpox two years later. It was so tragic, after achieving such heroism."

"His heroism is still being discussed, so I figure Charles Belliveau still survives in the memory of many."

"Certainly in mine, Major."

My education lasted throughout the summer and autumn whenever DesBarres and I had any spare time. He seemed to enjoy sharing the drawings and plans he drafted of the proposed fortifications that were required to defend Halifax from a French invasion. Britain was still at war with France, and in the summer of 1761 there was still no end to the conflict, despite the British hold on Louisbourg, Quebec, and Montreal. Governor James Murray in Quebec was insistent that the construction at Halifax be sped up and completed in case of a French invasion of the seaport. Finally, all was completed for the time being and we were permitted to return home for the winter.

Chapter 40

Before the first snowfall we all returned to our families at Fort Edward. My sojourn in Halifax had been the very first time I had been separated from my family in over thirty years. Jeanne and the girls were overjoyed to receive us home. My sons-in-law had barely spent any time as husbands to my three daughters. Jeanne remarked on how Jospiau had changed. I had to admit he was looking more like a man. Those who remained behind at Pisiquit observed the difference in the boy far more than I.

"It is such a blessing to have you all home. The time you were away from us, Piau, felt like such a long time. Your absence left us with such an emptiness," Jeanne grinned, before she continued, "I hope you have returned with the stone tablets."

I laughed heartily at her reference to Moses.

"The only mountain I stood on at Halifax was a large mound called the citadel, and my divine wisdom came from an unexpected source. I met and worked with a British officer, Major Frederick DesBarres, a Huguenot raised in France and Switzerland, who was such a fount of knowledge that I feel I have returned enlightened. He filled me with such learning that I am a changed man. This gentleman treated me like his equal and was generous with his knowledge. His understanding of science knew no bounds."

Jeanne looked mystified when I referred to the wonders of science.

"What is science, my love?"

"It is not easy to explain, but I can simply say it is the study of how things work. Science can explain how a wagon works, how a pulley and rope can make it easier to lift the bucket of water in a well. Everything in our lives, especially those things that help us build structures, can be explained by science. All things in our life are explainable and can be measured by mathematics. Is that not remarkable?"

"I am not certain I understand everything you say, but I see it fills you with great enthusiasm. That does not surprise me, for I have always been aware of your passion for learning new things. I can always feel your excitement when you master something or learn something brand new."

My return from Halifax also allowed me to renew my relationship with Samuel Mangeant. He had been made acting commander of the garrison at Fort Edward when Captain Gay left in the fall, promising to return after he had met with his superiors in Boston. Mangeant seemed genuinely pleased to see me on my return from Halifax.

"I missed you, Piau. Things were not quite the same here in your absence. Your congeniality was absent."

"You are kind, Captain. It is wonderful to be back in the bosom of my family and friends."

It was time for all of us to assist the New England planters in the yearly harvest. It was refreshing to be out in the fields collecting the crops and enjoying the camaraderie and fresh autumn air. It brought back memories of the harvest festivals celebrated years ago at Melanson Village and later Gaudet Village, resurrecting Uncle Pierre, Grandmama Marie, Mama, my brothers Charles and Jean, and of course Benjamin. Their spirits played amongst the corn like children in the warm autumn sun.

Not long after we returned from Halifax, another group of people came to the village. A ship arrived on the incoming tide carrying a human cargo that required more troops than would usually be necessary to deliver prisoners of war.

Those who disembarked that day did not appear fierce or hostile. But when one man appeared I could hear whispers travelling across the camp, murmuring "Beausoleil." I had heard his name many times. He was the leader of the Acadian resistance in the battles at Annapolis, Halifax, Grand Pré, Beauséjour,

and Restigouche. An almost mythical character, he was said to be fearless, a
fierce enemy of the British for the past eighteen years. The first time I heard of
him was back in 1744 when the French were attacking the fort at Annapolis.
Unlike the French troops under Duvivier, the Acadian-Mi'kmaq militia were
elusive, an army of ghosts attacking from every side, causing mayhem and fear
everywhere they went. Their leaders were Father Le Loutre and Beausoleil.

Most of my people had ambivalent feelings toward both men and their
Acadian-Mi'kmaq army. They fought the British supposedly on our behalf,
but we rarely reaped the benefits of their efforts. Their continued resistance
to British rule in Acadia made life for the neutral Acadians like us perilous.
We could not help but respect the Acadian resistance fighters, but they were
as much a problem for us as a help.

With the arrival of the resistance fighters came the news that the new
lieutenant-governor in Halifax was taking a harder line toward the Acadian
prisoners of war. Samuel Mangeant kept me informed as to the latest rumblings emanating from Halifax and Lieutenant-Governor Belcher's crusade
to empty Georges Island of its Acadian occupants. I had not been billeted
there but instead lived in the barracks at the citadel. In my discussions with
the captain, I felt he was not sharing everything he knew, and this created a
feeling of foreboding in me.

"What is likely to happen to all the Acadians at Halifax? Surely they are
not planning to deport them. I realize we are still at war, but many of these
prisoners have already taken the oath."

"I am not at liberty to relate all the details of the lieutenant-governor's
plans toward the Acadians, but I can tell you that with the arrival of the
resistance fighters at Fort Edward, the status quo has changed. Belcher is
determined to have them close to him because they pose a threat to our
colony. Although he participated in the 'burying the hatchet ceremony' and
has an assurance from the Mi'kmaq that they will no longer be a threat to
the British in Nova Scotia, he believes that the Acadian resistance should be
removed from the colony."

"What impact will that have on us at Fort Edward?"

"Should they deport the Georges Island Acadians, we would be required
to provide at least eighty men to the building project at the capital. That
would mean that the men here would be obligated to replace the workforce
that had previously been expelled from Nova Scotia."

"Captain, I fear if we leave this place and go to Halifax, we, too, will be on a ship to nowhere. Fort Edward has become a safe haven for us, but if we leave we may never return. These are very uncertain times!"

Mangeant gave me a troubled look. Perhaps he knew the truth at that time, perhaps not. Both of us were intelligent enough to know that once one is out of his place of safety, his vulnerability increases tenfold. It was early summer; perhaps we would be left in peace.

The members of the Acadian resistance were kept separate from the other prisoners of war, so we could only gaze at them from a distance. They were heavily guarded at all times, and therefore Beausoleil and his companions remained strangers to us. What I did know was that the presence of these fighters jeopardized our existence in Nova Scotia. The Acadians in my group began resenting these men rather than considering them heroes.

The day I most feared came in mid-July 1762 with the arrival of a large contingent of British soldiers from Halifax. Eighty Acadian men, many from my group, in addition to all the members of the resistance army, were paraded into the square and instructed to gather their belongings in preparation for an immediate relocation to Halifax. The women were extremely alarmed that their men were being taken off yet again. One could read the terror on their faces, for they dreaded the worst: that they would never see their loved ones again. That possibility certainly crossed my mind.

Alarmed that Jospiau would be included in the group, I beseeched Captain Mangeant to intervene and ensure my son remained behind with the women, for he would be needed as the man of the family. Mangeant gladly escorted Jospiau back to his family.

"It is done, Piau, so Godspeed."

"I will always remember your various kindnesses to my family. Every good deed done to us will negate the offences your father perpetrated upon my family at Grand Pré. I repeat, the son does not have to pay for the sins of the father. God bless you, Samuel."

Mangeant put out his hand to shake mine. I imagined I could feel his regret pulsating through the leather of his glove. He turned around and returned to his quarters, demonstrating his preference not to witness the sad scene that was playing out in the square.

Weeping and painful goodbyes filled the air with grief. I embraced Jeanne and each of my children, not knowing whether I would ever see their faces again. As we marched down the road, I began to sing "*À la claire fontaine*" so that Jeanne would have this final memory of me. As the sound of the melody soared above the river, I could hear the Acadians raising their voices in song, pouring their hearts out to heaven, asking God to intercede on their behalf, so their loving husbands and sons could be brought safely back to them.

The Acadian resistance fighters were still kept separate from the rest of us as we travelled the road to Halifax. We preferred it that way. I had my own bodyguards in my sons-in-law, the three LeBlanc boys, but despite their physical strength they too succumbed to the devastation of having to leave their wives, perhaps forever. To this day, I am able to resurrect the gut-wrenching pain we suffered as we marched away from Fort Edward in the summer of 1762.

Chapter 41

Our expectations on arriving at Halifax were that we would probably be reassigned to work duties related to the continued construction of the citadel. Those expectations were dashed when we were all placed on lifeboats and dropped off at Georges Island. There were close to a thousand Acadian men camped there, and they appeared to be packing up their belongings in preparation for a voyage. I asked some of the officers where we were being sent, and later I asked some of the Acadian prisoners. The former refused to answer, and the latter had not the slightest idea.

The number of British ships moored near the island was substantially greater than I had remembered in the past. I feared that these vessels were there for some greater purpose — we were being deported. After seven long years avoiding it, I found the reality that we were to leave our beloved Acadia horrifying and tragic. How could we be torn away from our loved ones, never to see them again? What form of cruelty was this? I then thought of the thousands who had already been forced into exile, not knowing where they were being sent until their arrival at a destination that was not of their choosing. They would have arrived there without money or belongings, and I could only imagine the horrific life they were compelled to endure. Now I was to join them in this appalling world of obscurity.

Destiny was not finished with me yet, however. As we boarded our vessel, my name was called. Having identified myself, I was directed by a ship's officer to step aside and wait until all the others were below deck. Another officer pointed me in the direction of a solitary prisoner being closely guarded by four armed soldiers. The man they were watching over was chained at the ankles, and his hands were bound tightly together by a thick rope; I did not know why. The first officer walked toward me across the deck bearing a paper on which, I came to discover, were special orders.

"Pierre Belliveau, you have been given special orders by the commander at Fort Edward. His Excellency the Lieutenant-Governor of Nova Scotia has signed his approval of these exceptional orders and we are fulfilling them. You are to occupy a berth with this prisoner for the duration of the voyage. Follow the soldiers below."

Surprised, I looked at the face of my new bunkmate before climbing below. The man looked dispassionately at me but seemed to possess a knowledge I did not. I stared at him for no more than a moment, but there appeared to be something familiar in his features. There are often times when you see someone who looks like a person you knew in the distant past and in trying to recall who it is you imagine a young face under the aging one. I stripped away the lines in my mind as I lowered myself below deck and discovered it was someone I had known as a young boy at Port Royal. It was Joseph Broussard, whom I had not seen since I was a child. He was four years my senior. What did not dawn on me until we were in our tiny cabin together was that the man in chains sitting on the opposite bunk was none other than Beausoleil!

"Well, well!" the man remarked in French. "So, you are the famous Piau. The fates have brought us together, finally."

"Apparently it was Captain Samuel Mangeant and not the fates, monsieur. Although I can hardly understand what Mangeant's motive was in having us placed together."

"Perhaps he wished to unite the two great resistance leaders of the Acadian people."

"Greatness should not be confused with notoriety, Joseph."

He was not expecting me to address him by his Christian name. It became clear to me that his only knowledge of me was one associated with my fame. I was Pierre, known as Piau Belliveau, but he did not remember me from his childhood.

"I have not been called Joseph for many years, monsieur. Why would you use a name from my past?"

"I knew you, Joseph, when we were young at Annapolis."

"You mean Port Royal. I have never recognized the British governance of Acadia. You have me at a disadvantage, monsieur. Who exactly are you?"

"My father was Jean Charles Belliveau, who fought and died in the Battle of Port Royal a year after my birth. My grandfather was Charles Melanson, founder of Melanson Village."

Beausoleil sat opposite me digesting what I was revealing of myself and my family.

"Your father was a hero and your grandfather was a traitor!" Beausoleil barked. "Which are you?"

"Neither, Monsieur Beausoleil," I replied sarcastically. "But surely you know that. After all, you say that you have heard of me."

After I challenged him, Beausoleil calmed down immediately. "Indeed I have. After the Battle of Restigouche, which, by the way, you did not participate in, you may have heard that my militia wandered about in the area, causing havoc for the British wherever we could find them until we landed in the Miramichi in 1760 after you and your group had left for Beauséjour. Those who remained along that river told tales of the great Piau. I believe they actually considered you their deliverer. The stories of Charles Belliveau, who I now understand was your brother, and his taking of the HMS *Pembroke,* and your taking of his schooner from the British at the mouth of the Petitcodiac, have become legendary. Many Acadians are inspired by such stories of heroism."

"I cannot object to anything that keeps their hopes alive. However, the heroes sitting here in this cabin have come to a sorry end, wouldn't you admit, monsieur?"

"Neither of us is dead yet. Who knows what trouble we can stir up in the British colonies?"

"From where I sit, monsieur, *'le beau soleil'* has set. Who knows when it will rise again?"

I could see that my comment had bruised his vanity. He remained silent, sizing me up like a foe who had to be vanquished. Again his mood rose to a slow boil.

"And what crusade have you led where your life was in peril time and time again? What army has followed you time and time again? How many battles have you fought in order to secure a land that respects your language and your religion?"

"My battles have been with my conscience and they have consumed most of my time, monsieur. I have risked life and limb for the safety of my family and friends. In every case, I have permitted those I lead to choose their own path. There were times they followed me and times they did not. With God's guidance, those who followed me have survived. Many that chose not to have perished. Perhaps this was by divine providence, but I believe that prudent decisions have allowed us to prevail, to survive until we had to make yet another choice."

"You are a philosopher, monsieur. However, extreme action is the only solution when those who govern you restrict your freedom and oppose your religious beliefs."

"I have the belief, Joseph, that my relationship with the Almighty cannot be violated by any living being. The spiritual realm is inviolate. There are times when one must fight for what one believes, but muskets and violence are not always the solution. Did not the Lord tell us to love our enemies?"

"Nonsense. You are beginning to sound like the bloody Protestants."

"I admit that there is Protestant blood flowing through my veins, but we Acadians are devout Catholics although we have never subscribed to the intolerance of the French Crown. I have been a British subject for most of my life. That is where we differ, you and me. You chose to leave Port Royal for the Petitcodiac years ago. You have lived most of your life in French territory, at a time when we preferred to fight our own battles of quiet resistance within the land of the English. We have been engaging in a war of peaceful coexistence with the British for fifty years and have defended our right to speak our language, practise our faith, and live in Nova Scotia without firing a single musket shot."

"And where has that got you, monsieur?"

"Precisely in the same cabin below deck as you, monsieur. And tell me, which of us is in chains? Extreme actions beget extreme consequences, would you not agree!"

Beausoleil observed me quietly for several minutes and then broke into a spontaneous laugh that I am certain could be heard all the way to the citadel.

"If nothing else, Piau, you provide me with amusing conversation."

"Perhaps this is the role Mangeant wished me to play, jester to the mighty Beausoleil!"

Again the man in chains convulsed with laughter.

"Oh, monsieur, I think I am going to enjoy bunking with you in this tiny hole of a place."

The anchor could be heard lifting against the bow of the ship and we heard the sails flapping as we set sail for parts unknown. I lay still on my bunk, tired from my long journey and even more exhausted from the spirited exchange with Beausoleil. I felt, however, he was correct in saying we would enjoy one another's company during the voyage, for the man was not without charm.

At mealtime I was commissioned to deliver Beausoleil's meals to him, for he was not permitted to fraternize with the other prisoners aboard the ship. I would remove the ropes around his wrists so that I did not have to hand-feed him. After he had finished his meal I would reverse the ritual by retying the ropes. After several days, I began to realize that I was becoming his caregiver.

It was not what I had imagined I would be doing on this ship, but it gave me a purpose and helped me overcome the severe pain I was experiencing in my heart. At times late at night I turned to the wall and wept uncontrollably. Most of these times my bunkmate was fast asleep. However, one night I could sense he was still awake, and although I attempted to control my grief and weeping, he responded to my flood of emotion.

"When one is living in close quarters with another, one senses the happiness and grief the other is feeling. Your sadness is plain to me, Piau. I suspect it is the loss of your family that pains you so."

There are times when one wishes to wallow in one's own grief without sharing the experience with anyone else. I remained silent.

Beausoleil respected my privacy and left me to my solitude.

On those days when we were permitted to go above deck for fresh air, the two of us stood at the side of the upper deck, alone except for the British crew who manned the ship.

"Piau, you know I have a large family, eleven offspring in all, but unlike you I have been on so many resistance campaigns over twenty years that I have hardly spent any time with my wife, Agnes, and the children. My sons and daughters are all scattered to the winds, and my wife passed long ago. So, you see, I only measure my happiness by how much freedom I possess. My suffering returns when I realize that I may spend the remainder of my life in bondage."

"Then you would describe your life as a military one. That is not an easy existence, but certainly it has its excitement and daring. In the past seven years I have experienced a different sort of excitement, eluding the British whenever possible and living the life of a nomad. Perhaps we are both nomads but travelling on different paths. You enjoyed the camaraderie of your troops and I the warmth of my family and friends."

"Does your faith in God sustain your hope of a future spent in the bosom of your family or do you foresee only a life of emptiness like me?"

"I have been thankful for the gifts I have been given in life and I accept the challenges that have been placed as obstacles before me with the hope that with perseverance they will each be overcome."

"So, it is your belief that you will be guided back to Acadia?"

"I am absolutely certain of it. I have not made this extraordinary journey leading my people to end it here and now. We have not yet reached the Promised Land."

"It is as they have described you; you actually fashion yourself as the new Moses. I wish I shared your faith in the Almighty. I once believed in divine destiny; otherwise, why would I have waged the war against the British for as long as I did? But one loses track of one's place on the eternal path of righteousness. Once you have been fighting for years at a time, I believe you lose sight of the purpose of your original crusade. Even Father Le Loutre began to waver in his faith and became more caught up in the power he was accumulating leading the Native people than waging God's war against the infidels."

Time passes slowly for those who are imprisoned. The days were not discernible to us below deck and we felt no compulsion to count them. Our vessel sailed into Boston Harbour after several days at sea. It lay anchor in the harbour, and by midday Beausoleil and I were above deck for our daily fresh air. On first witnessing the city of Boston, we thought we had arrived at some mysterious place. It made us realize that we had spent our entire lives in the wilderness. Even Halifax appeared small compared to this massive sea of buildings.

"I have often heard of Boston," I spoke, viewing what I thought a miraculous sight. "My great-grandparents spent their final years here and I had several cousins living in the city, but I had never imagined that this was where they lived. A life in this place would simply dwarf any existence we have had in Acadia."

"I once travelled to Quebec and spent a brief time there," Beausoleil added. "It, too, pales in comparison to Boston. I wonder what those streets hold for us. I imagine it will be some form of servitude, do you not agree, Piau?"

I pondered his question as we gazed at the city. Eventually, we were led away from the deck and back to our cabin. Typically, apart from delivering orders, the sailors who moved us made no attempt to speak to us. The officers and crew of our ship remained faceless to us. We knew no names and they did not relate to us as human beings, never addressing us by name. We were merely pieces of a human cargo to be unloaded and transferred to an undisclosed place. The officers came and went, some remaining on board, others going ashore for undetermined periods of time.

Weeks passed in the harbour without any change in our status. It was strange to be in this kind of limbo.

"Do you not find it odd, Piau, that we have been left here to rot, with absolutely no change in our situation? If they went to the effort to transport all of us to this place, you would conclude that the British officers would wish to dispense with their cargo. What good are we to anyone sitting here, week after week?"

"I have ceased wondering what our captors are thinking. I am more affected by the number of insufferably sweltering hours we endure below deck on these hot summer days. Never in my life have I felt such unbearable heat."

"Perhaps this is what hell feels like." Beausoleil began to chortle as was his custom. His persistent tendency to expel a nervous laugh began to wear on me and became as insufferable as the unbearably hot days. I began to seek my own solitude by turning my back on him.

To relieve the boredom of the resulting silence, he would fire questions at me to stimulate some form of communication between us. More often than not, I ignored them. One day, however, he asked a question that I was compelled to answer. It became a confession of guilt, and my willingness to answer him was perhaps a way of absolving myself of it.

"I suppose, Piau, you have never killed a man? I have shot many."

"I have shot a man, but only one. I took his life so that I and my kin could survive. When we captured my brother's schooner from the British at Beauséjour, it was either capitulate to the enemy or destroy them. There was only one choice for us.

"I shot the captain at close range, claiming justice for the death of my father. The thing that disturbed me most about that moment was that I felt nothing when I pulled the trigger, except a momentary twinge of vengefulness. The justification was we were at war and it was a matter of kill or be killed. We knew the British were hunting Acadians through the woods like animals and shooting them on sight.

"Are you surprised, Joseph?"

"I am more impressed than surprised. That was heroic, a great act of courage. Shooting a man, eye to eye, at short range, requires far more fortitude than firing indiscriminately on a field of battle. Did the captain die honourably?"

Of course this question recreated in my mind the image of the captain shamelessly pleading for his life, but I decided not to judge the dead.

"Yes, he did," I lied, in order to preserve the dignity of my victim, who had given up his life so I could live.

Despite the extreme heat, our food improved in the port of Boston. After a month passed — at least it appeared to be a month — we began to speculate as to why we were left to bake below the deck of our ship. When we were above deck, the same number of ships sat huddled in the harbour, stationary and stagnant. Beausoleil was the first to venture a guess as to why the "Acadian Flotilla," as he called it, remained in port with its human cargo intact.

"Wouldn't it be a joke of the gods if the people of Boston refused to have us and we were forced to return to Halifax?"

Was Beausoleil clairvoyant or was what he said the truth?

Whichever, the following day we heard a great commotion up on deck and heard the sound of the anchor being pulled up. Were the British organizing to move? When we went on deck, we noticed that all the ships were raising their sails and preparing for a journey at sea.

What could this mean? I could only imagine that we were being transported away from Boston to another destination. Having been told nothing by the crew, we heard no announcements either from the officers.

Our ship was finally out at sea again. For the first time since we left Halifax, we encountered severe gales on the open sea. Enduring storms on the ocean was a new sensation for me and I suffered from a stomach illness that I knew only from Bernard's descriptions. Beausoleil looked green as the ship rolled from side to side. For the benefit of the ailing prisoners, the captain allowed us more frequent visits to the deck. Considering that most of the Acadians on board were seasick, they posed little threat to the British officers and crew. I must say it was a relief to breathe the cool air, even on a tumultuous and windy sea.

There were times I was certain the ship would capsize and all those aboard would be swallowed up by the sea, just as Jonah had been by the great leviathan. Under these severe conditions, even Beausoleil began to pray for deliverance from this terrible tempest.

I saw this as yet another obstacle sent by God to test my faith. The sickness I was experiencing was far more concerning than the raging storm. This trial in my life seemed greater than any before because I was lacking the soothing balm my family had always provided me.

"Wherever this ship is bound for, Piau, it will be a relief to arrive, supposing even it is on the far side of the world."

"I always considered myself as someone with firm sea legs, but I find under these circumstances, they feel like they will never lift me up again!"

"Do you believe God has forsaken us?"

"Absolutely not! He sends these trials to strengthen our resolve to survive and prosper in His name."

"Piau, you are relentless!"

Our ship did survive the storm without throwing us savagely against the rocks along the seacoast. When the calm returned, we were surprised to be called to the upper deck as a complete assembly of prisoners. How happy this made me, for I was permitted for the first time to visit with my sons-in-law and my nephew Pierre. We rejoiced at seeing one another again. It had been over a month since we had been in one another's company, and witnessing family in the flesh made my spirit soar. The captain spoke when all were present on deck.

"Messieurs, it is my duty to inform you that circumstances have arisen, circumstances that I am not at liberty to share with you, but as a result we are forced back to Halifax, after which you will be escorted back to your families wherever they may be imprisoned. This is by order of the governor of Massachusetts."

A spontaneous roar rose from the Acadians on board. God had delivered us from exile and we were to be reunited with our families. What joy we felt!

PART 4:

THE TREATY
OF PARIS

Chapter 42

The winter of 1763 was long and cold, and we suffered more than usual from the inclement weather. However, good news came with the dispatches from Halifax in early March and warmed the atmosphere in our camp. The war between Britain and France was over and a treaty had been signed in Paris on February 7. The news arrived a month late, but the delay did not matter. Everything was about to change as a result of the peace agreement. France had relinquished all her colonies in North America, and now French-speaking peoples throughout the empire who were willing to take the oath of allegiance became subjects of His Majesty King George III. Acadians no longer needed to fear deportation. Freedom to leave the prison camps was close at hand.

"Well, Piau, this is excellent news for Acadians, is it not?" Mangeant asked.

"It certainly gives us much to ponder. What to do and where to go are not easy questions to answer. We have been either wandering or in bondage for the past eight years, so the prospect of living freely as British subjects is almost incomprehensible."

"Believe it or not, I am relieved at this outcome. Do not forget that I too have Acadian blood running through my veins. My mother grew up in Beaubassin."

"Yes, but you have never lived as an Acadian."

I still wasn't willing to include him in our suffering or our journey. Young Mangeant realized at that moment that I was not about to be patronized.

"And what is to become of Beausoleil, Captain? Does he have the same right to live peacefully in this colony?"

"He is a special case, to be sure. His treasonous past is far more damning than your peaceful resistance in wartime. He has not been executed to date, so I believe it is likely he will be forced into exile. I have orders already to have him transferred to Georges Island in Halifax where he will await further orders. It is more than likely he and his co-conspirators will be given the opportunity to face exile outside British dominions."

The news spread through the prison camp like a fierce wildfire. You would think this news would provoke rejoicing among my people, but instead it was bewilderment that plagued our entire group. Our homes on the Annapolis River had been destroyed and our lands were being given to others without payment to us for our loss. No reimbursement was likely; in fact, it was impossible. Where could we go and how could we live without land to cultivate? A quick decision could not be made, so we did not make one. Many of the prisoners refused to work for the New England planters any longer. They felt like slaves, and for them the wilderness with no prospects was better than being forced to work the land that had once been theirs.

At an assembly of friends and family I warned against a hasty move. "Over the past eight years we have been wise in our moves; each one has been well planned and considered. I suggest that we remain here until an opportunity presents itself. Who knows, it might be close at hand."

Most of my group respected my judgment and complied with my suggestion to stay until further opportunities presented themselves.

In April of that year, our deliverance came. It came in the form of Major Frederick DesBarres.

His unexpected visit threw the entire garrison into a tizzy. Such an illustrious military commander had never visited the fort, not even in its most glorious days.

On his arrival, he put everyone at their ease.

I was very excited that he had come to visit. I felt comfortable enough to parade my large family to meet him. They stood as formally as any line of soldiers ready for inspection. The great one approached us with Captain Mangeant following behind. It was evident Mangeant was not privy to our friendship.

DesBarres spoke in French for the benefit of those present.

"Piau, Piau. What a pleasure to see you! I have missed you, indeed I have."

He shook my hand warmly, having removed his right glove. "I am pleased you have not decided to flee from me before I delivered my proposition.

Greetings to you, Master Jospiau. You are becoming a handsome young man, for sure. And this must be your lovely wife. Madame, it is an honour to meet you." He bowed politely, removing his hat. "She is lovelier than you described, and all your daughters are as beautiful as their mother. What an exquisite family you have, Piau."

The meeting was overwhelming for my family and friends, especially being treated so respectfully in their native tongue. Their smiles could have lit up the world. This esteemed gentleman was someone they were prepared to adore, even though he was an English officer.

"Since you left us at the citadel, I have circumnavigated the island of Newfoundland and have spent the winter drafting the maps from that expedition. I will have to share them with you after I have gotten settled here."

"I look forward to it, Major."

Mangeant looked on in shock and wonderment. He wondered how this Acadian, who had been away from Fort Edward for only eight months, had gained the confidence and friendship of the great DesBarres, the hero of Louisbourg and Quebec.

DesBarres bowed to the Acadians, and then turned and marched toward the officers' quarters. His stay at Fort Edward was to prove an interesting one, and the lifeline he was throwing my way had the touch of divine providence associated with it. God had placed DesBarres in my path and now I would reap the rewards of the friendship I had cultivated in Halifax.

"Papa, Major DesBarres remembered my name."

"That is because you made a very favourable impression on him. Do you not agree, Jeanne?"

"I do, to be sure. You are truly favoured, my son. I have a feeling that this great man will bring us good fortune."

DesBarres sent for me not long after his arrival. He had a plan, a grand plan, to share with me.

"Piau, my expeditions mapping the coastline of Nova Scotia have truly inspired me. The land is rich and nearly uninhabited now that most of your people have been sent into exile. I have applied for land grants at Tatamagouche, Menoudie, Memramcook, Cape Breton, and here, the lands surrounding Fort

Edward. My vision is to restore the lands and dikes of Nova Scotia and settle them, not with New Englanders, but with Acadians, for it is my belief that many of your people will choose to return to their homeland now the war is over. My plan is to turn them into tenant farmers with a future prospect of owning the lands over time. What do you think of my grand scheme?"

No answer or response was forthcoming because I was overwhelmed by the prospect of farming the land again and what it would mean for my people. DesBarres did not wait for me to speak.

"However, for the short term I have decided to build an estate here in this area so I can spend my winters working on the mapping project commissioned by the Board of Trade in London. This is the only place in the province that has a direct, usable road to the capital. My land grant here is a *fait accompli*, so it is just a matter of drawing up the plans and beginning the development of what I will call 'Castle Frederick.' I want you to build it. Have no fear, my castle will be modest compared to those in England, but I rather fancy living in a castle.

"Ostentatious? Yes, I admit it, but one who seeks greatness must not only achieve it but promote it as well. And it will be you who will help me realize my great dream, Piau. Serve me well and I promise wonderful things will come to you, your kinfolk, and those who have followed you these past eight years. What do you say? I won't require you to make an immediate decision. Think it over, discuss this with your family and friends, and we will talk again. Good day, *mon ami*."

Smiling at DesBarres, I wished him a good day and I walked out of his quarters. That was the first time the great one had ever called me "friend." It had always been understood but never uttered. It augured well for the future.

Freedom is a feeling. It is a gift. It is a right. Acadians were suddenly, by an accident of time and circumstance, permitted to cherish that feeling, rejoice at such a gift, and be thankful that that right had been restored to them. The immense flood of emotions that followed only filled me with confusion. I was free to go if I pleased, but where? DesBarres was providing me with a solution. Work to build Castle Frederick and rewards would follow. How could I reject such an opportunity? From our first meeting, was I not certain that divine destiny had thrown us together? My people were free to leave or stay. Which would they choose? For once, I was not certain of the outcome. For the first time, I lacked the faith that they would follow me.

First I spoke to Jeanne. I explained to her in detail what DesBarres had proposed and what accepting that proposal would mean for our family. She was quick to respond.

"Piau, we have been nomads for so many years I have lost count — wandering endlessly in the desert, as you have always told us. Our journey has been long and difficult and yet we have managed to stay alive. I thought I had lost you forever when you were so cruelly taken from us and sent off to Boston. When you were lost to us, I thought I could not bear it. Only the children helped me survive the long days. Your return filled me with a greater joy than I have ever felt. We are now safely together, we have our freedom, and we have new prospects in our lives. I accept any decision you choose to make because I love you, I trust your judgment, and I am certain God is guiding you."

My eyes filled with tears as I embraced her.

"How blessed I have been to have you as my wife. With you at my side, I am able to endure anything. Let us gather all the Acadians together and we will trust in God that they will make the right decision, for it is finally theirs to make."

"What you are suggesting, Piau?"

The Acadian elder continued his questioning. "Are you suggesting that we go along with this plan to create a seigneury on the French model and build the Manor House for this Major DesBarres? And that we farm the lands of the estate as his tenants? And for this, there is a possibility that in time we will own our lands, as we did before the war?"

"That is what DesBarres has promised me, yes."

The elder continued to question me.

"Why has the great DesBarres chosen us rather than having the land settled and farmed by New Englanders?"

"I will not deceive you, monsieur. DesBarres is motivated by the fact that he owns great tracts of land throughout the colony and that he has plans to purchase as many more as possible. He requires manpower to farm them. The English-speaking Protestants refuse to settle land if they do not own it. Look at the New England planters here, for example. But we all know that the seigneurial system has functioned extremely well in New France for over a century. Governor Champlain himself established it, and the relationship between seigneur and tenant is advantageous to both."

"That may be so, but our ancestors arrived in Acadia owning their land from the start. The seigneury at Belle Isle failed to last more than fifty years. It has not been our tradition in the New World to be subservient to an overlord."

"What you say has some credence, monsieur, but can we not think of this new arrangement as a transition on the road to farming our own lands? We will have work and we will reap the benefits of our labour. Is that not enough?"

"This may be acceptable to some but not to others. For many of us, the only choice is to leave this place where we have been imprisoned these past three years. Living in the Miramichi puts a distance between us and the British. We will not live among the English again."

"So be it. I will honour any decision you make and may God grant you safety and prosperity. However, those who have followed me on the journey that God has chosen for us these past years have an unwavering belief that to stay here and see what materializes is the prudent choice at this time."

The debate quickly established who was remaining and who was going. Those who had travelled with me since French Cross unanimously resolved to remain with me and accept DesBarres's offer. Few joined us from the other groups. We respected that they were prepared to accept the vagaries of further wanderings.

Samuel Mangeant departed Fort Edward before our move to the DesBarres lands a few miles away. He was finally returning to his family in Boston. Perhaps his place in my life was preordained; he was not a casual contributor to its narrative. I was certain Cousin Elizabeth, wherever she resided in New England, would have approved of how things had turned out in the end and would have surely realized that much of what Samuel Mangeant had done for us was due to his long-standing and abiding love for her. I owed a huge debt of gratitude to both Elizabeth LeBlanc and Captain Samuel Mangeant — the sort of star-crossed lovers one only reads about in romances.

DesBarres's land was situated about eight miles from Fort Edward and consisted of five hundred acres of forest. Very soon after our acceptance of his offer to stay, horses and oxen arrived at the fort from Halifax to facilitate the clearing of the trees in order for a road to be built to the site. Besides the Acadians, DesBarres brought German settlers from Lunenburg to help assist in felling the trees. We marvelled at the tools being used to prepare the land for construction. A hundred men toiled diligently to clear the brush and trees from the land, and the Acadian women kept the food production at a maximum.

Granite stones were transported from the coastlines around Halifax. Limestone and sandstone from the coast of the Bay of Fundy arrived by boat at Fort Edward, where it was unloaded and conveyed to the building site miles away. A massive system of pulleys was provided by DesBarres, who borrowed these from the citadel. I had been involved in building construction all my life, but I had never witnessed a project on this grand a scale.

DesBarres kept his residence at the fort, and we maintained our temporary homes there as well. It was not long, however, given the numbers in the workforce, that we reached the heart of the major's acreage. Each day the whole company of workers journeyed along the new road to clear the forest so we could begin to erect Castle Frederick. By early July, the stone foundation was begun.

Frederick DesBarres visited his emerging estate every day until July, after which he returned to Halifax to set sail on his annual mapping expedition. He left me in charge of the building operations. It was splendid to watch the mighty LeBlanc boys place the massive timbers that would constitute the upper storeys and roof. Once the frame was completed, we set about layering and sealing the stone walls. DesBarres had drawn detailed plans for me and my team of masons. The spirit of Great-Uncle Pierre stood watching over my shoulder, whispering in my ear when something was not quite precise enough.

While I worked, childhood memories of the construction of St. Charles Church at Grand Pré came to mind. As we laboured, the Acadians sang ancient French folk songs. They filled us with a happiness we had not felt for a very long time.

> *V'la l'bon vent, v'la l'joli vent*
> *V'la l'bon vent, m'amie m'appelle.*
> *V'la l'bon vent, v'la l'joli vent*
> *V'la l'bon vent, m'amie m'attend.*

Sixteen-year-old Jospiau worked by my side and practised his stone-mason skills under my direct tutelage. The conversations we had enabled me to discover the man he was becoming. I chose to share my experiences aboard the New England–bound ship and my impressions of the great city of Boston. He was captivated by the stories I related about the great Beausoleil, whom he had only seen from a distance. Beausoleil's exploits as a freedom fighter fired his imagination. Although he was a cheerful boy, I had to wonder how his years in exile had truly affected him, for he had spent half his life as a refugee. I dreamed that someday this young man would own his own land and live in peace and harmony with his fellow man.

The most profound effect on all the young Acadians living in exile was the lapses it created in their education. They had all been taught to read and write in French when they were very young, but because in recent years it was a matter of just surviving one day at a time, they had few opportunities to read and write in their own language. The best they could do in the Miramichi was write sentences in the sand. I carried in my satchel only two books, Pierre and Priscilla's King James Bible and Benjamin's *Fables of La Fontaine*. The one was in English, so it was usually up to me to translate the stories found there; the other was in French, and each of my children had read its tales time and time again until they could recite them from memory.

When DesBarres returned to take up residence in his new but still uncompleted Manor House, I voiced my concern that my children and their children might descend into illiteracy. He was sympathetic and understood what I was saying.

"Piau, your concerns are not unfounded. Those who have an education in this life have good fortune follow them.

"When I studied mathematics and science at the University of Basel, and, by the way, my education was in French, a whole new world opened up for me. When I finally moved to England, that degree opened doors for me and finally the Duke of Cumberland recognized my intelligence and apti-tudes and supported me in my military education. I am what I am because he was my benefactor.

"The best I can do for you is, when my book collection begins to build here, you and your family can have access to those books that are within their grasp to read. I will make certain that there are volumes in both languages, with special emphasis on the easier pieces of literature. If you can wait until next spring, I should have the latest published books from England and France."

"I am particularly partial to *Robinson Crusoe*. Would you be able to get your hands on a copy?"

"Really? And how are you familiar with this book by Daniel Defoe?"

"Sir, it was the first book I read in English when I was a child."

"How did you acquire a copy of the book?"

"It was from a surprising source, Major. It was loaned to me by the governor of Nova Scotia!"

"Oh, Piau, you truly are one in a million!" He began to laugh with appreciation.

Throughout the following winter, Jospiau and I passed many hours working on the Great Room of the castle, completing the joining and other smaller constructions. Invariably we were interrupted by DesBarres, who invited us into his unfinished library. The bookshelves were still relatively empty, but the great one discussed with us the volumes with which he intended to fill the shelves in the upcoming years.

The maps of the colony, which he called the fruits of his labour, were scattered indiscriminately all over the room, on tables, on the floor, even hanging from the walls. His drafting was a lonely occupation, so he often shared the maps with us, describing the coastlines and the problems he experienced circumnavigating the colony in order to complete his enormous project. Jospiau was fascinated by the maps of Nova Scotia, never having seen one, let alone witnessed the creation process. Interesting stories were told and DesBarres appeared to enjoy entertaining us with the tales of his many expeditions. In later years, he housed a coterie of draftsmen to facilitate the completion of his mapping project.

During the winter of 1764, he was assisted by a young naval officer, James Cook, who had captained his ship while mapping the British colony of Newfoundland. Cook was cordial to us, but because he spoke only English he was often left out of our conversations, for DesBarres preferred to speak to us in French, his mother tongue.

By the late spring of 1764, the two were gone from Castle Frederick to parts unknown, not expected back until the autumn. For us, this presented the opportunity to complete the fine work outlined in the architectural plans of DesBarres. Although we continued to live near the fort at Pisiquit, we Acadians working on the estate built wigwams on the site so we were not forced to walk the distance to the Manor House every day. The Germans from Lunenburg initially kept to themselves, but because many of them had come from lands in Germany close to the border of France, they spoke French as well as German. I observed that these Europeans were outstanding and skilled workers. By the time DesBarres returned in the fall of 1764, his dream house had been, for the most part, completed.

In addition to the five hundred acres he had originally owned at Castle Frederick, DesBarres had increased his acreage by the thousands, thus opening up his estate to tenant farming. The construction of our farmhouses began in earnest in early autumn, and we were able to complete them before the first snowfall. This was achieved through a co-operative effort, an Acadian tradition that expedited the building process considerably.

My people became the tenants on the DesBarres estate, but our time there was to be short.

Chapter 43

Frederick DesBarres's homecoming in the autumn of 1764 did not include Captain James Cook. He arrived back at Castle Frederick with a comely young woman. Her name was Mary Cannon. On their arrival, Jospiau and I were summoned to the Manor House, where we caught our first glimpse of the lovely Mistress Cannon. Our first impression was that she was extremely young. We later discovered that DesBarres was thirty years her senior. What role she was to play in the life of the castle was soon to be revealed to us.

"Piau, I wish to introduce my housekeeper, Mary Cannon. She will be responsible for running the everyday workings of the household. This establishment requires a womanly touch to create the atmosphere of gentility that best befits my station in the colony. She will be responsible, with my assistance, for decorating the castle. We have transported furniture from England, some artworks that I collected before arriving in the colonies in 1756, and all the cookery and china necessary to entertain large numbers of guests."

"It is our pleasure to make your acquaintance, Mistress Mary," I declared, as Jospiau and I bowed politely to the young lady standing ceremoniously before us.

The girl gave us a quizzical look when she was introduced to us in the Great Room of the manor. I sensed she was struck by the unlikelihood of an Acadian dressed as I was, speaking the King's English like a country gentleman. She was neither charmed nor did she utter a single word of greeting. However, the charms of my handsome seventeen-year-old son were not lost on her.

Her figure was comely beyond her years, and her features were even but unremarkable. However, there was a spark in her eyes that more than compensated for the plainness of her face. Her hair was a bright strawberry-blond colour, which added to the fire burning deep within her emerald green eyes.

Throughout the introduction, I became aware that the young lady kept a constant gaze on Jospiau. To ease the discomfort my son was feeling, standing there equally unable to keep his eyes off the young lady, I introduced him to her.

"And this is my son, Jospiau, baptized Joseph Belliveau."

"Charmed, mademoiselle."

Mistress Cannon gave my son an interested look, which could have been construed as flirtatious. To confuse her attitude toward Jospiau at that first meeting as an example of girlish coyness was to underestimate Mary Cannon's extraordinary power as a woman. She may have been only fifteen, but there was no denying she was in every sense of the word an experienced woman of the world. It would not be long before we all became aware of her full capacity as an ambitious femme fatale.

DesBarres interjected with enthusiasm.

"Piau, as promised, I have acquired two books for you, one you requested, *Robinson Crusoe*, and one newly published this year, *The Castle of Otranto*. How appropriate is that, *The Castle of Otranto* by my close friend Horace Walpole, the son of the deceased former prime minister of Great Britain, Sir Robert Walpole, first earl of Orford. I have read the latter just recently, and the story will scare the britches off you."

I could barely contain my excitement at this news, not having read any book but the Bible since Benjamin's death.

"Major, I am so filled with gratitude. Thank you so much for remembering my request."

"It pleases me to do this favour for you, Piau. You are a true lover of literature and learning, and that is rare in this colony."

Jospiau produced a broad smile, feeling the excitement the gift had created in the room.

Mistress Cannon looked on with astonishment.

During the winter months, our life at Castle Frederick became intertwined
with DesBarres's. Jospiau and I continued to apply our woodworking skills
in the various rooms of the house, and Jeanne was brought in to assist and
instruct Mistress Cannon on the fine points of preparing food. Jeanne was
circumspect with her young student. My wife was straightforward and
without artifice; Mary was the exact opposite. This created a quiet mistrust
in both women. To make matters worse, every time Mary entered a room
occupied by Jospiau and myself, the atmosphere changed. Jospiau became
animated in Mary Cannon's presence. No words were exchanged between
them, but it was apparent that there was a quiet attraction between the
two, which only exists in the young.

Of course, DesBarres was oblivious to such things. His obsession during
the snowy months of winter was to draft the maps he had charted the summer before. There were several military assistants living at the castle by this
time, and they were engaged in the work that DesBarres was spearheading.
He treated Mistress Mary like a highly prized possession, showering her
with compliments and pretty gifts whenever possible. When he was compelled to journey to Halifax to meet with the governor, he always returned
with dresses and jewellery for his pretty mistress. Jeanne remarked that he
treated her like a doll, dressing her up to please himself more than Mary. The
Acadian women working at the Manor House disapproved of DesBarres's
mistress, most questioning the purpose of her presence at Castle Frederick.

"I do not think it is appropriate for a young lady to be living in the
home of a gentleman without a chaperone, even if she has the title of
housekeeper," commented Jeanne one evening while we lay in our bed.
"Usually one is hired to such a position when one has the required skills to
do the job. She arrived here with none of these skills! And I do not approve
of the way Jospiau and Mistress Mary look at one another. The attraction
between them is so obvious."

"On the first point, my love, it is not for us to judge DesBarres, for he
is a gentleman who knows what he is about, and on the latter point, you
are correct in your observation, but with any luck, it will remain a mutual
unconsummated admiration. It is wise that we keep our eyes peeled at all
times to prevent our son from becoming embroiled in a relationship that
could compromise our position at the castle."

"Perhaps you should speak to your son."

"Best not present him with the idea of forbidden fruit, my love, before it has been offered. Besides, I cannot discuss a matter with Jospiau that does not yet exist."

Not long after she arrived, Mary Cannon had been given her own set of rooms at the castle, where she spent her private moments undisturbed. Her tiny salon was comfortably decorated with upholstered chairs covered in needle-work done by Mary herself. She did have a talent for needlecraft, and her work began appearing throughout the castle. DesBarres was pleased to no end with her elaborate embroideries. What he did not know about his little flower, how-ever, was that she could neither read nor write. How this escaped him, I will never know. She obviously possessed other virtues that interested him more.

And so, winter flowed into summer, and summer into winter. We went about our lives and our duties much as we did before the deportation. There were many lost to us in time, but my grown children began to live lives that were productive and happy. New life appeared as families celebrated the births of babies. We Acadians began to celebrate our festivals again, and everyone, including the non-French inhabitants, joined in to give thanks to the Almighty for our bounty and our peaceful and harmonious exist-ence. Mary Cannon occasionally joined us, and it was not beyond anyone's notice that she invariably sat and chatted with Jospiau. But still all appeared innocent enough. After all, DesBarres was only in residence during the late autumn and winter. Who could blame her for wanting the company of someone young during the summer months? He was one of the few Acadians there who could converse in English, and she spoke no French.

One day, in the late summer of 1766, my daughter Theotiste was pass-ing by the castle on her way to the summer kitchen when she noticed her brother leaving the house through the back entrance. That caused no curios-ity in my daughter until Mistress Cannon appeared at the exit and followed Jospiau into the woodland behind the the castle. What we all feared seemed to be unfolding, or, as Theotiste suggested, it could have been happening for some time. This was the first time anyone had noticed them, but who knows how long the subterfuge had been going on.

No accusations were forthcoming, on my recommendation, for my son was now an adult and Cannon was, after all, officially a maiden nearing adult-hood. Caution in this matter had to be the path we chose but observing the path was absolutely mandatory. On rainy days, Jospiau would go missing for long periods of time and eventually, after constant surveillance by my daughters, he was spotted exiting Mistress Cannon's private quarters at the castle.

Major DesBarres arrived home in time to celebrate the harvest with us. He was accompanied by his usual military assistants, but to our surprise there were several others accompanying him, persons who possessed the darkest skin we had ever seen. We were informed that these were slaves the major had acquired on a sailing trip to the Carolinas during the summer. These poor souls were the sole property of DesBarres; we were told that they had originally come from a continent called Africa. We Acadians looked on in horror, realizing that we had barely escaped such a fate as these poor souls. They were forced to sleep in the barn until other quarters were constructed for them. Witnessing these poor men and women shed a different light on the question of whether Jospiau was romancing Mistress Mary or not. At least my son and Mary were free to seek one another's company. But that freedom also came with responsibility. For what would DesBarres think should he find out about their liaison?

With DesBarres on site, I breathed a sigh of relief, knowing that neither Mary Cannon nor my son would risk being caught in a clandestine affair while the master of the estate was in residence. Jeanne and I decided to postpone any confrontation with Jospiau until the following summer. Perhaps by then the ardour would have cooled somewhat, we reasoned.

Not only did it not cool, but throughout the winter Jospiau visited Mistress Cannon in her private quarters on a regular basis. There seemed to be no attention given to the regularity of their meetings. Then, on an evening the following spring, at a time when the tiny apple trees were in full blossom, Jeanne and I were summoned to the castle by DesBarres, who said that we were to be accompanied by our son, Jospiau. We were certain the time of reckoning had arrived.

Jeanne and I uttered a silent prayer and we informed our son that he was to escort his parents to the Manor House. He was unperturbed by the unexpected summons and appeared to be pleased at the honour of spending an evening with the great one and his guests. The closer we got to the castle, the more I began to sweat and imagine the worst.

I had spent the past two winters translating into French *The Castle of Otranto* for the family to enjoy. It was a chilling story of a prince, Manfred, who had chosen a woman named Isabella for his son to marry. In the story, his son dies suddenly before he is able to marry Isabella. Manfred, much

older than Isabella, desires to marry the girl himself, divorces his wife, and
Isabella is forced to escape from the old prince to seek protection at a monastery. A young man named Theodore chances on the monastery and decides
to be Isabella's protector. Ultimately, however, he falls in love with her. The
denouement of the story has Manfred deposed by Theodore, who is then
discovered to be the rightful king. This was known as a Gothic novel. It was
a spine-chilling story: the family could not wait for each episode.

My imagination started to run wild on the road to the castle. In my
mind DesBarres was Manfred, Mary Cannon was Isabella, and Jospiau was
Theodore. I was praying that the life of my family was not going to be transformed into a Gothic tale.

We were invited into the Great Room of the castle, where DesBarres
greeted us warmly.

"Welcome, Piau and Madame Belliveau. Come sit by the fire. What I
wish to discuss concerns your son."

My heart began to pound so loudly I was certain everyone in the room
could hear its every beat. Still, Jospiau remained calm. Mistress Mary sat
sedately on one of her embroidered chairs with a book in her lap. The cover
looked familiar.

"Everyone, may I have your attention, please? I wish to share a story that
I believe you will find immensely inspiring. The characters in this story are
none other than Mistress Mary and Joseph Belliveau."

I had never heard DesBarres call my son by his formal appellation. What
could this mean? I looked at Jeanne and she had lost all colour in her face.
DesBarres still showed no sign of anger and no evidence that he was about to
expose the two people in this room who had been engaging in a secret dalli-
ance these past two or more years. Perhaps his fury was still to manifest itself.

"Before I relate my story, Mistress Mary is going to entertain us by reading a passage from one of Piau's favourite novels!"

"I wish to begin with chapter one of Daniel Defoe's *Robinson Crusoe*."

What was happening here? I asked myself. I was certain that Mary
Cannon was illiterate. How could I have been so wrong? I had witnessed her
often unable to read the letters sent to her by DesBarres, and on many occasions she had asked me to read them to her. Perhaps she had memorized the
passage. However, she continued to read uninterrupted for the next hour.
No one could recite that long a passage from memory:

So we work'd at the oar towards the land, tho' with heavy
hearts, like men going to execution; for we all knew, that when
the boat came nearer the shore, she would be dash'd in a thou-
sand pieces by the breach of the sea.

With that last word, Mary raised her face to her audience and closed the book, giving all present a brilliant smile, filled with contentment and triumph.

Suddenly, DesBarres began to clap loudly. The others present in the room followed suit.

"Brava, Mistress Mary, brava! You have read to us beautifully and with such expression."

Mary responded to the ovation with a polite nod of the head.

"Thank you so much for your high praise, Major. But I must give credit where credit is due. I am able to read to you tonight because I have had a brilliant teacher these past two years. And that gentleman is none other than Joseph Belliveau."

Mary began to clap in Jospiau's direction. He simply gave her a beautiful smile and bowed. He remained silent.

"What Mary has said is true," DesBarres continued. "When she arrived here at Castle Frederick three years ago, she came as my housekeeper. She possessed many skills, but reading and writing were not among them." Desbarres let loose a barrel of a laugh. "At that time I approached the young man here, knowing he had been well schooled in English by his father, Monsieur Pierre Belliveau, and secretly requested he take on the tutelage of Mistress Mary. They have been diligently engaged in this enterprise for almost three years. I recognized her acute intelligence when I first spoke to her in Halifax, and my belief that she could be a competent writer and reader of the King's English has been realized. Brava, Mary, and my most sincere thanks to you, Jospiau. You both have achieved a great accomplishment."

The applause resumed for another minute, and we all were poured a glass of wine to celebrate. Once we all had our glasses in hand, DesBarres spoke solemnly.

"It just so happens that I have additional good news to share."

Again Mistress Mary began to smile broadly.

"I am happy to announce Mary here is with child and we are both overjoyed."

Those present lifted their glasses and toasted the couple.

"Hurrah, hurrah!"

When I looked at Jospiau to see if he had any previous knowledge of this, I was answered in the look he exhibited. His face had turned ashen. Jeanne and I knew at that moment that Jospiau was in love with Mary Cannon, but that their relationship had not been consummated. Poor Jospiau. He had not turned out to be as lucky as Theodore in *The Castle of Otranto*. Real life was not as kind as the stories with happy endings. The young woman had used my son, had most profoundly encouraged his romantic advances, and was now disposing of him like a used boot. She had achieved what she set out to accomplish. I began to dislike Mary Cannon at that very moment, and I have not changed my feelings toward her to this very day. Mistress Cannon was now the enemy, and we would lock horns many times before I finally decided to lead my people elsewhere in search of the Promised Land.

Just when one thinks life is settling into a peaceful state, people and things appear on the scene to disturb the tranquility one is enjoying. So it was with the arrival of Mary Cannon into our lives. The power of her disturbance was not felt for some time, though.

When DesBarres was in residence everything progressed as it should, with established domestic rituals both inside the castle and on the estate. We were nicely settled into our new homes, working diligently to clear the land and cultivate the soil. Livestock had been shipped in from Halifax and from other places throughout Nova Scotia and from as far away as Quebec. This livestock was equally distributed among the Acadians on the larger part of the estate, and it was our responsibility to make sure they bred and multiplied.

DesBarres introduced other settlers, some Scottish, some German, and they were responsible for the estate itself. They dwelled in residences in close proximity to Castle Frederick. There were also the slaves from Africa, who now lived in the simplest of barracks near the barn. Although DesBarres was a benevolent slave owner, they were still, in our estimation, humans who were being treated like beasts of burden. Their presence at Castle Frederick filled us with profound sadness on their behalf.

We Acadians felt privileged that we had been granted greater independence here. This was a brilliant strategy on DesBarres's part, for it encouraged a greater pride in maintaining the land and enhanced our desire to increase crop production. DesBarres was the beneficiary of our hard work, of course, but we felt pride in our work

This happy arrangement began to unravel, however. After several years of living with Mary Cannon as mistress of Castle Frederick, while the major was off on his mapping expeditions during the summer, she began not only to manage the household but also the estate and everyone on it. It was time to leave.

My family had nursed Jospiau back to health after he had been so cruelly treated by DesBarres's mistress. He was now healed and eager to embark on new adventures. When I told him of my plans to depart DesBarres's estate he readily agreed, especially glad to leave it now that Mary Cannon was inserting herself more and more into our daily lives.

We remained on at the Castle Frederick estate for another year, however, waiting until the spring of 1768 to make any momentous changes in our lives. That is when I spoke to the master of the estate with a proposal I believed he would approve of.

"Sir, you have often mentioned lands throughout Nova Scotia that you have acquired by grant and by purchase. Each of these estates requires families to cultivate the land, restore the ancient dikes, and raise livestock in order to increase your wealth. You have been especially kind to my family, a noblesse oblige, you might say. Our gratitude to you knows no bounds, but I think it is time for us to leave this place and find a new life elsewhere. Despite being free for the past five years, this area still possesses memories of our captivity that we would like to erase from our minds and hearts. Should we venture to one of your new properties, there would still be many Acadians living around Fort Edward who would gladly take over the care and productivity of the farms we have established on this estate. It should not be lost on either of us that you would have everything to gain by sending experienced farmers to these lands you own elsewhere. You have to know that, given your many kindnesses to my family and friends, you can count on us to be good and competent stewards of your lands."

DesBarres pondered for several moments then responded calmly. "Your proposal, Piau, has some merit. You know that I personally would hate to lose your company. I value it so. But change is always good to restore one's creativity. Where had you thought you might wish to settle?"

"There is a special place that holds a poignant memory for me. When we were in flight following the expulsion in 1755, we sailed into a beautiful river called the Petitcodiac, and it provided us with a great deal of safety and good fortune. Its beauty and richness have never left my mind for a minute. I believe God has ordained that we settle there and prosper."

"Indeed. It happens that I own the land in the Memramcook River Valley that is situated in the vicinity of the great river of which you speak. It possesses neglected dikes and land already cultivated by previous Acadians, and it would be a brilliant spot for raising my Holsteins. I would arrange your passage by sea and transfer as many cattle as is possible to enlarge my herds in as many of my lands as I can disperse these livestock. I will arrange your departure for late spring. You will require some time to organize your people, for, as you always say, this journey will at last take you to your beloved Promised Land."

"God bless you, sir. We shall not fail you, I promise."

DesBarres and I shook hands to seal the deal. Amen!

PART 5:

THE PROMISED LAND

Chapter 44

B y June of 1768 the vessels promised by DesBarres to transport us
away forever from Castle Frederick and Fort Edward set sail with a
huge number of Acadian families and a herd of livestock. The Avon
River was calm, and the sun shone more brightly than on any day that I could
remember. As we approached Grand Pré, on the port side of the ship, a pink-
and-white cloud of apple blossoms hovered over the landscape. The farms
once owned by our relatives and friends had long since fallen into the hands
of the New England planters who were now working diligently to cultivate a
land that had once felt the ploughs of an Acadian community. Strangely, it no
longer provoked a surge of melancholy in us, for we had our sights on another
place, one that was new to us and one where hope and happiness would reign.

Even the Bay of Fundy was unusually peaceful that day, reminding us
of the parting of the sea in the Book of Exodus. On this day, though, there
was no pharaoh's army in pursuit of us, and the excitement we were feeling
was joy and expectation.

By nightfall our ship laid anchor in Beaubassin. The captain rowed
ashore to inform the British authorities at Fort Cumberland of our arrival.
Some of the Acadian families on board were to venture on by sea, with
the captain at the helm, to DesBarres's lands at Menoudie. The rest of us
waited patiently while the major's agents, who had accompanied us on the
trip, mapped out land directions for us to follow into the Memramcook
River Valley. By morning, all the families in our group had disembarked and
were organizing their belongings and herding the cattle for our day's journey
across the Tintamarre salt marshes.

We Acadians were energized by the prospect of reaching the Memramcook River by sundown. With each step we took on our day's journey, we felt the cool breeze of freedom penetrating our bodies and filling our spirits with sublime expectation. This was a day I had longed for my entire life: no British authority watching our every move, an independence that was never afforded us because we were Acadian, and a homeland that only we were responsible for. As we walked north over the marshes, where dikes still embroidered the landscape, we purged our souls, driving out the suffering and hardships we had been forced to endure for most of our lives.

Native people met us along the way and welcomed us to the land of their fathers. We shared our food with them and requested they accompany us on our journey. They guided us across miles and miles of marshes and dike lands, only departing from us when we reached the east shore of the Memramcook River. There my people stood fixed on the spot, visualizing what their lives would be like once they had crossed the river. I could imagine how joyful Moses must have been when he first caught sight of the River Jordan. God, however, was affording me something that Moses did not experience; I would cross the Jordan to the Promised Land with my people and would be permitted to settle there until the end of my days.

On the eve of our deliverance we built huge bonfires that lit the summer sky with flames and sparks that seemed to reach the stars. We sang the ancient songs and we played music for our dancing — even the elders joined in. Looking around, I saw a sea of young faces filled with hope. It was their time to begin a new life, nurture their children, and create a bright future for their descendants. Tomorrow would be the dawning of a new day, *une belle époque*!

When the sun rose on the following day we gathered to pray by the river. I recounted the story of the children of Israel entering the land of Canaan by crossing the River Jordan. They cheered when I declared that, unlike Moses, I was being allowed by the Lord to enter the Promised Land with my family and friends. The Acadians gathered on the eastern side of the Memramcook River began to chant my name.

"Piau! Piau! Piau!"

I began to weep tears of happiness that I should be so honoured by the people I loved. Jeanne took my arm and squeezed it out of pride. The children danced around me and shouted the same.

"Piau! Piau! Piau!"

I was so overcome with emotion that for the first time in my life words failed me.

No words were required.

Once the cheering subsided, I suggested that we construct a large raft made of logs to transport the ladies at high tide rather than submit them to the mud of low tide. With many hands and new tools provided by DesBarres himself, we built a large barge with ropes on two sides to convey as many provisions and people as we could. The livestock would ford the river further up, where the river bottom was rockier. By mid-afternoon we were safely standing on the opposite bank of the river, ready to begin our new life.

And so we built our community on the west side of the river. We restored the dikes to their previous state, and we planted our crops early enough in the first season to harvest them in the autumn. We built our homes in the old-fashioned way, with wood fences and vegetable gardens alongside. The settlement we established was larger than Melanson Village and Gaudet Village combined. All the cultivation of the land and tending of livestock was done co-operatively so that all could share in the results. The benefits of our labour ensured that everyone prospered equally. They called this community Piau's Village.

Need I say more? It only remains to say that families reproduced themselves tenfold. Before long the barns were filled with cattle, oxen, and chickens, and the stables housed ever more horses. In time, this valley we lived in became famous for breeding fine horses and cattle.

We made the newly designated Colonel DesBarres proud. He never visited us at Piau's Village, but we felt his presence. Many years after DesBarres returned to England, Mistress Mary Cannon, now known infamously as Polly, travelled throughout the DesBarres domains to collect her rents and cause mayhem. Living so far from Castle Frederick, we enjoyed an independence that closer regions did not. When she finally arrived to terrorize us in the Memramcook Valley, Polly and I locked horns — and, may I say, it was not the lady who won the day. She was a determined woman, but she surely met her match in me. She never returned.

As a last communication with me, before Colonel DesBarres left in 1774 for England, where he would remain for many years, he had one of his land agents deliver me a letter. I read the letter on its arrival.

My Dear Piau,

I have missed your company these past six years since you departed Castle Frederick. You will be happy to learn that the estate has expanded to such an extent that there are now ninety-three persons administering to the advancement and maintenance of the Manor House and grounds. Mistress Mary has borne me several children since you left, and they are thriving. I have finally completed my mapping expeditions and have drafted a book of comprehensive maps of the eastern colonies of Canada. You would be astonished at their accuracy. I must return to England to present my book, *Atlantic Neptune*, to the Admiralty and the Board of Trade at Westminster. I have heard that the young king himself is interested in having a copy printed for his library. This is a very high honour.

Now to the reason for this missive. Your contribution to the building of Castle Frederick cannot be quantified, for no calculation could measure its value to me. On a more personal note, your son, Joseph, did me a great service assisting in the education of my lady. For these favours, I wish to return one in kind. On my lands along the eastern side of the Petitcodiac River, near its mouth and in the shadow of the Beaumont Hills, there is a large acreage that I wish to grant to your son and his heirs.

You will find a legal document enclosed that will certify his ownership. It is the least I can do to repay you for your friendship, unwavering loyalty, and exceptional service to my person and my interests.

May you and your family enjoy great prosperity in the coming years.

Yours most sincerely,
Frederick DesBarres, Col. His Majesty's Navy

And so it was, without divulging the contents of Colonel DesBarres's letter to anyone but Jeanne, I asked Jospiau to accompany me on a walk over the Beaumont Hills to view the great Petitcodiac at high tide. He agreed willingly, although he gave me a curious and mischievous look. Perhaps he thought I was going to discuss his upcoming marriage to Marie Josephe Gaudet, a descendent of Jeanne's Uncle Denys. And so we stood at the top of the hill and viewed the river and its mighty tidal bore rushing to its destination at Coverdale. He smiled as I described my courtship of Jeanne and our marriage. He seemed charmed.

After much discussion, I motioned him to follow me to the bottom of the hill to the place that DesBarres described in his letter. As we reached the land that was to be his, I recounted to Jospiau what the great DesBarres had bequeathed him. He was overwhelmed with emotion.

"Is this possible, Papa?"

"It is, my son. Remember, from every good deed comes another good deed. In your case, you paid dearly for your generosity. But God has delivered you a gift, and Colonel DesBarres has heard His wish."

As the tide rose higher and higher, we could see the sunbeams dancing on top of the water. It was at that magical moment that I drew a sack from my belt and presented it to my son.

"Open the sack and pour the contents into your hand."

Jospiau gave me a broad smile and did as I asked.

"What are these, Papa?"

"What do you think they are?"

"They are apple seeds, Papa. The sack is filled with them. What does this mean?"

"Many years ago, when you were only four years old, I collected these seeds from the apples growing in the orchard at Melanson Village. My ancestors planted those trees when they arrived in Acadia. I felt that if I harvested and kept these seeds I would possess a little piece of Charles Melanson; Marie Dugas; my father, Jean; my mother, Madeleine; and all those who had gone before them. By planting these seeds here on your new land, you honour your ancestors and me."

Tears appeared in our eyes and we embraced.

"I love you, Papa."

"And I you, my son."

Epilogue, 1806

Here I sit in my son's apple orchard overlooking the mighty Petitcodiac River, comfortable beneath the blossoms, in a birch chair surrounded by my descendants, who have gathered to celebrate my hundred years of life. My son is now the patriarch of Belliveau Village and I am my people's living ancestor. Soon I will join the ancient Acadians, the pantheon of those who, by the grace of God, created Acadia at great cost to themselves so we could live here in peace. The new generation does not remember the Deportation, but the elders will never allow them to forget the sacrifices of those who have gone before. I longingly look out at the Bay of Fundy, imagining a return to Melanson Village, wondering whether someone has resurrected my homeland from the ashes of time.

It is now time to close my eyes and sleep. Perhaps I will have visitors.

Appendix 1

PLACE NAMES

Acadia — Nova Scotia

Annapolis Basin — Mouth of the Annapolis River, Nova Scotia

Beaubassin — Amherst, Nova Scotia

Belliveau Village — Community on the Petitcodiac River, founded by
Joseph (known as Jospiau) Belliveau in 1774

Castle Frederick — Falmouth, Nova Scotia

Chebuctou — Halifax, Nova Scotia

Cocagne — New Brunswick community on the Northumberland Strait

Fort Beauséjour — French fortress between Amherst, Nova Scotia, and
Sackville, New Brunswick

Fort Edward — British fort at Pisiquit

Fortress of Louisbourg — Louisbourg, Cape Breton Island

French Cross — Morden, Nova Scotia — Village on the Bay of Fundy

Gaudet Village — Bridgetown, Nova Scotia

Goat Island — Island in Annapolis Basin

Grand Pré — Acadian village in the larger community of Minas

Île à Piau — Major's Point in Belliveau Cove, St. Mary's Bay, Nova Scotia

Melanson Village — Melanson Settlement National Historic Site near
Champlain's Habitation of Port Royal

Memramcook — Town in New Brunswick near Moncton, formerly known
as Piau's Village

Minas — Acadian communities on the Minas Basin

Miramichi — River on the eastern coast of New Brunswick

Petitcodiac River — River in New Brunswick flowing into the Bay of
Fundy

Pisiquit — Windsor, Nova Scotia

Port Royal — Annapolis (Annapolis Royal after 1713)

Restigouche — New Brunswick community north of Miramichi

St. Croix Cove — Cove on the Bay of Fundy coast

St. Mary's Bay — Bay between Digby Neck and Nova Scotia mainland

Appendix 2

PIAU'S GENEALOGY

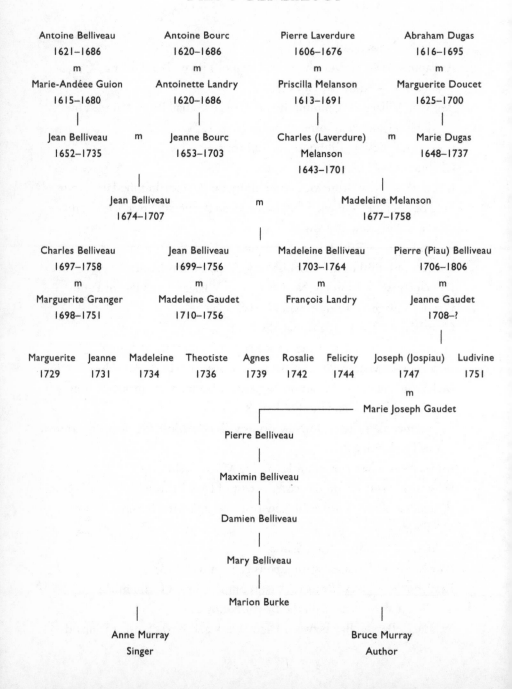

Antoine Belliveau 1621–1686 m Marie-Andéee Guion 1615–1680

Antoine Bourc 1620–1686 m Antoinette Landry 1620–1686

Pierre Laverdure 1606–1676 m Priscilla Melanson 1613–1691

Abraham Dugas 1616–1695 m Marguerite Doucet 1625–1700

Jean Belliveau 1652–1735   m   Jeanne Bourc 1653–1703

Charles (Laverdure) Melanson 1643–1701   m   Marie Dugas 1648–1737

Jean Belliveau 1674–1707   m   Madeleine Melanson 1677–1758

Charles Belliveau 1697–1758 m Marguerite Granger 1698–1751

Jean Belliveau 1699–1756 m Madeleine Gaudet 1710–1756

Madeleine Belliveau 1703–1764 m François Landry

Pierre (Piau) Belliveau 1706–1806 m Jeanne Gaudet 1708–?

Marguerite 1729   Jeanne 1731   Madeleine 1734   Theotiste 1736   Agnes 1739   Rosalie 1742   Felicity 1744   Joseph (Jospiau) 1747   Ludivine 1751

m

Marie Joseph Gaudet

Pierre Belliveau

Maximin Belliveau

Damien Belliveau

Mary Belliveau

Marion Burke

Anne Murray Singer

Bruce Murray Author

Appendix 3

Historical Acknowledgements and National Historic Sites Related to this Work

Regis Brun — Acadian historian, author, and archivist, Centre for Acadian Studies, University of Moncton

Harry Burke and Edward "Ned" Belliveau — Family historians who provided full details and family lore about Piau and Colonel Frederick DesBarres

Placide Gaudet — Acadian genealogist and archivist, National Archives of Canada

Henri LeBlanc, Marguerite Michaud, and Edouard Richard — Acadian historians who mention Piau's life and exploits

Stephen A. White — Chief genealogist, Centre for Acadian Studies, University of Moncton

National Historic Sites Visited in Massachusetts

Massachusetts State Archives — Letters of Charles Melanson (Piau's maternal grandfather) to Governor Stoughton of Massachusetts, 1690–1696

National Historic Sites Visited in New Brunswick

Cocagne
Restigouche

National Historic Sites Visited in Nova Scotia

Belliveau Cove
Fort Anne at Annapolis Royal
Fort Beauséjour
Fort Edward at Windsor
French Cross Park
Georges Island
Grand Pré
Halifax Citadel
Fortress of Louisbourg
Melanson Settlement
Memramcook Institute

Acknowledgements

First of all, I would like to acknowledge and thank those who are no longer with us, whose contributions to this book have been incalculable: my uncle, Harry L. Burke, for introducing me to Acadian history and, more specifically, to Piau and Colonel Frederick DesBarres; historian and cousin Edward "Ned" Belliveau, who resurrected Piau just in time to inspire my interest in him; Regis Brun, renowned Acadian historian, author, and archivist at the Centre for Acadian Studies, University of Moncton. Our two-year correspondence enlightened me on all aspects of my Acadian family history. Nineteenth- and early twentieth-century historians Placide Gaudet, Henri LeBlanc, Marguerite Michaud, and, notably, Edouard Richard, whose two volumes on Acadia introduced me to the relationship between Lieutenant-Governor Armstrong and the antagonist in my book, Mangeant. To Albert Belliveau, who I interviewed at age 103 and who had a keen remembrance of the stories told to him as a boy growing up in the Promised Land (Memramcook, New Brunswick). And, finally, my Acadian mother, Marion (Burke) Murray, who accompanied me on trips to graveyards, churches, and any number of ancestral sites, providing her memories and insights into our Acadian family history.

Those still with us, Stephen A. White, chief genealogist, Centre for Acadian Studies, University of Moncton, whose genealogical work made this book possible. Thanks also to Mr. White for pursuing the quest that led to my discovery that Piau was among the Acadian prisoners who were shipped to Boston from Halifax in July 1762. Fellow Cumberland County native, Brenda Dunn, whose book *A History of Port Royal/Annapolis*

Royal, 1605–1800 kept me on track chronologically and, most import-
antly, led me to the Massachusetts State Archives, where I discovered the
Charles Melanson (Piau's grandfather) letters to Governor Stoughton of
Massachusetts, 1690–96.

Many thanks to Laura Boyle, senior designer at Dundurn Press, for
designing an inspiring cover, featuring the art of my favourite Nova Scotia
painter, David MacIntosh. I could not have dreamed of a more appropriate cover to accompany my story. To my sympathetic and dream editor,
Dominic Farrell, whose suggestions made everything clearer and better, leaving the author's voice beautifully in tact. His support has been pivotal.

I wish to especially thank my agent, Arnold Gosewich, for his wise
counsel and for finding my book the ideal publisher.

Thanks and love to those who support my work on a daily basis:
Corinne Murray for listening and advising, Donna Murray for reading the
manuscript, and Anne Murray for agreeing to support me on this author's
journey with a gracious foreword.

Finally, I must acknowledge publisher Kirk Howard and all the diligent
and helpful staff at Dundurn Press for their assistance and continued commitment to promoting Canadian history.

Also Available from Dundurn

A Dark and Promised Land
Nathaniel Poole

When Orkney woman Rose is shipwrecked on the shores of Rupert's Land, she quickly falls in love with Alexander, a half-caste man who is guiding her people into the dark heart of the continent. But after the death of her father at the hands of another Native, Rose turns against Alexander and all his kind.

Heartbroken, Alexander returns to his wild life of running buffalo on the prairie. Although parted from Rose by endless miles and hard fate, his heart remains bound to hers, and on the eve of war he is compelled to reclaim her love, setting himself against his people amid a conflict that will help form a nation.

Matrons and Madams
Sharon Johnston

Clara Durling, a British widow of the First World War, arrives in Canada as the new superintendent of the Lethbridge Hospital just as wounded soldiers stream home. Lily Parsons is a young, widowed schoolteacher from Nova Scotia who ends up in the same city, managing a brothel called The Last Post.

Set against the backdrop of love, union organizers, amorous bachelors, gamblers, drinkers, and prostitutes, the lives of these two women unexpectedly intertwine when Clara, in the heat of local politics and responding to the highest incidence of venereal disease in the province, establishes the first venereal disease clinic in the province, with Lily's help. In this sprawling saga, Lily and Clara must confront the city's conservative thinkers to bring help and compassion to wounded veterans.

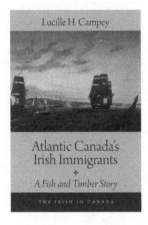

Atlantic Canada's Irish Immigrants
Lucille H. Campey

In this major study, Lucille Campey traces the relocation of around ninety thousand Irish people to their new homes in Atlantic Canada. She shatters the widespread misconception that the exodus was primarily driven by dire events in Ireland. The Irish immigration saga is not solely about what happened during the Great Potato Famine of the 1840s; it began a century earlier.

Although they faced great privations and had to overcome many obstacles, the Irish actively sought the better life that Atlantic Canada offered. Far from being helpless exiles lacking in ambition who went lemming-like to wherever they were told to go, the Irish grabbed their opportunities and prospered in their new home.

Campey gives these settlers a voice. Using wide-ranging documentary sources, she provides new insights about why the Irish left and considers why they chose their various locations in Nova Scotia, New Brunswick, Prince Edward Island, and Newfoundland. She highlights how, through their skills and energy, they benefitted themselves and contributed much to the development of Atlantic Canada.

This is essential reading for anyone wishing to understand the history of the Irish exodus to North America and provides a mine of information useful to family historians.